M000202867

WAKING UP NAKED IN STRANGE PLACES

TALES OF THE ROUGAROU BOOK 1

JULIE MCGALLIARD

GOTH HOUSE PRESS

Waking Up Naked in Strange Places

First published by Per Aspera Press
Copyright © 2015 Julie McGalliard

This edition published by Goth House Press
Copyright © 2019 Julie McGalliard

All rights reserved. No part of this book may be reproduced, stored in a retrieval system, or transmitted in any form or by any means, electronic, mechanical, photocopying, recording, or otherwise, without the prior written permission of the publisher, except as provided by U.S.A. copyright law.

Edited by Shannon Page
Cover Art and Design by C.S. Inman
and Julie McGalliard

ISBN:978-1-951598-02-0

For Ulysses and Carol
If they got sick of me hanging around their apartment while I wrote the
first draft of this book, they never let on.

1

BEHIND THEE STALKS A BEAST

The demons flee in a rush, leaving my body limp and dark as mud. Brother Justice senses the change and hesitates before lowering the cane for another blow against the back of my legs. "Sister? Art thy will surrendered at last? Is the beast gone from thee?"

"Yes, brother." My voice comes out in a whisper.

"Praise Him! Welcome our sister Self-Abnegation back into our hearts!" Justice and Great Purpose, the oldest boys, call out to the congregation.

"Praise Him! Welcome, sister!" the congregation calls back. But one voice seems to be missing: the deep rumble of Father Wisdom. He was there at the pulpit when my chastisement began, and his absence now troubles me. I try to let it go. All that thinking and wondering, that's what gets me into these situations, right? I need to learn to just do what I'm told. That's what all this chastening is supposed to get through to me, but I don't think it's working.

Justice undoes my shackles while Purpose comes to help me climb down from the Mercy Seat. They reek of sweat, nearly as tired from delivering the strokes of the cane as I am from receiving them. Supported between them, I half walk, half stumble down the aisle of the chapel, while broken colored light streams in from the stained-glass Jesus. I lift my gaze up to focus on the window, my favorite thing here in New Harmony. It shows Jesus carrying a lost lamb home on his shoulders. Jesus appears to be caught mid-laugh, while the lamb, black-wooled, wears an expression of almost comical bewilderment. The Lamb Jesus is the good Jesus, the one who is pleased with you. My father used to talk about him more often back when Mother Blessed was still alive. Now he's mostly interested in Wrathful Jesus, but we don't have a window for that.

I trip over the threshold of the chapel, so intent on the window that I forget to look where I'm going. Purpose wraps his arm tighter around my shoulders. "Careful, Abnegation. You are still weak."

"Mortal flesh is always weak, is it not?" Justice sounds very much like Father.

The cold outside shocks me, like a hail of icy needles stabbing through my flimsy, sweat-soaked gown. Right away my toes go numb, and I lean heavily on my brothers as they lead me through the heart of New Harmony, an irregular circle of what they call log cabins, heavy dark wood now dusted with frost. My mother told me this was built to be a church camp, a place for kids from the city to get out and stay in God's real country for a while. My brothers leave me propped, shivering, against the outside of the girls' cabin. I make my way inside and collapse face-down onto my cot, where I will be allowed to rest until first light tomorrow.

Well, the Mercy Seat is horribly painful, but at least it gets me out of afternoon chores.

The thought dances impishly across my mind, daring me to laugh at it. Father isn't here to see, but I struggle to keep my face neutral. My demon of inappropriate humor is almost as bad as my beast, the demon of rebellion and temper. Jokes are a trick of the devil, to mock holiness and make sacred things seem trivial or absurd.

I'm not aware of falling asleep, but the next thing I know is the sensation of dragging myself out of darkness while my sister Chastity shakes my arm. "Wake up, Abnegation. Please wake up. I can't carry her by myself."

"Her?" The worry in her voice finally penetrates and I find myself sitting up straight, heart pounding. "What's wrong? Who?"

"Sackcloth with Ashes," she says, tearfully, eyes wide in the dim light. "She's burning up and not breathing right. I want to get her to the bathing room and see if water will help cool her down." Chastity, the oldest girl, has always been the one to tend the sick, and as the second-oldest girl, I'm usually the one to assist her. At nearly sixteen, post-Humbling, post-menses, I am an adult the way we reckon things at New Harmony. But Chastity at seventeen actually looks the part of a woman. Sometimes she reminds me of Mother Blessed, even though she is the child of Marybelle, Wisdom's first wife.

I swing my legs down to the floor and try standing up. Everything aches, but they'll hold me all right. When I draw near Ash, her breathing is harsh and ragged, and she exudes a pungent odor of something -- illness, wrongness. Something bitter and terrifying. Her eyes flutter as if she might be awake, but she doesn't react when I pick her up. In my arms she's hot and weightless, as if I hold sunlight.

Chastity frowns at me. "You're going to carry her all by yourself? You're hardly bigger than she is."

"I won't drop her."

She nods, still frowning, and blows out her breath in a heavy sigh. "No, I guess you won't. Follow me then. I'll open the doors and make sure there's nothing for you to trip over."

Outside, a nearly full moon illuminates our path with cold pale light. The freezing air bites at us, and the night sparkles.

"Frost coming," Chastity says. Our bare feet grow numb quickly, and Ash stirs.

"'Gashun?'"

"It's okay, beloved. I've got you."

"I'm sorry I got the letters wrong."

"Shh. It's all right. You don't have to worry about that now."

We're nearly at the washroom, a plain structure of concrete bricks at the edge of the village, when a long shadow falls across us from behind. My heart squeezes with dread. "Chastity. Self-Abnegation." Father's voice booms out and a chill races down my back.

"Father."

He walks around to stand in front of us, blocking our way. "And where do you girls think you're going?"

"A demon of heat has come upon our sister Sackcloth with Ashes," Chastity says. "We hope cool water will drive the demon away."

He takes a step closer. "I see thou art recovered most swiftly from the Mercy Seat, Abnegation. Perhaps thy brothers were weak in their conviction and spared thee of the true cleansing pain?"

The beast of anger leaps in my heart. He knows very well I tend to recover quickly, no matter how severe the chastisement. My shoulder prickles with the memory of the one time I didn't, when the wounds burned for days and left scars. I stifle the beast and bow my head.

"Father, I was gifted with such a powerful spirit of submission that the Lord has blessed me with a quick return to health."

He takes another step forward and places a big hand on Ash's forehead. "She is indeed very hot. Abnegation, look at me." I raise my head. His eyes burn darkly into me, like the coals at the bottom of a fire. "Beware, child. Behind thee stalks the terrible shadow of thy beast. He waits for his chance to devour you, should you ever leave the protection of my spiritual covering."

"Yes, Father Wisdom."

He places his hand under my chin to turn my head this way and that. He sighs and looks very grieved. "You speak as one compliant, but there remains a demon of stubbornness deep in your eyes. Thy demons grow ever stronger. I am afraid I must devise another correction. You test my powers of invention. I will pray on it."

"Yes, Father Wisdom." Damn it all to hell. The words sound in my head, oddly satisfying for a moment, but then my stomach shudders in sick panic. Blasphemy is a grave sin, even if never spoken aloud. Unable to hold his stare any longer, I close my eyes and lower my head. "Thy will be done, amen."

"Withhold not correction from the child; for if thou beatest him with the rod, he shall not die." He rests a heavy hand on the top of my head, shaved as part of my chastisement, only a fuzz of red remaining. His hand is hot in the cold air. "Go thou and help your sister cast the demons out of Sackcloth with Ashes. I will share thy new correction when the Lord has shown me what it must be."

"Thank you, Father," Chastity and I say together. He continues on his way.

Inside the washroom, I lay Ash down on the steel table we use to fold clothes. She gasps. "Cold." Her voice is small and plaintive.

"It's all right, beloved, the cold is to get the heat demon to leave." Chastity kisses her on the forehead. "Abnegation, go to the pump and fill a tub with water."

I obey, and rush back with the sloshing plastic tub. "Do you have any idea what's making her sick now? She was fine when I went to the Mercy Seat." Went in her place, although I don't mention that.

Chastity dips a sponge in the cool water and drizzles it

across Ash's forehead. "This will go better if her skin is bare. Lock the door and help me remove her shift."

I do, and notice with alarm that there are dark spots across the back side of her body, like bruises. "When did she get sick, Chastity?" My voice breaks.

"Abnegation, don't."

"Don't what?"

"Don't get angry. Please."

"Why would I get angry?" But I know. "He beat her anyway, when I was at the Mercy Seat. Didn't he? He beat her and it made her sick." My voice trembles with suppressed rage, the demon flamed to life in an instant.

Chastity hardens her expression and continues to squeeze the sponge. "No. He chastised her. Later on, the Lord made her sick."

"But I took her punishment onto me! I offered myself in her place!"

"No. She was chastened for her reading mistakes. You were chastened for defying Father Wisdom. Do you understand?"

"He lied!"

"No. You misunderstood. I'm sorry."

Panic makes me reckless, and my voice rises in obvious frustration. "But you were there in the classroom. You heard him say it. He said, 'Abnegation, dost thou offer up thyself to atone in thy sister's stead?' And I said yes."

She turns to me, eyes flashing. "Stop it. Just stop it. This is all your fault. He beat her to punish you." Her voice never rises above a whisper, but the fury of it shocks me, makes me feel slapped across the face. "What on earth led you to cross him like that?"

"But it wasn't fair of him to punish her! You know she has trouble with the letters. You know she always tries her best. She didn't do anything wrong! It was wrong to let him punish her for it!"

"And who are you to say what's wrong and what's right?" She glares at me. "That's not your place, little sister, and you know it. But none of that matters now. She's ill. We have to save her if we can."

"And if we can't?" I think of Mother Blessed, who we tended in much the same way six years ago.

"If the Lord wills, He takes her. If anything can truly save Ash, it is our faith. Pray with me now. The Lord is my shepherd, I shall not want."

I join her in the familiar words, but they remain only words. When Mother was sick, I prayed for real, with all my soul, without ceasing. I made atonements. For three days I didn't eat or sleep. I wore a hair shirt and itched and ached under my dress. I shaved off my long, red braids and burned them stinking on the altar.

But she died anyway.

Since then, I have never been completely sure in my faith. Did I not do enough to please the Lord? Did I do the wrong things? Was God even watching? Did He care? Why did He remain silent? Was it a test?

The night grinds on, dark and seemingly endless. Ash falls eventually into what seems like a peaceful slumber, then slips away from us entirely. No breath, no heartbeat. Chastity sighs, and I think she's about to say a prayer for Ash's soul, but instead she turns toward me and forces my chin up so that she can meet my gaze. Her expression is firm, and her eyes are bloodshot. "Sister. I'm going to try some outsider medicine, a thing called CPR. Promise me you will not speak of it outside of this room."

"I promise." I watch in fascination as she tries to force her breath into Ash's mouth, and presses against her heart, in rhythm. I don't know where she learned such a thing. She tries this for a few moments, and it seems exhausting. She turns toward me.

"Abnegation, you saw what I was doing, with her heart?" I

nod. "Do you think you can do that same thing, while I do her breath? I'll tap out the count for you."

The physical exertion comforts me at first. I'm glad to have something useful to do. But then I feel a bone crack and nearly run screaming from the room. "I broke her! Please, God, please—"

"No, it's all right, that's just her sternum, it happens sometimes." She closes her eyes and sighs deeply, swaying on her feet as if she's about to fall asleep standing up. "By my count we've been trying for twelve minutes. I believe, if this were going to work, it would have worked by now. She's gone."

We place our hands against her body and say a prayer for the safe passage of her innocent soul up into Heaven. My eyes fall on the silver flash of a pair of scissors, part of the kit we use for mending clothes. Without thinking, I obey the impulse to braid a small lock of Ash's pale hair, tie it with a length of thread, and snip it off. Chastity watches me and I expect her to berate me again, but instead she nods, and does the same thing. We coil her braids into the pockets of our aprons, and carry her body to the chapel to await burial.

BECAUSE OUR SISTER ASH IS PURE, LIKE THE LAMBS, WISDOM decides she will be burned as an offering to the Lord. We carry her to the altar, an open stone ring at the bottom of a half circle of sloped concrete that faces the dense, swampy woods beyond. Rotten boards seem to indicate there were benches here once, but they're long gone and Wisdom would probably make us stand anyway. Plus, it's too cold to want to sit. The hard ground sucks warmth from my bare feet.

Ash's body, shrouded in white, rests on a bed of dry moss, atop a raised latticework of wooden sticks. Below that lies a pile of wood with more dry moss and shaved bark as kindling. Purpose, Justice, Righteousness and Unity, all the boys older than twelve, help Wisdom stack more wood and kindling underneath her. Then each one is given a white candle, lit by our father. The boys kneel and use their candles to ignite the kindling. But the fire doesn't want to catch, and soon dies to a smolder. Acrid smoke engulfs us as we struggle to suppress our undignified coughing.

Wisdom exhales with barely suppressed rage and strides toward the pyre. He produces a silver flask from his pocket and shakes its contents, a pungent liquid, over the sputtering wood. Hot red flame explodes across the surface and everyone flinches away. Kerosene, I think. It's what we use in the lanterns. But it does the trick. Soon the fire is burning too intensely for comfort, and fragrant smoke curls up into the freezing air.

All of New Harmony is gathered here. With Ash gone, I count thirteen of us, including the little ones. A chill runs down my back as I think of Judas, the thirteenth disciple, the number that is forever cursed.

You could leave, and then they would be twelve.

The thought comes to me almost as if I heard it spoken aloud.

Father begins to preach, reading from the Bible, talking about Ash's life. Now it is permitted for us to weep, silently, like Jesus. I won't be able to cry without screaming, so I hold back, hand in my pocket where I can stroke the soft lock of hair. When I cry for her I want to be alone.

The flames begin to lick at my sister's flesh, bringing forth a roasting meat smell that nearly makes me hungry. No, that's wrong. It makes me feel sick.

This is all your fault. He beat her to punish you.

Chastity's words come back to me, guilt sinking in painfully like a blow from the heaviest cane. Yes. It is all my fault, isn't it? Everything would be perfect here without me.

After a while, Meekness, his wife of five years, takes the children younger than twelve away, back to the main house for prayers. They're not expected to stand vigil, to go without food and drink and trips to the outhouse for the hours it will take the pyre to consume Ash's body entirely. But I'm glad to do it. It gives me time to meditate on my own sin, my own failure. I tried to protect her from Wisdom's wrath, but brought it down on her instead. When the full moon rises, and her body is nothing but bones and soot, I know what I have to do.

I have to leave.

2

MARKING THE FLESH IS SINFUL

I think I'm lost.

I intended to head toward the highway, guided by a distant memory of its direction, from the old days when we used to sometimes take the van into town or to outsider churches. But there are no clear paths through these woods, just endless meandering trails that end in tangled branches and muddy pools. Maybe I'm wandering in circles, right back to New Harmony. It's not too late, is it? I could head back there. They won't know I'm gone until the morning. I won't be in trouble yet.

Arooooooooooo

An animal howl wavers through the bitter air. I whip around, see nothing. I'm imagining things. He told me there was a beast, and now I'm conjuring a beast.

Arooooooooooo

Closer now, the howling comes again. Do I hear the rustle of paws through dead leaves, the panting of a dog in chase? I turn, and see, yes, the amber flash of eyes in darkness. Four eyes, two beasts. I break into a reckless sprint, crashing through the underbrush, stomping right into shallow puddles of water. Soon I'm covered in small cuts and mud.

But the creatures are fast, and soon they're right behind me, hot breath tickling my ankles, razor teeth snapping at the hem of my dress. A man's voice calls out, "Daisy! Buttercup! Heel!" I hear the words, but fail to process their meaning.

I stop. Before me, a canal or drainage ditch stretches about five feet wide, full of dank water and pale trash. It looks to be only a couple of feet deep, but it's hard to be sure. The highway lies just on the other side. I look both directions along it, searching for a break in the canal, without finding one.

Roaring, and a piercing light, indicate an approaching car. With a deep inhale, I hike up my skirt and wade in, wincing as the water's unclean touch reaches higher and higher. I have the thought that this is like a reverse baptism: plunging into filth, emerging into a profane unsaved world. This is the point where I can no longer go back.

At its highest point, the water reaches barely above my knees. I slog up through the mud, then run to stand on the other side of the highway. Still following me, the dogs plunge into the ditch without hesitation. The rapidly nearing head-lights reveal them to be ordinary hunting dogs, and not the hell-hounds of my imagination.

"Daisy! Buttercup! TO ME!" The man's voice is shrill now, desperate. Oh, he's afraid they're going to run into the road, heedless of the car. I judge I have enough time to run back across the road without getting hit myself, and do that. Now they have no reason to run across the road. The lead dog jumps up on me, playfully I think, but with enough weight and force that she knocks me down backwards, right into the path of the car again. My tailbone thunks painfully onto the hard asphalt, and then I'm smothered by hot meaty breath and a wet tongue in my face.

The car is still coming at us in a blaze of noise and light. I try to stand, but my legs, exhausted by the run and still aching from the Mercy Seat, refuse to obey me. Now we're all going to be crushed. This is my punishment for rejecting Wisdom's authority. Hell awaits me now and I close my eyes tightly, bracing for the meat grinder, for the pain that never ends.

The car emits a high-pitched squeal and stops getting closer, although I can still hear the engine running. No pain. Well, no new pain. I think I'm still alive. I open my eyes. A woman has emerged from the car, her silhouette curvy and black against the glare. "Please, God, please tell me I didn't hit anything." She comes toward me until I can see her face: sooty eyes and scarlet lips, a painted Jezebel. "A girl. But I thought—are you all right?" She kneels beside me, giving off a cloud of perfume and sweat. Her fingers brush my forehead and the warmth of her hand reminds me how cold the night is.

Their master approaches and the dogs bound up to him joyfully, unperturbed by their near-death experience. They stop to shake themselves dry, showering us all with canal water. "Thank you, miss," the man says to me. "I saw what you did, to try to stop them running across the road, and Daisy knocking you down like that. Sometimes those dogs don't have the sense God gave a grasshopper." He skritches under their chins, and they bask in his love. "What's a little girl like you doing out here all alone this time of night, anyway?"

Fear jumps in my throat. Does this man know my father? Was he hunting me after all? I'm still trying to formulate an answer when the woman says, "Hon, can I give you a ride somewhere?" I nod, and she helps me to my feet and walks me to her car. "Oh, you're all wet and muddy." She hands me a roll of paper towels. "Here, dry yourself off." She lays more paper towels down on the seat and floor, then helps me to the passenger seat and straps me in.

The man watches us with a frown. "You gals gonna be all

right there, on your own?" The dogs have become fascinated by a dead nutria. They nose at its tawny, decaying fur, sending a puff of sweetish foul rot our way.

"We're fine!" the woman calls back, waving. "Don't worry! I'll take care of her!" She closes my door with a slam, then climbs into the driver's seat and fastens her belt. She drives slowly at first, possibly fearing the dogs will run into the road again. Toward her nose she pulls a strand of hair, inky black and flame red at the tip. She sniffs, grimaces. "Ugh, swamp water." She glances at me. "Now, sweetie, you want to tell me what's going on? Are you hurt? Do we need to call somebody?"

I clear my throat. "No, ma'am." My voice comes out in a dry croak.

"Ma'am? Don't ma'am me. I'm only twenty-eight. You can call me Steph. What's your name?"

"Self-Abnegation in the Service of the Lord."

She barks out a surprised laugh. "Seriously?" Then she looks thoughtful. "Wait, that man with the dogs, does he make you dress up like that? In the pioneer dress, with the shaved head and all?"

"Oh, no, m—Miss Steph, I don't know that man. My father is the one who—" I break off. I don't want to talk about my father.

"Ah. I think I get it. Mind if I call you Abby? Where are you going?"

"Baton Rouge. My aunt is there. I'm going to stay with my aunt." I don't know where that lie came from, but it seemed to be reassuring to her, that I know where I'm going.

She nods. "I'm passing through there. I'll drop you off." We drive on in silence. I stare hypnotized at roadside trees as they loom briefly into sharp clarity, throw back long, distorted shadows, then disappear. A vent in the dashboard blasts warm air, like the breath of a dragon. I lean forward and bask in it. Then, abruptly, the warm air stops. I glance over at Steph, who has wriggled out of her overcoat.

"Sorry, I was getting too hot. If you're still cold, though, you can have my sweatshirt." She takes off her next layer of clothing, a bulky black cardigan, with a hood and a zippered front, and holds it out to me. As she reveals her arms and the top of her chest, I see that her bare skin crawls with bright pictures: flames, devils, spiders, skulls, symbols of gambling and drinking, all the wickedness you could possibly imagine. Marking the flesh is sinful, according to my father. That's why he devised his chastisements to leave no scars.

The scars I have are a judgment from the Lord.

She catches me staring, and laughs. "Yeah, kid, I got a lotta tattoos. And I can tell you that each and every one of them seemed like a good idea at the time."

I take the sweatshirt from her and consider the image on the front, a grinning skull in a top hat. Some kind of demon? Will I be summoning him by putting on this garment?

No. If I was going to worry about that kind of thing, I should have stayed at New Harmony. I don't think I believe in demons anymore. No, I don't. I definitely don't. I don't believe in demons, or beasts, or heaven, or hell, or God, or Wisdom, or any of it. Not anymore.

The sweatshirt is soft and thick, like wearing a blanket. It smells strongly of Steph, and her perfume.

"Hey, you want some water? There's a bottle around here somewhere." She gestures toward the floor of the car. I locate the container where it rolled under my seat. The liquid inside is warm and stale, tainted with plastic. I drink until I have to pause for air, then drink again until it's empty.

Steph smiles. "Thirsty, huh? There's more water, if you want to try pawing through that mess in the rear." She points a thumb toward the back seat, which is piled high with bags and boxes. "Oh, you want some jerky?" She tries to hand me a plastic package, full of pinkish brown strips that have a sticky look about them, like dried fruit. But when the package nears my face, I inhale the sickening odor of desiccated flesh.

"No." I clear my throat. "I mean, no, thank you. I can't. It is meat, isn't it?"

She chuckles. "Beef jerky was meat the last time I checked, hon. Are you a vegetarian?" I'm not sure I've heard the word before, but it sounds right, so I nod. "Well, okay. But you look hungry. I got some trail mix in that shopping bag, peanuts and raisins and M&Ms, why don't you get yourself some of that?"

I locate the trail mix and eat greedily, fast enough that I almost choke a couple of times. The M&Ms turn out to be candy, brightly colored nuggets with a firm outer shell that crunches lightly under my teeth, bursting into a rich, creamy sweetness. I can't remember the last time I had candy. Years ago now. Mother Blessed was still alive.

"You know, it's the weirdest thing. When I stopped back there, at first I thought I saw three dogs, not two dogs and a person. Maybe I've been driving too long. They say you can start to hallucinate." She chuckles. "Of course, the moon is out tonight. You're not a rougarou, are you?"

"I'm sorry, m—Miss Steph, I don't know what that is."

"Oh, it's just a ghost story my Cajun granny used to tell. It's like a werewolf." Her voice takes on an imitation of age and a musical accent. "Li'l Stephanie, you best behave now, come right inside when Mama calls, or that rougarou gon eat you all up, hey?" She returns to her normal voice. "According to Granny, every full moon they have a big fais-do-do where they barbecue a whole wild boar. They start out wearing nothing but their human skins, then at midnight they put on their wolf skins and go running all over, terrorizing folks." She laughs. "Of course, once I was old enough to be interested in the idea of naked werewolf boys, I used to go out looking for that party. Never found it, though."

She gives me a big grin, and I smile in return, face hot as I try not to think about the concept of naked boys of any kind. Obviously, she expects me to already know what a werewolf is. Is it all right to ask? But as I try to work out how to phrase the question to avoid giving offense, the rumbling of the engine lulls me down into sleep.

"SHIT." STEPH'S VOICE WAKES ME WITH A PROFANITY, AND I look around in panic and confusion. Where am I? Colored lights flash inside the car, hellbeast coming to seize me in its terrible jaws. I shake off sleep a bit more, realize that red and blue lights mean police, not monsters. Still, I'm nervous. Would my father have called the police? He never previously had much use for outsider authority. But I don't think he ever had one of us run away before.

We pull over to the side of the road. "I was probably speeding or something." She looks at me and sighs."If the cops ask about you, what should I tell them?"

"You're taking me to Baton Rouge. I'm going to stay with my aunt." My voice comes out in a fluttery panic. I wouldn't believe me either.

"Uh-huh." She smiles wryly. "And your aunt's name?"

"Please. Please don't take me back there."

"It's okay." She puts a hand on my shoulder. "I'll take you wherever you want. But I still need a story for the cops. 'Hi, this is the runaway I picked up after I almost hit her with my car' is probably not going to cut it."

"Why don't you be my aunt? And I'll pretend to be asleep and maybe they won't say anything."

She nods. "Okay. I guess we'll try that."

I close my eyes and sink into the seat, curl up into the sweatshirt, try to keep my breathing relaxed. I hear tapping on glass, a muffled male voice, then the whirr of a window lowering, letting in a blast of icy air. Cologne, masculine sweat, and a hint of stale tobacco smoke waft inside the car as the officer leans toward the open window.

"Do you know why I pulled you over, ma'am?"

"I'm sorry, I don't."

"That stuff you got piled up in the back there, can you see anything at all through your rear view mirror?"

"A little bit?"

I feel the heat of a flashlight on my face. "Is that your kid?" the cop asks. I make a show of yawning and blinking awake.

"My niece. She helped me clear out my stuff in New Orleans and we're heading to stay with my brother for a while." Steph sighs, and waggles her left hand. "Recent divorce. Still got the ring on. I'll probably have to get it cut off, unless my finger shrinks again after I have the baby."

"Baby? You got a divorce when you were pregnant?" I can hear the frowning disapproval in his voice.

"Yeah, I know. Classic bad timing. He finally showed his true colors by beating up on me, and I left. But a few weeks later I finally figured out why I kept puking first thing in the morning."

"Maybe it was good timing." The cop sounds sympathetic now. "At least you got him figured out before he could hurt the baby."

"I do try to tell myself that. And my family is very supportive. We're close. My mama is definitely going to help me when the baby comes."

The flashlight continues to study my face, as I shield my eyes from its glaring light. "What's your name, kid?"

I hesitate, two names hovering on the tip of my tongue, before answering, "Abby." I stifle a real yawn.

"Ever been to New Orleans before?"

"This was my first time."

"How'd you like it?"

"The old buildings were pretty." I hope I'm remembering

right, that pictures I've seen of fancy antique structures, with balconies of iron lace, are New Orleans. Then something else pops into my head and I smile. "Aunt Steph bought me a frozen Cafe du Monde, but we're not supposed to tell Mom about it. She thinks I'm too young for coffee."

The cop snaps off the flashlight, revealing himself to be younger and cuter than I would have guessed from his voice. He's smiling in return. "Sounds like fun. Now, Ms. Marchande, I'm going to let you off with a warning this time, but before you get on the road again, please rearrange that junk in the back to give you a clear view of the road behind. You got two kids in that car there you need to protect, okay?"

Steph thanks him profusely and he pulls away, no longer flashing the lights. She watches him go, then blows out her breath and plops her head onto the steering wheel. "Whew, that was terrifying. I was so sure George had found some way to sic the cops on me." She gives me a sad smile. "Hey, you want to help me get that stuff in the back sorted out?"

We turn around, kneeling on the car seats, and start moving boxes and bags down from the rear window. For a while we work in silence, then Steph says, "Abby? How old are you, anyway?"

"Almost sixteen."

She frowns. "That old? You poor thing. You're so tiny I thought you were closer to twelve. Now, I can make a stop in Baton Rouge, take you to Child Protective Services."

I find my voice. "I want to stay with you. I want to go wherever you're going."

"You sure about that? I'm headed all the way to Seattle. That's where my brother's living right now. It's thousands of miles away. I'm going to be there at least until the baby is born." She sighs. "Then I guess I'll figure the rest of my life out after that."

"But I can help with the baby! I helped with all my younger brothers and sisters, and I know how to clean house, and cook, and take care of sheep, and dogs—" I break off. I sound desperate, pathetic. People on the outside, people in cities, they don't need somebody to take care of their sheep. Still, Steph is smiling. She seems about to say something, when her repacking efforts dislodge a bottle partly full of golden liquid. She catches it and stares at it for a long time, her face troubled. The label indicates it's something called SINGLE MALT SCOTCH.

"I shouldn't have taken this," she says. "Why did I pack this? I'm not thinking." She turns to me, holding out the bottle. "All right, Abby. Maybe we can help each other. You come with me to Seattle, and I'll take care of you. And I need you to not let me drink any alcohol while I'm pregnant. Okay? Not even a beer."

"I will. I promise."

She searches my face for a moment. "You sure? It's going to be harder than you think." I nod, certain that nothing I face in Seattle could be harder than what I've just been through. "Well. I guess that's settled. You can start by getting rid of this." She hands me the bottle.

"You want me to pour it out on the ground?"

She winces. "Oh, hon, don't do that. Leave it by the side of the road. Maybe somebody will find it and think it's a Christmas present."

3

BUT THEY LOOKED SO HANDSOME

I wake up, body already standing in a defensive crouch, voice howling in dread. A strange man stands in my room, reeking of sweat and brimstone. Blood and tissue coat his hands, smeared over the silvery gun he holds.

"What the hell? What's wrong?" he shouts, panic in his voice. His voice, with Steph's accent. His face, with Steph's dark coloring. His shirt, red checked flannel open over black cotton knit, white letters that say

MEAT IS MURDER
TASTY, TASTY MURDER.

I stop screaming, as my brain catches up to the rest of me. This must be Steph's brother Morgan. We arrived last night, late, after he was already asleep. I relax a little, then cold air on my legs reminds me that I'm not wearing any pants. Frantically, I cast my gaze around for the sweats I wore last night. There they are, draped across a cardboard box. Why did I take them off? Oh, the cuffs are muddy. Still, I snatch them up and hold them in front of me, which probably calls extra attention to the fact that I was previously half naked. When

Steph helped me set up my sleeping bag in here, she assured me this little room was my own private space, and nobody would come in without knocking first.

I give him an awkward smile. "I'm sorry. You're Morgan, aren't you?"

"And you're Abby. Sorry I can't shake." He holds up his gory palms. "I was making sausage. What was all that noise about? Why were you screaming?"

Huh. I thought I was screaming because a strange man with blood-covered hands came running into my room with a gun. "Nightmare?" I guess.

He nods, and tucks the gun into a holster under his left arm, hidden by the flannel shirt. "Steph is out for a while. I can make you some lunch if you want. She said you're a vegetarian but you eat eggs and dairy? Is that right?" I nod. "Great, I'll make you an omelette. If you want a shower, use the one upstairs. The one on this level is kind of torn up right now." His smile turns apologetic. "I don't know if she told you, but this is our grandma's place, a crappy little house with a million-dollar view. I'm hoping to fix it up well enough to get us that million." He leaves, whistling a tune. The melodic whistle, more than anything else, convinces me that I'm really here. Wisdom couldn't abide music, not even church hymns. Demons could get at you that way, he always said.

But I don't want to think about that. To think of Wisdom is to think of Ash, to think of my shame, to want to collapse into a puddle of grief and never move again. I check the pocket of my borrowed sweatshirt, where I placed the lock of her hair. Still there. Still pale and silky, still smelling of her. I look around the room for somewhere safe to put it, and find a little wooden box where it will just fit. There. Let my guilt rest, until I can bear to look at it again. Someday I will atone.

In the kitchen, Morgan has cleaned up most evidence of his sausage-making, although the air still holds a thick, meaty odor. I recognize the metal grinder as a small version of the one I saw once, when Father took us into Baton Rouge so that we could tour a butchering operation, and understand why those who welcome the New Kingdom must shun animal flesh.

It worked. I came to know the terrible secret behind those things outsiders call hamburgers: that harmless-looking brown patty is the actual flesh of a once-living animal that has been slaughtered, hooked, drained, gutted, skinned, dismembered, and finally pulverized in the contraption they call a meat grinder. Large slabs of red tissue, still barely recognizable as muscle fibers, were fed into the hopper at the top. A white-coated man turned a huge crank, and out the front, ropes of homogenized pink oozed and fell into a huge metal bowl. My father pointed to the pink glop piling up in the bowl. "Without His salvation, that fate awaits us in Hell, to be pulverized in torment and consumed by demons. For what are we, without the soul? We are meat."

Morgan turns a knob on the stove, and blue flames rise up to lick the edges of a deep black cast-iron skillet. He drops a generous pat of butter inside, and the aroma instantly fills the room, making my mouth water. I can't remember the last time I had butter. He glances over his shoulder at me, with a quick grin. "You're absolutely sure you don't want any bacon in this?"

"Bacon is a kind of meat, isn't it?"

He laughs. "Of course it's meat. So how does a kid like you end up as a vegetarian, anyway?"

"It's how I was raised."

"You're not ready to try something new?"

"I would prefer not to, thank you, Sir."

"Have it your way, kid. But let me know if you ever change your mind. We don't eat that disgusting factory bacon around here. It comes right from the butcher, right from the farm. I could probably tell you the name of the pig."

I shudder at the thought of eating a pig with a name.

The front door slams open. I recognize Steph's perfume all the way from here. She joins us in the kitchen. "Oh, Abby, you're up. How did you sleep?"

"Fine, thank you."

To Morgan she says, "Mmmm, mushrooms. You still have that smoked bacon?"

He jerks a thumb at me. "I'm frying that up last, out of consideration for your little vegetarian there. So, did you manage to get that job?" He dumps sliced mushrooms into the foaming butter and begins stirring.

She smiles, and I notice that she's dressed with particular care: hair coiffed, lipstick precise. "I did. It's in the old quarter. Pioneer Square, I guess they call it? It's a place called The Nola Bar & Grill. The owner died recently and they needed somebody who knew how to make the classic New Orleans cocktails, and could manage a bar."

Now the kitchen fills with the sharp, sweetish aroma of—alcohol? I look at the freshly opened bottle in Morgan's hand. It says DRY SHERRY.

I get up and put a hand on his arm. "Morgan, no!" He glares at me, perplexed. I remove my hand, suddenly shy. It's not my place to correct him, is it? "Steph can't have alcohol right now. The baby." He glances at Steph, then back at me. He nods, corks the sherry, and reaches for a bottle labeled BALSAMIC VINEGAR.

"What?" Steph laughs. "Abby, I didn't mean for you to—I mean, cooking sherry isn't—"

"No, she's right," Morgan says. "I wasn't thinking."

A few notes of music come from Steph's pocket, made by a device she calls her phone, a small rectangle of smooth black operated by touching the glass screen. We used it to play music, take pictures, send messages, find gas stations. Sometimes she even uses it to talk to people.

"Mama? Yes, I made it to Seattle okay. Morgan says 'hi.'"

She listens in silence for a moment, then her face turns furious. "What? That asshole came by the house?"

Her fury and casual profanity shock me. I shrink down into my chair, willing myself to disappear.

Steph seems to notice me flinch, and gives an apologetic smile. "S'cuse my French, Abby. I'm—what? No, Mama, she's just a girl from the neighborhood." She heads out to the back porch, phone at her ear, long, angry strides that resonate on the linoleum floor. "Just tell me you didn't let him inside? Tell me that much."

She slams the door behind her, but the wood is warped and doesn't latch, leaving a gap through which we can still hear her voice raised in anger, although we can't make out all the words. Morgan and I stare awkwardly at each other.

"You know you don't have to call me 'sir.' Makes me sound like my dad."

"I'm sorry, um—Uncle Morgan?"

He laughs. "Not your uncle, either, but it'll do. So, Steph didn't tell me much about you, except that she picked you up hitchhiking on Highway 61?" I nod, although I'm not sure what hitchhiking is. "And you're, what, thirteen? Fourteen?"

"Fifteen."

He nods. "Sorry if this is an awkward question, but sometimes my sister does things without thinking them all the way through. Is there somebody back in Louisiana who's looking for you, Abby? Calling the cops, anything like that?"

"I don't think so, Uncle Morgan. If my father wants me back, he'll trust the Almighty to do it." But I feel a tug of apprehension, as I remember all the stories we used to tell. People who left the faith and something terrible happened to them. A car accident, or cancer.

The back door slams open again and Steph stalks in, shouting. "She almost let him inside the house! She still thinks we're maybe going to get back together!"

"You know how charming he is when he wants to be.

Mama's still charmed." He shrugs. "Anyway, they'll both get over it eventually. What's the big deal?"

"The big deal? She might accidentally tell him where I am! She could mention Seattle! He might see a piece of mail with the address here!"

Morgan makes a scoffing noise. "Yeah, but he's not going to come all the way to Seattle just to find you."

"Not me, you idiot. His son. Doesn't anybody in this family ever listen to a word I say?"

"No, not really." But he's grinning when he says it.

LATER IN THE DAY, STEPH TAKES ME OUT SHOPPING. "WE NEED to get you some everyday clothes. Do you mind walking to the store? I hate trying to find parking around here."

"Of course." I never hesitate to walk, although I'm still not entirely comfortable in the heavy, stiff shoes Steph gave me to wear. At New Harmony, only adults wore shoes. It was wasteful to shod children with growing feet. I wore shoes only when we went to outsider churches, and they were always too large for me and had rags stuffed in the toes to keep them from falling off.

Outside, I get my first look at Seattle in daylight, although "daylight" seems to be a bit of an exaggeration. The sky is a uniform silvery white, the air full of chilly mist that turns everything damp. It's not icy, like it was when I left New Harmony, but I shiver as the moisture seems to suck all the warmth from my skin. When I inhale, the air has a sharp gray-green tang to it that I think is the smell of the ocean. Thick evergreens tower over our heads, huger than any trees I've ever seen. We seem to be at the top of a hill, the sidewalk steeply angled, plunging into unseen depths. All this up and down makes me dizzy.

As we descend, we rapidly leave behind the detached

houses and the looming trees. The buildings become taller, closer together, and the sidewalks fill up with people. I cringe in anticipation, remembering the curious stares and suppressed laughter that we New Harmony folk used to face on trips into town. But the people here don't take any special notice of me. Instead I'm the one fighting the urge to stare, at people with more tattoos than Steph, or hair dyed fantastical colors and teased into astonishing shapes. They wear sparkling jewelry plunged into unlikely places: noses, eyebrows, lips. They give off strong whiffs of coffee, alcohol, tobacco smoke.

Two men pass us, walking very close to each other. They strike me as looking oddly like a matched set: similar in height and build, but one with very dark skin and black hair, the other with pale skin and light hair. I do a double take as I realize they're holding hands. One kisses the other on the lips.

"Come on, Abby, don't stare." Steph puts a hand to my cheek and forces my gaze away.

"Were they sodomites?"

Steph groans. "Don't use that word, hon. It makes you sound like a nutty TV preacher. Yeah, they're gay."

"But they looked so—" I search for the right word. Happy? Normal? Non-demonic? "So handsome."

She smiles and ruffles the fuzzy stubble of hair on top of my head. "They were, weren't they? There's a lot of that in this neighborhood. It's Seattle's major gay district. You'll get used to it."

"They have districts?" I look around, expecting the buildings or the sidewalks to seem different somehow, more perverted.

"It's a tradition. Improves dating potential and cuts down on bigotry." She folds her arms and gives me a stern look. "Abby, I know you're young, and I know you come from a strict religious upbringing, but I won't put up with anti-gay bigotry from anyone. I've even got my brother trained out of it. So, if you have any further thoughts about 'sodomites,' you'd best keep them to yourself. Are we clear?"

I nod, cringing under the sense that Steph is mad at me. But how was I supposed to know it was rude?

Giant plastic letters proclaim the store to be VALUE VILLAGE. Steph gets a metal shopping cart and leads me through narrow corridors overstuffed with goods of all kinds. The vastness and abundance shocks me. For the last few days traveling, we've stopped at what she calls convenience stores, but they were nothing like this.

Steph holds up a black skirt, asks what I think, and I nod, and she adds it to the shopping cart. We repeat this ritual several more times, and after a while, she stops in obvious frustration.

"Abby, you're saying yes to everything."

Now I feel shamed, guilty. "I'm sorry, Miss Steph, I wasn't trying to be greedy."

"That wasn't the point. I'm trying to figure out what you'd like to wear, now that you're not—" She gestures, unable to find the words. "You know. Now that you can dress however you want, how do you want?"

"I don't know, Miss Steph. I really don't." I hear an edge of desperation creep in my voice. Even the tiniest things in the outside world are turning out to be so baffling and complicated.

She smiles reassuringly. "All right, sweetie, it's okay. Why don't you try on what we've got so far and see what you think?"

The changing room startles me when a huge, full-length mirror occupies most of one wall. At New Harmony mirrors of any kind were vanity, and even though I don't believe any of that stuff anymore, it still feels weird to see myself like that, and I turn my back to it. But then I keep whipping around, with the feeling that I'm going to catch someone behind me. It's always just the movement of my own reflection, caught in my peripheral vision. Eventually, I drape a long raincoat over the mirror.

I leave the room and show Steph my "yes" pile.

She frowns at my choices. "Really? Nothing but dark-colored flannel and sweatpants?"

"I'm sorry. I didn't mean to do it wrong."

"No, they're your clothes, it's fine. If I can get you into Saint Sebastian we'll shop for uniform pieces separately." She notices my look of confusion and smiles. "Sorry, Abby. Didn't we talk about this in the car? It's a girls' school not too far from here. I went there myself, after I managed to get myself suspended in New Orleans. I thought my parents were sending me to live with my grandma in Seattle and go to a girl's school as some kind of punishment, but I ended up loving it. I think we can get reduced or free tuition, and they do a customized curriculum that might work better for you, with your home-schooled background." She stops, frowns. "You were home-schooled, right?"

"I've never been to an outsider school, no." Father Wisdom often spoke about what he considered the evils of public schools, and I have the vague impression that they're a bit like church, only they talk about evolution and sex instead of God.

"That's what I thought. Anyway, a smaller private school will probably work better for you."

"But why do I have to go to school at all? I already know how to read and do sums. I was already teaching the younger kids…" I trail off, having just reminded myself of the last time I taught the younger New Harmony children, when Father Wisdom showed up and caught Ash flubbing her letter recognition.

"Abby, is something wrong?"

I take a deep breath, holding back a flood of emotion that threatens to break through. Not here. I put all that in the box.

"No, Miss Steph. I'm a little nervous, is all."

She gives me a quick hug. "Of course you are, sweetie. It's scary to do new things sometimes. But I think you'll like Saint Sebastian. Now, let's go look at housewares. We need some cheap stuff you can put in a microwave."

We study coffee mugs and dinner plates, when I notice something bright out of the corner of my eye. Painted pictures. We had a few of those while I was growing up, usually depictions of Bible events or images of Jesus. But these are pictures of strange landscapes, monsters, women in opulent gowns and skintight leather. Fiction books. That's what those are. Fantasies. Lies from the imagination of men and not the mind of Almighty God, Wisdom would say.

Furtively, I check the price sticker on a book with a cover that shows a spectacular fire-breathing dragon. It's fifty cents. I'm not sure I've got outsider finances entirely figured out, but that seems affordable.

"Miss Steph? Can I get a book?"

Absorbed in studying a teapot, she barely glances at me. "Sure thing. Get as many as you like."

I nod, and start to assemble a pile of books. As the pile grows, I feel more at ease. It's all right that I'm doing this. Books are just words. Anyway, my father is worlds away—

Without warning, his face is before me.

For half a second I'm sure he's really here, manifesting the mysterious spiritual powers he always alluded to having. He sees, he's watching, he knows. He's come to take me back, chastise me for leaving. In a moment of pure unreasoning revulsion, I take a step backward without looking where to place my foot.

The ground slides, as if a pit to hell is opening up ready to swallow me whole. My arms flail for balance, smacking right into a tall free-standing shelf. It rocks, threatens to tip over. I right myself and stabilize the shelf. I inhale, thinking for a moment that everything is going to be all right. Then dishes and glassware cascade down, exploding as they contact the unforgiving tile floor.

"Oh, no, Abby!" Steph turns toward me, her eyes wide. This whole disaster has played out in a few seconds, and now I stand still amid a rubble of broken dishes, afraid to move or touch anything. A young store employee appears and I wince, certain I'm about to get into trouble.

"What happened?" he asks.

I look down, to where I lost my footing. "I stepped on that." I gesture toward a small, wheeled toy. "I almost knocked over the shelf."

"Stay right there!" he orders. "Don't move. Let me get the glass cleaned up first."

"Abby, are you okay?" Steph asks, taking a step toward me.

"Don't get any closer, you'll track broken glass every-where," the employee tells Steph. She glares at him, but does what he says.

"I'm fine." Terror drains away, leaving behind shame and embarrassment. I can see exactly what happened, now. One of my father's books is on the shelf, back cover out, so I saw his face. The same book was in our library at New Harmony.

Steph follows my gaze to the book rack, and frowns. "What are you staring at over there? You look like me watching a big spider."

"My—" My voice breaks. I clear my throat. "My father. He wrote that book. *Perfect Obedience.* That's a picture of him, on the back."

"Really?" She plucks it off the shelf and frowns at it. "John Wise? Wait, I think I've heard of this guy. Back when I was a teenager, didn't he make a big deal out of predicting the end of the world? Some of my friends got really freaked out by it. Of course it didn't happen. It never does. I always wonder where guys like that go afterward."

"He changed his name to Wisdom in the Service of the

Lord, and took his family out to try to start a farm called New Harmony."

"Of course. He's Wisdom, you're Self-Abnegation. Some things are so predictable." She returns the book to the shelf. "You know, he really doesn't look much like you." She frowns at me. "Oh, Abby, you're bleeding."

I reach up, wipe dampness away from my forehead, see the bright smear of scarlet. "It's all right. It doesn't hurt."

We pay and leave. As we head back to the house, the misty rain grows slightly heavier, and Steph complains about the paper shopping bags. "Can you believe a city where it rains all the time passed a ban on plastic bags? These things are going to disintegrate on the way home." But the rain is so gentle that the little droplets seem to gather on the surface of the paper without soaking in.

We set our bags on the front porch while Steph unlocks the door. She picks up her own bag and heads inside, but I'm distracted by activity on the front porch of the house next door, and pause for a moment to make sense of it. They're taking down strings of lights and sparkly things in red and gold. Christmas decorations. At New Harmony we didn't celebrate Christmas, because it was pagan, but sometimes we would visit outsider churches that decorated for the season.

Oh, no. Our neighbors are the two men who passed us holding hands. The sodomites. Did they hear me call them that? Are they offended? They seem intent on their activity and I plan to slip into the house before they notice I'm here. But they have a pet, a small white poodle, and she's already picked me out. She runs to the edge of their porch and stands at attention, barking furiously in my direction. It's almost funny, because she's so small and fluffy. Still, her fury is a little alarming.

"Emily! Bad girl!" The darker-skinned of the two men comes up to grab the dog. "Sorry, miss. She's usually a better dog than that." He holds her trembling form and flashes me a white smile. He's not acting upset. Maybe he didn't hear what I said before. I hope he didn't.

I smile back. "It's okay. Her name is Emily?"

"Emily Barkinson, the poet," he says, with a grin. "You are new, yes? New neighbors?"

I nod. "I'm Abby."

"I am Paul Singha, and my husband there is Harold Davidson."

Husband? Did he really say husband? A sense of unreality overwhelms me, as if I'm imagining all this. It's a fantasy I'm having, as I sit in the hard New Harmony pews for hours on a Sunday, listening to a sermon about the men who burn with unnatural lusts toward each other and pervert God's plan for marriage. But these men seem so cozy, with their little dog and their Christmas lights.

"Nice to meet you," I tell Mr. Singha, and scurry inside the house.

"Abby? Who were you talking to out there?" Steph asks.

"The neighbors. They're nice. The two men we saw together before. They're married."

And I remembered not to say "sodomites."

4

THE GIRLS OF SAINT SEBASTIAN

"Y ou're going to be fine." Steph tucks my white Saint Sebastian shirt into the back of my black Saint Sebastian slacks. Both items have been washed, but remain strongly reminiscent of former owners and their laundry detergent. "The kids are going to make fun of you, but that's just what kids do, okay? It's nothing you did wrong."

"I know." Steph and Morgan decided that the best way to prepare me for this day was to give me a crash course in the mythology of the American high school as depicted in movies and television. So, I spent the last week or so learning about mean girls and queen bees and cliques that turn into witch-craft-practicing covens. I know about pranks and set-ups, nerds and jocks, popular and unpopular, and how mean prac-tical jokes are dangerous, because you might target a girl who turns out to have deadly telekinetic powers (Morgan showed me that one when Steph was at work). I know about lockers, homework, note-passing, crushes on cute boys, and cheer-leading camps that turn into bloodbaths (Morgan again).

When my father ranted about the evils of Hollywood, I never knew quite what to picture. I thought movies and televi-sion would be like our passion plays, except about wickedness instead of Bible stories. I never pictured lighting, and camera angles, and what they call special effects. But the strangest part is the way they have music all the way through. I can't always follow the stories, but it seems like the music is there to tell me how I'm supposed to feel about what's going on. Just because it sounds a certain way, the music can make me want to laugh, or cry, or cower, or jump around. It frightens me a little. It makes me worry that my father was right about one thing, that demons exist and can get at you through music. When the tunes go through my head later, I don't know what to make of them.

In spite of my confusion about the finer points of plot, I do get the underlying repeated message: some kids are mean to other kids, especially if they think those other kids are weird. We all know I'm going to seem weird. Raised out in the middle of nowhere, in a hyper-religious environment, far from the pop culture everyone else grew up immersed in, I won't talk like them or get their jokes. I'm small and freckled and not very pretty, and I don't know how to wear makeup and polish my nails. My hair is in a buzz cut that makes me look, as Morgan so elegantly puts it, like a plucked chicken, and its fierce red color clashes with the burgundy of my Saint Sebastian uniform jacket. I'm exactly the kind of kid they target. Steph and Morgan have been trying to warn me. I'm as prepared as I can be, but I'm scared, too.

Steph begins walking me to Saint Sebastian. My outsider tennis shoes still feel like bricks strapped to my feet, but it's cold and damp outside, so I wouldn't enjoy going barefoot either. We don't talk much. I think she's almost as nervous as I am. Then, abruptly, when we're still well away from the school, she stops and kisses me on the top of the head. "I'm going to let you go the rest of the way on your own. You just keep going down this street for a few blocks. You can't miss it."

"What? Don't you have to come along and help me sign papers and things?"

She smiles. "I already did all that, kiddo. Anyway, trust me, it will not help you fit in if the kids see your aunt walking you to school. Even your cool Aunt Steph."

She hugs me. "Before you go, this was mine when I was a student here." Into my hands she presses a number of small round stones, smooth and cool to the touch. I look down and see that I hold a necklace of deep, rich blues and greens and reds. "The beads are only semi-precious, but I always thought they were pretty."

"They are, thank you." I hold the necklace up to the light and see that it has a cross dangling from it. More than a cross, a crucifix, the kind of cross that shows Jesus dying on it. The kind Catholics use. I swallow over a lump of panic. Of course. This is a Catholic school. How did I miss that before? The "Saint" name should have tipped me off. I can hear my father's voice shouting: *Papists! Idolaters! Blasphemers! Witches! Flesh eaters!*

I don't believe any of that. But I'm still worried. Are they going to expect me to know how to do Catholic things?

Steph grins. "You've never seen a rosary before, have you?"

"Not in real life." Although they figured prominently in some of the spooky movies Morgan showed me, which does nothing to lessen my apprehension.

"Well, you don't have to do anything special with it. Nobody is going to make you pray the rosary if you don't want to. It's just, all the other girls will have one of their own, and I thought maybe you should too."

"Thank you." I move to put it on, and she stops me, with a small laugh. "Sorry, sweetie, you don't wear it. Not at school, anyway. Keep it in your pocket or bag."

The rosary goes into my jacket pocket, reminding me fleetingly of the lock of Ash's hair. The stones clink together in a way that seems oddly satisfying. More hugs, then Steph leaves. I'm really on my own now.

As I get closer to the school, I start to notice more girls in Saint Sebastian uniform. They walk in small groups of twos and threes, most of them wearing the skirt variant, with knee socks. They seem like they must be cold, but maybe they're used to the weather here. They have long, straight hair, and their faces are made up. Clouds of perfume hover in the air behind them, and I sneeze a couple of times passing through their wake. If they recognize me as a new student, they give no sign. In fact, they give no sign they notice me at all. So far so good.

The school is a stately brick building, huge trees enclosing the landscaped grounds. I step outside of the crowd for a moment to get my class schedule and map out of my backpack, study it before stepping through the front doors, which are swung wide open. To the left side of the entrance, a glossy white statue of a robed, smiling woman welcomes me with her arms outstretched. On the right, a white statue of Jesus opens his heart to me. Is it really all right that I'm doing this? A sense of unreality overwhelms me.

I cross the threshold. Nothing happens.

I make my way to the first classroom on the list. A woman is seated at the desk at the front of the room. She looks like an ordinary woman except for the veil over her hair, marking her, I think, as a nun. I stand in front of her for a while, but she doesn't look up. I clear my throat. She glances at me. "Can I help you?"

"I'm Abby Marchande." We gave me Steph's last name for all the forms, but now the lie makes me nervous. What would happen if the teacher found me out? Steph seems to think that private schools are allowed to be lackadaisical about that kind of paperwork, but I don't think she really knows.

"Oh. Right. New girl. Let's see, that desk by the window is open, second row from the back. Why don't you sit there?"

I take the seat, not reassured by her manner. She wasn't mean, but she wasn't friendly, either. She barely seemed to realize I was there. I study the other students as they enter, try to watch them without obvious staring. Pretty girls with shiny hair, tall athletic-looking girls, sullen girls with dark-dyed hair and a reek of cigarette smoke, all of them seem to find their own groups, eyes flickering across a sea of indifferent faces until they spy a friendly one, then smiles and words of greeting. But if any of them notice me, they give no sign.

This is what they call my homeroom class, and we study Washington State history. This feels familiar. We studied American history at New Harmony, reading from one massive book called *A True and Complete History of the United States*. The book *History of Washington State* is very much like that, without the references to God.

Pre-Algebra is my next class. The girls seem different here, most of them obviously younger than I am, but one girl seems older. She glares at me with fierce sullenness through limp brown bangs. She's tall and broadly built, seeming to overflow the confines of her desk. I was disturbed to be invisible, but now I'm disturbed to be noticed.

In my next class, English Literature 3, I'm completely invisible again. Invisible at lunch, I read a book about dragons and eat a peanut butter and jelly sandwich that I made. Invisible in physical education, I tuck myself into the corner to change into exercise clothes, hoping that, naked, I stay invisible.

If the instructors didn't say a few words to me now and then, telling me where to sit, giving me assignments, I would suspect I was being Shunned. Shunning was both the least painful and the most painful correction we had at New Harmony. The idea was simple: everyone had to pretend you didn't exist. Most Shunnings lasted a day or two, but once I was Shunned for an entire moon. If I spoke, they ignored me. If they saw me, they would unfocus their eyes and pretend they couldn't see I was there. They brushed my touch away as if I were an annoying fly. I ate the gleanings of the fields, wilted leaves and moldy fruit. A

Shunned sister or brother was a ghost, a wind, a shadow. By the end of the moon, I began to fear I really was dead.

I'm almost relieved when I finally get a bit of genuine bullying. As I'm changing from gym clothes back to the uniform, the girl who glared at me in math seeks me out in my corner and makes a point of looming over me. "Hey, new girl. Are you shy?" She lingers on the word "shy," in what seems to be an attempt to make shyness sound like something to be embarrassed about.

It strikes me as a stupid question, but I answer honestly. "Yes."

"Hey everybody!" she barks out to the room, pointing at me. "The new girl is shy. She doesn't want us to look at her." Some of the girls glance over and laugh, but in an offhanded way. They don't seem interested in joining her to gang up on me. "What are you shy about, new girl? Is it your gross freckles? Or your complete lack of tits?"

I think about what I learned in the movies. If you don't respond they get bored and go away. I shrug.

"How old are you supposed to be anyway? I thought you were fifteen but you look twelve." Steph told me the same thing, but she was full of sympathy, assuming it was from misfortune. This girl acts like it's a personal failing, which is so ridiculous I can do nothing but stare at her for a moment. "What are you staring at? You feeble-minded too? I bet you're a retard." She grabs my shoulder. "Retard. Why don't you talk?"

I slap her hand away, which makes a startling sharp clap. "Don't touch me." My voice comes out in a shout. My heart pounds. Am I angry, or afraid? I can't even tell.

The gym teacher rushes over. "Hey! Are you girls fighting?"

"She started it."

The teacher looks from her to me and back again. She

folds her arms and shakes her head. "Lorinda. Abby. You two stay away from each other or I'm sending you both to the principal's office."

Lorinda smirks at me, apparently pleased at her power to get us both in trouble. I go to my last two classes of the day fighting to suppress the smoldering outrage of the unjustly accused.

At the end of the school day, my backpack is bursting with books and papers to carry home, and I have a few more in my arms, wrapped in a plastic bag in case it begins raining again. I pass a group of girls in black and white and burgundy, Saint Sebastian girls. One calls out, and I tense, apprehensive of more bullying.

"Hey, new kid. You got a cigarette?" Her voice is low and crisp. She has dyed-black hair and darkly made up eyes, several facial piercings, colorful tattoos peeking out from the edges of her sweater.

I smile nervously. "I'm sorry, I don't smoke."

"Don't be sorry. Smoking sucks." She laughs. One of the other girls hands her a cigarette, which she lights, with a burst of sulfur and smoke. "Where you from anyway? You got kind of an accent."

"Louisiana."

"What? No way. That's not a southern accent. You from New Orleans?"

"Near there. But not the city. More of a farm."

"She's from gator-rasslin' country," says one of the other girls, and they all laugh. Are they making fun of me? It seems like it, except their eyes aren't mean, not like Lorinda.

"Hey, yeah. You ever watch Swamp People, new girl?"

"I'm sorry, no."

"You're always sorry. What are you so sorry about?"

"I don't know." My heart is pounding now. She's definitely making fun of me. Isn't she? I feel surrounded. "I'm sorry, I've got to go." I start walking away, the sound of their laughter and the stench of cigarettes trailing after me.

When Steph asks me how I liked my first day of school, I tell her it was fine.

IN A MATTER OF DAYS, MY WORLD TURNED COMPLETELY UPSIDE-down. But, now that things have changed, each day passes much like the day before: school, housework, homework. Everything in Seattle that once seemed terrifying or magical becomes routine, then dull. Grocery stores with vast arrays of food and fresh produce even in the winter? No big deal. A kitchen stocked with food nearly all the time? Ho-hum. Central heating? Of course. Electric lights? Trivial. If I feel like it, I can make tea every day. Assuming the pipes are work-ing, I can shower in hot water every day. Every night I sleep on a real padded mattress, under a big pile of clean blankets, in my own private room. That's just life, isn't it? Of course I have my own mobile phone, read fantasy novels instead of the Bible, find myself surrounded by rock music, television, the Internet. Why did these things ever seem so amazing?

Of course our next-door neighbors are two men married to each other. That's just how things are out here, right?

At some point, I realize I have genuinely stopped waiting for the beasts and demons to show up.

LATE ONE SATURDAY NIGHT, STEPH COMES HOME FROM WORK to find me at the kitchen table. "Hey, kiddo, what're you still doing up?" She sets a pint of chocolate chip ice cream on the kitchen table and eases herself into the chair across from me. I can tell by her movements that she's starting to find her pregnancy awkward, belly too heavy and always in the way. Her due date is soon, I think.

"Studying." I sweep my hand to indicate the piles of textbooks and notebooks spread before me on the table.

"Oh, honey." She reaches out to ruffle my hair, now about five inches long, and completely unruly. At New Harmony it would have been bound up in a head scarf. Steph keeps offering sprays and gels to tame it, but the perfumes make me sneeze, and I don't like the way they make my hair feel like it's made out of plastic. "Are you having trouble in your classes? Do we need to get you a tutor or something?"

"No, I'm fine. I just need to study harder, I think."

She frowns. "Abby, please. If you're staying up until two in the morning on a Saturday, there's no harder you can study. Look, I know you're shy, but if you're having trouble in school, you need to speak up."

I sigh, force a little smile, and lie. "I know. I will." She likes to tell me I should stand up for myself, let my teachers know when I don't understand, let my fellow students know when they bother me. But I can't even manage to tell Steph how impossible I would find it to do any of that.

"Hey, you want some ice cream?" She gets two spoons, and opens the carton, pushing it to the middle of the table halfway between us. I accept one of the spoons, even though I don't want any ice cream. I'm pretty sure she's planning to eat the whole pint herself, and wants me to have a spoon so that later she can tell herself we shared it.

"Is school going well, otherwise?" she asks. "Are you getting along? Making friends?"

"Yeah. It's good. School is good." I lie again, gently, without enthusiasm. I think of Cigarette Girl, who has called out to me a few times since that first day, but I'm still not sure if she's trying to make friends or trying to make fun of me. Lorinda sometimes goes out of her way to bump into me exaggeratedly, then pretend it was an accident. That's about it for my social interaction.

"Well, if you have friends, you should do something with them. Movies, go to the mall—do kids still go to the mall? You ever been to the mall?"

"I don't think so. When we went shopping, was that the mall?"

She laughs. "No, honey, that was a thrift store. Anyway, you don't have to go to the mall, that was just one idea. You could go to a movie, or an all-ages rock concert, or anything you want."

Anything I want. What do I want? At New Harmony we were never supposed to want anything except what God wanted us to want, which is to say, what Wisdom claimed God wanted us to want. I tried to want that, and failed. I wanted to save my mother and my sister, and I failed at that too. Then I wanted to leave, and now I'm here. This is the only thing I ever got right.

I take her hand. "Steph, I want to do well in school. You told me that was how people succeed in the outside world."

"Oh, honey, that's not—I never meant for you to stay up all night doing homework. When I said school was important, I meant that it was important to do your best. I didn't want you repeating my mistakes."

I wonder if she's thinking the baby was a mistake. She's never talked to me about the details, not much more than she told that cop the night we met. George showed his true colors by hitting her, she divorced him, and a few weeks later found out she was pregnant. But I wonder why she kept the baby. Because she was raised Catholic? Or did she want to have a baby, even if it was half George?

"Ouch!" She drops the spoon and begins to massage her belly. "Tadpole's started to kick. Maybe he doesn't like chocolate."

"Maybe he kicks because he does like it."

"Maybe so." She gives me a long, thoughtful look. "I know what you're thinking. Yes, George was a mistake. Only I thought he wasn't a mistake at the time. I thought I was finally doing something right. I met him through somebody I knew from AA, that's Alcoholics Anonymous. I only went to one of the meetings, though. I hated it. You have to stand up in front of everyone and say, 'My name is Steph, and I'm an alcoholic.' It didn't seem right. I didn't want to be an alcoholic, you know? Like it was my identity? I just wanted to not drink so much.

"I don't blame Sheila, that's the friend from AA. She didn't know George very well. She thought he seemed like a nice guy, and he was a nondrinker, so she invited me and him out with her husband for an alcohol-free double date. It was my own fault that I said yes when George asked me out again. He always made it really easy to say yes. But the whole thing lasted only two years. We dated, we went to Vegas and got married, we moved to Baton Rouge, we started trying to have a baby. I told myself I was finally getting real, acting like a grown-up, but really I was letting him make all the decisions. I was barely there. Wait, I have a picture." She pulls out her phone, taps at it, then shows me.

In the picture she looks diminished, her body small, her hair small, her makeup small, her clothes small, all tattoos covered. She's smiling with pink, pretend-natural lips, but the smile doesn't reach her eyes. Next to her, a crude splotch of black hovers. It's creepy, like an evil spirit. She laughs. "I kept this one because I was so skinny there. I lost a lot of weight at first when I stopped drinking. Then when I got pregnant it all came right back." She puts the phone away. "Anyway, one day he comes home from work and says he thinks I should go to the doctor, that I might be infertile. We'd been trying for a year at that point. Honestly I'd kind of forgotten that we were supposed to be trying to have a baby. The relationship wasn't so great by then, and I was already thinking about divorce. So that pushed me to make a decision. I told him point blank that I didn't want to have a baby with him anymore. That's when he hit me. It was the strangest thing. It wasn't like he lost control or anything. He didn't even seem mad. He just decided to hit me, then he did."

"Right. He was chastising you," I say, to show I understand, but she gives me a look of such utter perplexity that I know I've said something strange. "I mean, that's how my father did it. He didn't chastise us when he was full of wrath, because wrath is one of the deadly sins. He was training us to obey."

Her frown deepens. "Abby? Were you hit a lot by your father?"

"Not hit. He never used his hand. The hand is the instrument of fatherly love, so you must never chasten with the hand. You use the rod—" I break off. Her unhappy stare is making me feel disoriented. I don't want to be talking about this. "You didn't like it. I didn't like it either. So we left. Right?"

She nods. "Right. George hit me, but he didn't give me any legal trouble. We went to Vegas again, and got a divorce just as quick as the wedding. I was already back home and staying with my parents in New Orleans, when I started feeling lousy in the mornings, almost like I was drinking again. Then I started feeling all bloated, like my period was coming, only it didn't.

"My mama figured it out. I thought I was all secret with the home pregnancy test, but apparently not secret enough. She was so thrilled. It was grandbaby this and grandbaby that. I told her over and over that I didn't want George to know about the baby, and she agreed not to tell him. But she must've spilled the beans, or George might have been stalking me. Anyway, he shows up at my parents' door all apologetic and friendly, telling me everything that went wrong in the marriage was his fault, wanting to take me to the fanciest restaurant in town. I almost fell for it. But something had changed. It was like I was seeing him clear for the first time, how he was always putting on an act, lying and trying to manipulate people.

"He said he'd pay for an ultrasound, so we got one. That's when things got really bizarre. He asked, 'is it a boy?' and the techs said it was too early to tell, and he said, 'but do you think it's a boy?' They went on like that for a while. Afterward he took me out to another nice dinner and kept talking about 'our son.' The next day he took me to spend the night in a fancy hotel, and I just knew, he was going to propose again. All romantic this time, none of that weekend in Vegas stuff. When he pulled out the ring, a real diamond, suddenly it all made sense. And it made me so mad. I told him, you don't love me, you just think I'm a walking incubator for your precious son. Well, he's not your son. He's my son, and I'm going to keep him far away from you.

"He was mad then, but cold, like a snake. I tried to leave, but he grabbed my arm and threw me down on the floor. That's when I realized how strong he was. He didn't really look like such a big guy, but I could feel that if he wanted to hurt me, there wasn't much I could do. I got scared. I thought he was going to kill me for sure. But he let me be. He said, 'You can't keep my son from me forever,' and walked out. Then I got it figured. He wasn't going to hurt me while I was still pregnant with his precious son. But afterward, who knows? That scared me bad. I threw some things into the car and set out that very night. I didn't even tell my parents I was leaving, just called them from the road."

She finishes the story and the ice cream, setting the empty carton on the table. "Anyway, that's why I think he might come after me. Because he has this weird obsession with having a son."

"But you still don't know for sure it's a boy."

She shakes her head. "I started consulting with a midwife

here in town. We got another ultrasound. And it turns out George was right. I am having a boy."

She grimaces, and puts a hand on her upper belly. "Ugh, Abby, why did you let me eat all the ice cream?"

"You told me not to let you drink alcohol, not to not let you eat too much ice cream."

She laughs, and pushes her chair back from the table. Then she stops, a look of intense pain on her face, but a little smile too. She braces both hands against the table and breathes heavily. "Oh, God, Abby, I don't think this is the ice cream. I think it's the baby."

5

TERRANCE ANDREW MARCHANDE, 7.3 POUNDS

"This is going to turn into a sitcom episode where I give birth in the parking garage in the back of the car, isn't it?" Steph says. But of course nothing like that happens. I call the Capitol Hill Birthing Center, and they take over with practiced smoothness. The journey from first labor pains to Steph holding little Terrance Andrew Marchande, 7.3 pounds and a full head of dark curly hair, is swift and, for childbirth, relatively painless.

Of course, that's the last easy thing about having Terry in our lives.

For his first two weeks out in the world, he rarely stops crying. Sometimes it's a siren wail, a passionate endless howl. Sometimes it's a gentle whimper, with a look of infant distress that threatens to erupt in noise at any moment. The midwife tells us he has colic and will grow out of it when his gut bacteria adjust to life in the outside world. Morgan gets a restoration job that takes him out the house a lot. Steph seems dazed and haggard. Caring for Terry falls on me, much of the time. Visceral reminders of caring for my sister Ash keep overwhelming me: holding a baby, feeding a baby from a bottle, changing a baby's diaper. I open the box to check on her lock of hair, make sure it still exists and smells of her. Is this my atonement? Caring for a new and much more difficult baby?

The cleanliness of the house begins to deteriorate. So does my school performance.

Whenever the rain lets up, I put Terry in a sling and take him for walks around the neighborhood. Outside, his cries seem to blend in with the noises of the urban environment: rushing traffic, mournful seagulls, barking dogs, music thump-thumping out of the dance clubs. In spite of everything, right this moment, I feel happy. The air smells sweet and rich and intensely green. I can feel the approach of summer. The ground is still muddy and the sky gray, but the yards have exploded with flowers and greenery, the vacant lots turned to a jungle riot of vines and bushes. I walk Terry up to the highest part of the hill, where we stand under graceful metal towers, red lights blinking a warning. The sun drops below the clouds, its light bathing everything in gold. A crow glides past, black wings spread out majestically. I spin around to show Terry Seattle from every angle.

"We're on top of the world, top of the world," I sing at him. "What does the crow say? Caw! Caw!" Distracted, he stops wailing, and I spin him some more, feeling I've won some kind of victory.

The back of my neck prickles, and I whirl around. A man stands on the sidewalk, his back to the setting sun and his face in shadow. He seems an ordinary man, in a gray suit and a hat, the kind of man I see downtown where the skyscrapers are. A lawyer, or an accountant. But why is he staring at me? My heart begins to thump and I clutch Terry closer. He senses my distress, and whimpers.

The man tilts his hat, gives me a little bow. He says, "Sorry to be caught staring, miss. I thought you looked familiar, but now I don't think we've met, after all." His accent is courtly, very southern, Texas?

"That's okay," I reply, out of habit. I tense up, certain that something terrible is about to happen. This is finally it, the urban crime that Morgan is always warning about, the reason he tells me I should carry a gun. This is the disaster at last. This man is the beast.

But he simply walks away, continuing down the sidewalk. I watch until he's out of sight, then head home. I was being paranoid. He thought he knew me. That kind of thing happens every day in a big city, doesn't it?

Still, I'm determined to tell Steph and Morgan about it when I get home. But back at the house, two people I don't know are sitting on the porch. They look harmless enough: a tall woman with black hair and a short, dark-skinned man, both of them dressed in nice casual garb. But when the woman rushes me, heading straight for Terry with her arms spread out, my instinct is to step back and keep him away from her.

"Who are you?" I demand.

The woman gathers herself up, affronted. "Who am I? Who are you? That's my grandbaby you got there, hand him over!" Her words, plus her accent, clue me in finally. These must be Steph's parents. The woman looks a little like an older, heavier version of Steph, and sounds a bit like Steph did when she imitated her Cajun grandmother telling the rougarou story.

"Of course." I maneuver Terry out of his sling and pass him to the woman. The movement wakes him and he starts wailing, the siren wail, with his little face all screwed up and scarlet. Steph's mother starts bouncing him up and down, chucking him under the chin, cooing, trying to calm him.

"How do you do, miss? I'm Roderick Marchande, and this is my wife Emalee." The man comes forward, with a bright smile, to shake my hand. He's much darker-skinned than Steph and Morgan, and has a different accent. A Seattle accent, I guess. He was raised in this house.

"I'm Abby."

Mrs. Marchande glares at me. Terry has not stopped wailing. "You that au pair girl Steph told me about?"

Au pair? I think that's like a nanny. "Yes. I help take care of the baby."

"Where is that girl Stephanie at, anyway? And my boy Morgan?"

"They're both at work, ma'am. Morgan should be home in a bit, but Steph won't be back until late. Did they know you were coming?"

"Not back until late?" Mrs. Marchande harrumphs. "Is she working in a bar again? I thought she was gonna get herself out of that scene."

"It's more of a restaurant, really. Why don't you come inside?" I unlock the door and usher them in, suddenly conscious of the neglected state of the house, dust and food waste and that persistent odor of diaper pail and air freshener it seems impossible to do anything about. "Would you like something to drink?"

"You got a beer?" her father asks.

"I'm sorry, no." But truthfully I don't know if Morgan might have a beer stashed away somewhere. He's been good about that, about not drinking in front of Steph, ever since that first day with the cooking sherry. But he does spend a lot of time in the basement.

I move some newspapers off the couch and stack them in the corner, freshly conscious of the lack of furniture in here. Most of their grandmother's things have been sold, except for a few pieces too big and awkward to move easily. The only place to sit, other than cross-legged on the rug, is a mammoth couch in brown leather. In spite of its size, it only seats two adults comfortably.

I move some folding chairs from the kitchen into the living room, and sit down. We stare at each other awkwardly for a few moments, while Terry cries. Then Mrs. Marchande stands up. "I'm taking the baby for a walk, now. Get him calmed down." She glares at me, as if his wailing is my fault, and leaves the house.

"I'm sorry," Mr. Marchande says. "That wasn't actually about you." I nod, and we stare at each other awkwardly for another while. Then he asks, "Do you like jazz, Abby?"

I answer honestly. "I don't know, sir."

"Well, why don't we have a listen, then?" He opens his bag to pull out a phone and a pair of small, flat speakers. The phone connects to the speakers, and soon we're hearing music, which I guess must be jazz. Mr. Marchande keeps up a low murmur of explanation about it, the instruments we're hearing, the name and history of the musicians. I've never figured out how I feel about music. It still seems strange that it has the power to summon such strong emotions from nothing but noise. If there are any mysterious spiritual powers in the world, music is the only sign of them I've seen.

"...how I ended up in New Orleans," he says.

Embarrassed, I realize I lost the thread of what he was saying. In New Harmony, it merited a serious chastisement if we were caught with our minds wandering. Lucky for me, I know how to cover that up. "That's fascinating, sir," I say.

He laughs. "Sir! Listen to that. Do you have any idea what I just said?"

"You were talking about how you ended up in New Orleans."

He folds his arms in mock sternness. "And how did I end up there?"

My heart pounds. Shoot. Time for an educated guess. "Jazz music?"

He shakes his head, laughing. "You're good at this, kid. You'll do well in college. Yes, it was jazz music. When I was in high school, our jazz band spent a year earning the money to go to New Orleans and march in one of the Mardi Gras parades. When our plane touched down at Louis Armstrong International, it was the farthest away from home I'd ever been. I had no idea what to expect. But it was—I mean, we were still in the airport, and there was already—" He gestures with his hands, as if trying to explain something he doesn't have the words for. "It was amazing. Music everywhere. The air hums with it. Makes the hairs on your arm stand up like there's a ghost in the room. All kinds of jazz, all kinds of blues, funk, soul, gospel, zydeco, African, Caribbean, things I can't even describe, and they've got the pop and the rock like you've got everywhere. It's like the city is a heart, and it beats with the music. It sounds crazy, I know, but I got off that plane and fell in love. I knew someday I had to go back to New Orleans and play music there."

"Wow." I stare at him, heart jumping in my throat, and ask a question I've been dying to ask somebody, "Do you think music has some kind of supernatural power?"

"Oh, yeah. You bet." He answers without hesitation.

"But—" I search for the right way to ask, and settle on the wrong way. "Isn't that bad?"

He raises his eyebrows. "Bad in what way?"

Demonic. But I can't say that. Steph says it makes me sound like a nutty TV preacher. "Demonic. I mean, not that I'm saying you're demonic yourself. That's not what I mean."

He smiles, full of pity, and takes my hand. His palms are warm, callused and very dry. He pats me reassuringly. "Somebody's messed with your head pretty good. Music has spiritual power, that's true. But demonic? No way. You tell me, how do you know the difference between a demon and an angel?"

I try to recall everything Wisdom had to say on the topic. "I guess I don't know. My father always talked about things being demonic. Nothing was angelic except—" My throat closes off for a moment. I cough. "My mother. He called her an angel sometimes. Especially after she died."

He squeezes my hand. "I'm sorry you lost your mother young. I grew up without a father, but I never had to lose him. He was already long gone." Another squeeze, and he turns his attention to the phone for a moment, fingers moving over the screen. Abruptly the music changes, and he turns back to me with a twinkle in his eyes. "How about a little Mahalia Jackson? If you're worried about what kind of spirit is in the music, you can always listen to some gospel. That way you know it's got to be the spirit of Jesus." He looks so amused, I'm worried that he's making fun of me. He thinks my concerns are absurd. But that's okay, don't I think my concerns are absurd?

"It's nice." I smile at him in return, sincerely. I do like it. I like the singer's voice, its richness and warmth, the way it caresses the tune.

"Now, if you want to know what I think—do you want to know what I think?" I nod. "Okay. I know power can be dangerous. But it's like the sun. You've got that pale skin, right? You know if you lie out there in the sun with no protection, you'll burn right up. But that doesn't make the sun a demon. Without it, there would be no life on this earth. So I think the sun is a good thing. And I think the power in music is a good thing. What does it say in the Bible? By their fruits you shall know them? Nothing's bad just sitting there minding its own business. A devil does bad things. An angel does good things. And we're human, so, sometimes we're angels, and sometimes we're devils. I try to be an angel if I can. So, now, what do you think about all that?"

What do I think? I think I'm still not used to the way outsiders are always asking for my opinion. I nod. "Of course. That makes a lot of sense."

He laughs. "You don't have to flatter me, kid."

Footsteps on the porch and the door opens. We stand up. Morgan stands in the doorway and goggles at his father for a moment, then shouts out, "Dad! Is Mama around? What are you doing here?" They embrace, then pull back.

"We drove up with the trailer. It's parked in back while I play a couple of gigs in town. Emalee's taking the baby for a walk." He drops his head and gets a conspiratorial look. "Son, I don't know what your sister told you about it, but she and your mother haven't been getting along so well. A lot of angry phone calls, then she stopped taking your mother's calls at all. She sent a text when the baby was born. A text! You did not want to be in our house when that happened."

"It had a photo, Dad. I don't see the problem."

"The problem is that your mother is a little old-fashioned. A text with a photo is fine, so long as you also get the phone call. You see what I'm saying? She interpreted the lack of phone call as a snub. Are you telling me she's wrong?"

"Okay, fine, you're right. It was a snub. But it's Mama's fault. She's the one who keeps trying to push George and Steph back together."

Mr. Marchande nods. "Of course. I didn't say Stephanie was wrong to be upset. But I think it's time they patched things up, now. Don't you?"

Mrs. Marchande comes back, Terry sleeping in her arms. "We're all going to take the baby down to that restaurant to see my daughter," she announces. She points at me. "You come along, now, au pair girl, and keep him quiet."

Steph's parents stick around for a week. Everyone seems to get along with everyone, and the name of George is not mentioned. Her mother warms up to me eventually, I think. She stops glaring at me, anyway, and is quick to hand the baby over if he's crying or needs a diaper changed. On their last night in town, Steph's father takes us to a fancy jazz club where he seems to know everyone and the staff won't let us pay for anything. I catch Steph staring longingly as everyone else in her family gets free drinks. Finally she grabs Morgan's beer and takes a sip.

"Steph, no!" I blurt out.

She glares at me. "Abby, I'm not pregnant anymore, it's okay if I have a drink."

"But—" Does this mean our contract is ended? I never thought about that before. Steph agreed to take care of me. I agreed to not let her drink while she was pregnant. But she's no longer pregnant. Will it hurt the baby now if she drinks? "You're nursing."

"It's okay to have a couple of drinks and then nurse. I asked the midwife." She tries for a sunny smile. "It's all right, Abby. Don't look at me like that. One drink is all I'm going to have."

I glance around at her family, at the table. They look troubled, but nobody says anything. I don't know what Steph's life was like, before she started trying to drink less, before she met George, before she got pregnant. I don't know if her having this one drink is a bad thing or not. I take another sip of my Shirley Temple, a pink and intensely sweet soda that begins to stick in the back of my throat. I spoke up, didn't I? If she doesn't think the bargain applies anymore, what can I do about it?

Early the next morning Steph's parents leave, with many hugs and promises to stay in touch.

"They got that video conference thing now that you can use, on the Internets," Steph's mother says. "Some of the ladies at church, they see their grandbabies that way every week. Works from anywhere. You gotta get that thing set up now." She points at me. "Get that little girl there to help you. The kids today, they know all about that stuff, yeah?"

Steph and I exchange a glance and a suppressed giggle. No matter how many times we told her mother that I was raised on a farm with almost no modern technology, she can't seem to remember that I'm not exactly a "kid today." Steph seems to get it, but maybe that's because she knew me before, brief as it was. She saw me in the long, pink old-fashioned dress, heard me give my name as Self-Abnegation in the

Service of the Lord. She asks me about my past sometimes—
little things, like did my father hit me a lot, or do I know about
tampons—but I don't want to talk about it, and mostly she
respects that. Still, if our bargain is over, what does that mean?
Do we have a new bargain, based on me taking care of the
baby? Or will she expect me to go back where I came from?

No, I'm never going back. Not even if Steph wants me to
leave.

Steph's father presses a small device into my hand. "There
you go. It's all loaded up with some of my favorite music I
think you might like. You listen to that and when we come
back around here, you can tell me what you think about the
spirit in the music."

"What is it?" I study the device but it doesn't look like
anything I've seen before. It's a tiny square of red-tinted
metal, with a round control in the middle. I do recognize the
tiny earphones hanging off of it. "It plays music?"

He starts laughing. "It sure does." He laughs some more.
"Kids. Hah. A few years ago this was the hot new thing, now
you don't even know what it is."

"It's an iPod," Steph says. "It plays music like my phone,
but music is all it does, and it doesn't connect to the Internet,
so you have to load all the files on there. But see how small it
is? You can clip to your sweatshirt and listen while you move
around." She demonstrates.

"Thank you." More hugs, and they take off. We wave
goodbye to their departing trailer. Morgan glances up at the
sky, a pale early-morning blue. "It's supposed to be good
weather today, for once."

Steph, holding Terry, shivers. "Really? But it feels so cold."

"That's the dew, the dampness. Always makes it feel
colder, but it'll warm up later. You think you girls will be okay
on your own tonight if I go out to the cabin?"

She makes a scoffing noise. "Of course we'll be okay. Why
wouldn't we be okay?"

He shrugs. "I don't know. I figured you'd tell me. With the folks gone, it's going to seem pretty quiet around here."

Steph snorts laughter. "What, nobody around to critique my housekeeping? That's the kind of quiet I like."

The morning does warm up as promised. By the time Morgan leaves for the mountains, the sun is strong and feels almost hot. Steph and I take Terry for a walk through the neighborhood. Everybody has a dog, it seems, a neat little apartment-sized big-city dog: pugs and toy poodles and needle-like whippets and one dog that looks like a miniature husky. Most of the dogs ignore us, or point noses in our direction for one sniff and then move on. But one tiny white poodle comes tearing out of a local park, yipping at my heels at the top of her lungs.

Emily. The dog next door. I remember her. She's terrified of me. I can tell this in her scent. It never occurred to me before that sometimes dogs act like that, very aggressive, because they're afraid.

"Emily, no!" Mr. Singha emerges from the park and lunges to scoop her into his arms, where she trembles, whining slightly. "Sorry, miss. I don't know why she is such a monster to you. She really is a good dog most of the time."

He turns back and joins Mr. Davidson—his husband, I must remember that—on a spread-out blanket, picnic basket between them. Mr. Davidson waves, but stiffly. I think he must have been bothered by the sodomites comment, even if Mr. Singha wasn't. It makes me want to go over and confess everything, tell them about my strange upbringing, tell them I'm sorry, that I didn't know any better. But it would sound like I was making excuses.

Steph and I stop for ice cream, iced coffee, window shopping, listening to street musicians. Terry doesn't cry once, and I start to feel almost giddy with happiness. But as morning meanders into afternoon, the weather turns moist and sticky. The blue sky fades to bright white, and the sun disappears, but it stays hot. Sweat trickles under my arms. Then the sky darkens, and I notice a pinching ache at the center of my forehead.

"This feels like a thunderstorm coming."

Steph shrugs. "Morgan told me they don't get them in Seattle very often, but they probably do sometimes. We can start heading back home."

The wind picks up, blowing first one way and then another. A couple of fat, heavy raindrops splat against my face. Above us, the sky has gone entirely purple-black, an uncanny color that fills me with a dreadful anticipation. I feel tense, afraid, for no reason I can point to. Even if it is a thunderstorm, I'm not afraid of those. Am I?

A flash of light, gone in an instant, then thunder engulfs us, a vast rolling, like boulders grinding against each other. All at once the scattered raindrops gang up into a downpour, and everyone on the sidewalk scurries and splashes for shelter.

Home is only a few blocks away, but the heavy rain soaks us down to the skin long before we get there. Terry whimpers as Steph tries to shelter him under her coat. On the porch we shake ourselves off like dogs getting out of the water. Again, the lightning flashes and the thunder rumbles over us. Terry starts wailing as we head inside.

"I hate thunderstorms." Steph hands Terry to me, and rushes around turning on every light, and the television. She grabs a big towel and begins rubbing off her ruined makeup and drying her hair. The scent of her favorite hairspray bursts forth, reminding me keenly of the first time I smelled it, the night we met, when I assumed it was perfume. Outside, the flashes get closer together. The thunder seems like a solid thing above, ready to crush us. Then, a flash so intense and bright that Steph yelps. We hear a cracking, popping sound in addition to the thunder, and all the lights blink off. Steph yelps, then shouts, "Damn it! We got hit by lightning! The lightning hit us!"

We head out to the porch and see that the lights on the entire block are dark. Mr. Davidson appears on the porch next door, peering out into the rain. "I think that last stroke must've hit a transformer or something."

"I bet it did." Steph seems calmer, although Terry is still very upset, his wailing turning to a desolate hiccoughing cry.

"Are you going to need candles or anything over there?"

"No, thank you, we're good. My brother has camping equipment."

The storm gradually dies out as the afternoon wears on. Steph falls asleep on the couch, holding Terry, both of them snoring lightly. I find myself too restless to do anything except pace aimlessly through the house, like a dog waiting for its master to come home.

"Oh, no, I have to get ready for work," Steph calls out. "Abby, why did you let me sleep so long? Is the power back on yet?" She stands up and passes me Terry without waiting for an answer. He remains asleep while I put him to bed. Steph dashes around, getting dressed and putting on makeup by the light of a single cinnamon-scented candle. The strong, chemical perfume makes my eyes water and the inside of my nose itch.

"Shoot, you need something for dinner." Steph stops in the kitchen with a frown. She opens the darkened refrigerator, then quickly shuts it again. The smell of room-temperature meat wafts out. "Right, no power, the stuff in the refrigerator is probably spoiled."

We didn't even have refrigeration at New Harmony, so I'm dubious. "But it's only been a few hours. Are you sure the food isn't good?"

She grimaces. "Oh, honey, no. No, you don't want to eat a room-temperature veggie dog. Why don't you order a pizza?"

I nod, excited now. Pizza is one of the many marvelous things in the outside world that I never imagined until I encountered it. On our road trip it was a staple food, when cheese pizza was the only thing Steph could think of to feed a vegetarian teenager. I thought it was the best thing I'd ever eaten.

She examines the refrigerator door and plucks a pizza coupon flier from under a magnet, hands it to me. "How does this one look? The Pizza Power guys are always leaving these ads on the front porch, large veggie combo for fifteen bucks. I know you can't eat the whole thing by yourself tonight, but we can have it for breakfast if they don't get the electricity back on."

It sounds good to me. She calls, and they tell her it might be as long as an hour, that they're backlogged because of the storm. She leaves me a twenty-dollar bill and pauses on her way out the door. "Abby, are you sure you're going to be all right here by yourself? In the dark?"

"Of course."

"No, not of course. It's okay to be scared."

"I'm not scared."

"Are you sure you don't want to take Terry and go over to Mr. Singha's and Mr. Davidson's house?"

"It's dark there too."

"I know, but—" She shakes her head. "Forget it. It's Saturday night, they probably want their privacy. Look, your phone has plenty of charge, right? You call me if you need anything. Well, send a text, I can check that while I'm working. Okay?"

"Okay." We hug, and then she's gone, hairspray whispering in the dark.

Steph hasn't been gone long when Terry wakes up crying. Indigestion crying, I think. He needs to be burped. I take him out to the back porch, where it smells green and wet, and we can watch the sun finish sinking, red and sullen under the black clouds. The rain has diminished to a typical Seattle mist. The clouds thin, and I see a bright full moon in the open space, turning the clouds to ragged edges of silver with dark hearts.

"Look at that, Terry." I show him the moon. He seems unimpressed. "Did you know that on the night of the full moon, the moon rises as the sun sets? It's a thing called a syzygy. Means everything lines up. Can you say 'syzygy'?" I blow raspberries on his belly and he laughs.

A strong, smoky aroma drifts toward me. In the yard next door, Mr. Singha tends a barbecue. He notices me and waves, then drops a skewer of marinated lamb on the grill. The odor makes my stomach lurch unpleasantly. Nausea, or hunger?

It's okay. I have a pizza on the way. I wave at Mr. Singha and go back inside. I put Terry down to bed again and hunt through the kitchen looking for something to snack on while I'm waiting for the pizza. An hour, did they say? But there's nothing in here I want. We have crackers, carrots, peanut butter, but none of it sounds good. All I really want is those lamb skewers. Their aroma is a twisting ribbon of hot, silken copper, wrapping itself around me, tugging, as if it would drag me over there against my will.

I don't want it. I don't want it. I find myself out on the porch again. No. Back inside to the kitchen. There's no food that wasn't there before. I don't want anything except the meat. But I don't want the meat. This is driving me crazy. How long am I supposed to keep waiting for this pizza? It better be good when it gets here.

Finally! Heavy footsteps on the porch, scent of a stranger approaching. Not a perfect stranger. I think I've encountered him before, though I can't place where. His sweat is over-whelmed by the enticing aroma of the pizza, garlic and cheese and tomato sauce and fresh hot bread.

My stomach lurches painfully in hunger, and gurgles so loud that I wonder if he can hear it through the door. I pick up the twenty-dollar bill Steph left for me. It smells like the place she works, the odors of booze and food that cling to her clothes and hair when she comes home. I never noticed before.

I fling open the door before the pizza guy has a chance to ring the bell. He seems startled by this and several things go through my mind all at once. I notice that he seems older than most pizza delivery guys, even though he wears the expected orange and white uniform. The uniform is too tight across his broad chest, as if they couldn't find one that would fit, and I think, it's because he's not really the pizza guy, he stole the pizza guy's uniform. But that kind of thing only happens in the movies, doesn't it?

Then I realize why he seems familiar. He's the man who was staring at me that day a week ago, the one who said he thought he recognized me. Right, I was planning to ask Steph and Morgan about that, but the arrival of their parents drove the whole incident right out of my mind.

Dread grows in my chest as I notice the cold look in his handsome gray eyes. I try to shut the door again, but it's too late. He pushes his way through, and shuts the door behind him.

"Hello," he says, in a deep, resonant voice. "My name is George. I believe you're taking care of my son?"

6

I PROMISE IT WON'T HURT

G eorge. Oh, no. No, no, no. Stupid. I should have known who it was, that day he was staring at me in the park. Staring at me and the baby. Why didn't I know? Why didn't I remember to talk to Steph about it later? Panic rises in my throat, choking me.

"Abby." His voice caresses the syllables pleasantly, almost seductively. How does he know my name? He's been stalking us. He knows everything. A river of ice crawls down my spine. He's going to kill me and take Terry. Kill me and take Terry. The words repeat in my head, like the chorus of a tuneless song.

Song, phone, wait, where's my phone? I cast my eyes around the room, find it on a small marble-topped table near the door, on the other side of George Why did I ever set it down? It should be in my hand right now, dialing 9-1-1, but all I've got is a twenty-dollar bill that smells like the bar where Steph works.

I stare at the money, and the sight brings a rush of helpless shame. Money, money is greed, greed is bad, bad is me. I brought this on our heads with my own wickedness, my beast, and now we're all going to be punished. "Get out." My voice emerges in the lowest growl I can manage, but still I sound like a small whining puppy. Tears sting my eyes, squeezed out by the pounding in my forehead. I don't know what to do. My guts flutter like a maddened bird. Am I going to throw up? Would that be good or bad if I threw up on him?

"Abby." He says my name again, with more force, as if he could command me by it. Abby, sit. Abby, stay. "It's okay. He's my son, I can take care of him now. Just let me take my son and go, and there won't be any trouble." Big, big smile. A line from one of Mr. Marchande's songs pops into my head: *oh the shark has, such pretty teeth, dear, and he shows them, pearly white.*

A shark, how do you fight a shark? Harpoon? Well, I'm pretty sure we don't have one of those handy. I choke back a hysterical giggle that turns into a shuddering gasp. His smile broadens as he pulls some thin white cord out of his pocket. He takes a step toward me, while I'm rooted in place. Every breath catches on the edge of a sob. I know I look powerless to him. This thought brings more shame, more weeping. I can't stand the idea that he's going to win.

"Abby, you don't have to be afraid. Just do what I say, and I won't hurt you."

He echoes my father's words: Just be a good girl and I won't have to chastise you. Why can't you behave? Do what you're told, Abnegation. Stop rebelling. Stop listening to the beast in your heart. Submit yourself to the Lord. Submit yourself to me.

I blink rapidly, tears rendering the world an incomprehensible blur. For fifteen years, Wisdom tried to beat all that out of me—the beast, and its demons of anger, outrage, and stubbornness. Not demons, as I know now. My own emotions. They pound red in my blood, but still I can't seem to move. Maybe Father Wisdom succeeded better than we knew. I never stopped feeling all those things he wanted me to suppress, but I stopped being able to do anything about them.

What could I do anyway? George is a huge man, easily

twice my size. I'm going to lose no matter what I do. I should just give up now. Get it over with.

He touches my hands, his skin hot and rough, and without thinking I step backward and shake myself free of him. He drops the cord, but he's still not worried about me. He laughs. "Aw, sugar, you don't wanna get tied up? I promise it won't hurt."

It won't hurt. That assurance again. Does he think I'm afraid of physical pain? Obviously he doesn't know me very well. Laughter burbles up. Inappropriate humor was always the most powerful of my demons. I let the laughter out in a short bark, and he looks confused, then angry. "What's so funny, kid?" He glances over his shoulder, as if I might be laughing at some threat behind him.

He doesn't like it when I laugh. This makes me laugh harder. But just when it seems like he's so mad that he's going to explode, he laughs a little himself, dismissing me with a wave of his hand. "You're nuts, kid."

He takes a step toward Steph's bedroom. I put myself in between him and the baby. My hands curl into fists. Every inch of me wants to fight him, all of a sudden. But I can't. I'll lose, and then what?

Then what what? If you fight him, and you lose, then he wins. If you don't fight him at all, he wins. So why not fight him? Maybe you'll win.

The strangely separate inner voice sounds an awful lot like the one that suggested to me, so many months ago, that I should leave New Harmony. And just like then, it seems so reasonable, in spite of the craziness of what it's saying. Except, it was right before, wasn't it? Wasn't I right to leave?

The outside world slows as my thoughts race. I'm holding Terry in my arms, and he becomes Ash. I'm whispering a promise to take care of her, now that her mother has gone to be with the angels. I'm looking into my father's eyes, as he asks me, *Abnegation, dost thou then offer up thyself up to atone in thy sister's stead?* I'm watching my sister burn on the altar. I'm holding Terry in my arms. Wisdom is preaching from Genesis, telling the story of Abraham and Isaac, reminding us that a man who serves the Lord will sacrifice his own children if God demands it. A line from a song, *God said to Abraham, kill me a son.*

I'm chained to the Mercy Seat, awaiting chastisement, tensing for the pain of the rod against my legs. *It is the beast in you. The spark of rebellion that will not die. Release it. A spirit properly chastised and obedient is healed, freed. Withhold not correction from the child; for if thou beatest him with the rod, he shall not die.* But my sister Ash is dead, burning on the altar. Look close and you can see the bruises on her flesh. *Flesh without soul, what then are we, Abnegation?* Meat, sir. On the barbecue, all meat smells the same: the skewers next door, a slaughtered lamb, my own sister. My mouth waters in hunger as I watch her body eaten by the flames. I bow my head, and know myself to be the most shameful wretched thing that ever crawled upon this earth.

George lunges to the right, as if to go around me, and I block him. To the left, and I block him again. He chuckles. "You wanna dance, sugar? I can do that. You're kind of a little skinny thing, but you got that wild red hair, I bet I could dance with you."

He reaches out to caress the back of my head, wrapping his fingers into my hair. His voice comes in a hiss. "I don't want to hurt you. But I will if I have to."

I thrill with terror and fury all mixed together, no way to tell where one ends and the other begins. We learned about this in science, the fight-or-flight instinct, an adrenal system that evolved to help us cope with saber-toothed tigers and giant prehistoric wolves. Now it causes problems when we stress out in situations where neither fighting nor running will help, things like pre-algebra tests and traffic jams. But this is real. George is a saber-toothed tiger.

If Abraham does not yield up his child, in the end, what

happens? God takes his child anyway, only now, Abraham has lost favor with God. *You defied me, and now your sister is dead. Do you see why the voice of the beast in your heart is a dangerous lie?*

I do see.

My mistake wasn't defying him, it was that I didn't defy him soon enough. I could have saved Ash, if I'd taken her and run away months before. That's what I should have done.

Now I know. If God himself stood before me and said, "Give me that child, that I might slaughter him," I would tell him,

"BITE ME!"

I tear myself away from George, leaving strands of bright hair caught in his thick-fingered hands. He laughs. "I might do that, sweetie." He has the rope in his hands again, and reaches out, as if he would lasso me with it.

A terrible dark excitement begins to race along all my nerves. I decide to scream, hoping to alert the men next door. It comes out in a funny wordless howl. I rush George, fast enough that I take him by surprise, get the rope out of his hands.

He retaliates, lunging back, pushing a fist into my mouth to shut me up. I reel backwards, falling to the floor, but as I do, I kick out and tangle my legs with his, so that he falls too, crashing heavily, making the dishes rattle. One of the buttons on the too-tight shirt pops off and rolls away.

"Crazy bitch." For the first time he seems truly angry. The smile goes away and his smell changes, becoming dark and spiky. He rises to his knees and hits me in the gut, a deep-fisted punch that robs me of air for a moment. He leans in closer, exhaling hot pepperoni breath right into my face. I rise suddenly to bash my head into his mouth. This hurts me a little as his teeth crack on my skull, but it hurts him a lot more. Blood in his mouth and he spits it at me. Hands wrap around my throat, big hands, closing off all my air with an iron grip.

I flail at him, my own hands so small and soft, nothing to

them, no claws, no power. I try to kick up, but can't seem to get any leverage. Squeezing harder and harder, could he kill me this way? The world fades to gray for a moment, retreats, tempting me with oblivion. I tried to fight, and I failed. Who can blame me for giving up now? *Ah, and does that not prove the futility of the fight? Thou arrivest at the same place in the end, only thou hast taken the reins of thine own life and pushed God away.*

Gah, shut up Father Wisdom, shut up God, shut up George, shut up shut up shut up, let me talk let me scream. My throat jumps and writhes, trying to get air, while deep in my guts another voice, rises, howling.

Slip out of his grasp. Pant heavily, teeth scraping against lower teeth. Pounce, snapping fangs at his throat, but he blocks with his arm. Teeth sink deep into his flesh. Enemy makes loud angry noises, human howls. DAMN YOU BIT ME!

She doesn't understand or care, and moves in for the final kill.

Neighbor man is here. The man howls OH NO. Now the little one howls too. He's afraid. Distracted by the instinct to comfort the little ones, her attention wavers. Enemy notices, starts to run. She brings him down with an easy leap, teeth barely missing his throat. Opens her jaw for the killing bite—

Neighbor man holds the little one now. Two enemies? She turns her attention to him and growls a warning. His scent spikes in fear as he cradles the little one, his posture protective, his voice crooning in a low purr, IT'S OKAY SHHH IT'S ALL RIGHT SHHH TERRY SHHH

He backs away slowly, eyes fixed on her the entire time. She is still trying to make up her mind if he is a friend or an enemy, when the first enemy strikes again, beating her shoulders with some large and heavy object.

Enraged, she turns all her attention back to the ENEMY, squirming and twisting to seize his arm between her teeth. Jolt of satisfaction from the taste of his blood and the sound of his agonized screaming. He drops the weapon. Now she goes for the kill again.

Machine noise, loud rumbling, air moves against her face, carrying familiar person smell, the male who lives here, the one who is almost pack. Her thought is joy, they can now fight this ENEMY together. He howls MY GOD

Noise and light and stink and PAIN PAIN PAIN PAIN PAIN

She roars and rushes toward him, all fury. He has the stick that explodes, and he used it to hurt her. He goes down under her leap, stick clattering away. He gazes up in wide-eyed panic, as her jaws snap inches from his face. The yellow scent of his alarm conflicts her. He's almost pack. Surely, when he hurt her, it was a mistake, and not the act of a true enemy.

She snaps her teeth at his neck, warn him to be more careful in the future. The pain begins to drive out other thoughts. She hungers. Time to hunt, find meat and then a place to lie low and heal. With a final warning growl, she leaps down into the night. The impact on her injured haunches sizzles pain through her body and she roars with it, a final challenge to the world. *Look out. I will eat you.*

7

WAKING UP NAKED IN THE PARK

I wake up.

Chilly air moves across my skin. I shiver, draw into myself, realize I'm not wearing any clothes, not even underthings or breast bindings. Did I fall asleep in the middle of a dirty chore? Burying the dogs, or Mother's bones? Father is going to discover me naked in the daylight, punish me with torments beyond anything I can imagine.

But no, that's not right. This is Seattle air, gray and fresh, smelling of the ocean, of spring flowers and sweet forest pines, stale recycled water and seagull droppings, car exhaust and coffee brewing, early-morning joggers and their dogs. We stopped at this park yesterday, was it only yesterday?

Eyes shut, I cherish the illusion that this is a dream, even while the world draws itself around me in lines of scent that grow brighter and more solid. The last thing I remember— the last thing I remember is—George. He came for Terry. I decided to fight him. His hands wrapped around my neck, and then—

Something electric, something big—

My stomach twists painfully. I lurch to my knees, eyes snapping open in spite of myself. Vomit spews out, sour lumps of meat and blood, choking hardness of feathers and delicate bones. No, I must be dreaming still. Why would I be throwing up meat and bones? I close my eyes again and wipe my mouth with the back of my hand. The slimy feel and the persistent foul odor start to convince me I must be awake. Awake, and vomiting something which seems to be a partially digested bird, eaten raw.

A seagull? One of them screams mournfully in the sky overhead. Or a duck, ducks probably taste better—

No. This isn't real. It can't be real.

A jogger approaches in a swirl of perfume and rubber, little pug dog in tow. The dog snarls and snaps at me when they get close.

"Curry, no," she tells the dog. "Miss? Are you all right? What are you doing here?"

I've forgotten how to speak. My throat is the wrong shape and nothing comes out but a pitiful little whine. I clear my throat, noisy and painfully.

"Should I call 9-1-1?"

"Please," I manage to choke out.

The jogging woman keeps one eye on me while she calls the police. I half-listen to her side of the conversation as reality slides back into place. She frowns in my direction. "Are you Abby Marchande?" I nod. She smiles. "I'm Veronica." She goes back to conversing with the police. The words, "They got him? Are you sure?" jump out at me. She pulls the phone away from her ear and directs her attention toward me again. "Abby? Your neighbors Mr. Singha and Davidson have the baby, and George is in jail, does that make you feel better?" I nod. "Are you willing to talk to the cops? Your evidence could be an important part of convicting George." I nod vigorously. A few more words with the cops, and she hangs up the phone.

"It's all right. They're sending a lady cop. I told her you were—uh—you know, without clothes." She stares at me with a frown, then unties the sweatshirt around her waist and drapes it over my shoulders like a blanket. Her little pug comes over to sniff at me, seeming to have decided I'm all right now that I'm wearing some clothing that smells like his mistress. He presses his nose into my hand for a wet snort. I pet him for a while, comforted by his warmth and the texture of his short, velvety fur. I think about calling Steph, but realize I'm not sure of her number. It was stored in the phone she gave me and I never had to memorize it. I hope she knows to call the cops if she's worried.

"Do you live around here?" the woman asks.

I nod. I think about pointing, but that would require uncurling, suddenly make my nakedness more obvious, and cold. "Back up the hill," I say instead. My voice feels harsh, like it's full of gravel. I clear my throat again.

The pug leaves me to investigate my immediate surroundings, and discovers the puddle of vomit. "Curry, leave it!" Veronica commands. She looks from the vomit to me. "Before the cops get here, uh, is there anything you don't want them to know about? Drug use, anything like that?"

I glance morosely at the vomit. The bones and feathers don't seem quite so obvious, now that everything is sinking into the grass. Please don't look too closely. "No. Nothing like that."

The police arrive, with a distinctive flash of red and blue lights, short siren burp as the car pulls to a stop on Pine Street outside the park. Two cops get out, one male, one female. They have a short conversation. The male gets back in the car while the woman approaches us. She's tall, pretty, very dark-skinned, hair cropped close to show off the elegant curve of her neck. She holds a bundle of black cotton in her arms and her gun is holstered.

"You're Veronica West?" she asks the jogging woman, who nods. "I'm Louanne Kaffa. Officer Lou." Her voice is rich and pleasant, a comforting voice, like being snuggled under a blanket. She crouches in front of me and smiles, a big, friendly smile. As she leans in close I notice that she smells strongly of another woman, that she lives with a cat and a dog, that she recently drank a mocha. Underneath, crisp odors of laundry, brimstone and machine oil of her gun, which reminds me of Morgan, reminds me of—

No, it's gone again.

"Can I have your name, hon?" she asks me.

"Abne—Abby. Abby Marchande."

"And how old are you, Abby?"

"Fifteen."

"Abby, I'm going to ask you a few questions, and if you don't mind, I'm going to record your answers, would that be all right?" I nod. "Could you say it out loud for me please?"

"Yes. You can record me."

"Thank you." She smiles, fiddles with something on her belt, then turns back to me. "Do you know how you got here, Abby? Here in this park?" I shake my head. "Can you say it out loud for me please?"

"No. I don't know how I got here."

"Do you know why you weren't wearing any clothes?"

"No, I don't know why I wasn't wearing any clothes."

"What's the last thing you do remember?"

"George." My voice breaks a little and I clear my throat. "It was George. He pretended to be the pizza guy. He tried to take the baby."

"George. That would be George Brooks Dunham?"

Is that his name? I realize I don't know. "The George who is Steph's ex-husband. I opened the door because I thought he was the pizza guy, I even smelled pizza. If I knew—I would never—" I break down into choking tears.

She puts a hand on my shoulder. "Honey, it's okay. Nobody's upset with you. We're just glad you're okay. We've been out searching for you most of the night. Everybody's been so worried. Nobody had any idea where you were. Understand?"

I nod, and try to continue. "All right. George tried to take the baby and I tried to stop him. We fought. Then—I don't know, something happened. He hit me, I think—" I remember a grayness, a sense of moving outside my body, my throat closed off. "He tried to strangle me. That's it. I was about to pass out because he was strangling me. That's the last thing I remember."

"So you passed out while he was strangling you?"

"Yes." I pause, vague flashes like dreams, a memory trying to come through. Morgan was there, with a gun, but that's not possible, he was in the mountains. It's a dream. I'm confused. "I think so. That's really all I can remember until I woke up here."

"Okay. Thank you, Abby. Now, why don't we get you to the hospital?"

"The hospital?" I hate the whine in my voice. "But I'm not hurt."

She gives me a sympathetic look. "Abby. I know this is going to be hard for you. But we still don't know everything that happened. If he knocked you out and then removed your clothes, your own body might provide important evidence against him."

I close my eyes. I don't want to see anything, not even her beautiful, serious, understanding, friendly-cop face. "You think I was raped." My voice comes out flat and harsh.

"We don't know. But if he did do that, don't you want him to go to jail for it?"

Of course I do. Even though I really want to go home. I open my eyes. "Okay. Take me to the hospital."

Lou smiles and hugs me with one arm. "That's my girl. I brought you some clothes. DARE T-shirts, nothing fancy. But you can take the big one and kind of stretch out the neck and wear it like a skirt, see?" I stand up, and discover this trick works surprisingly well.

I return Veronica's sweatshirt and follow Lou to the police car.

EVERYONE AT THE HOSPITAL IS FRIENDLY AND PROFESSIONAL, but it's boring, and smells weird. Medicine, disinfectant, rubber, plastic, all these tickle my nose and make me feel nauseated. But even worse, it almost seems like I can actually inhale the misery of the people here, that their pain and fear and grief creates an ugly miasma, the sick muddy brown that you get when you mix all the paint colors together.

I was not sexually assaulted. At first I'm relieved, but then I start to think, what if that means George gets off too easily? What if they can't prove he really tried to kidnap Terry?

Morgan comes to get me, bringing a bag of my own clothes to wear home. He gives me a fierce hug, much more enthusiastic than I expect. I always get the feeling he doesn't like me much. "Thank God," he says. "Thank God. We had no idea what happened to you. We've been out looking all night. What happened?"

...feathers, feathers and blood and little bird bones...

"I don't know. The last thing I remember is George strangling me."

"Strangling you? Really? Are you sure? That bastard." He clutches his hands in a burst of fury.

"Why aren't you camping?"

"The weather turned nasty in the mountains too. Come on, let's get you home."

In the car, he keeps coming back to wondering where I've been all night, but I can't tell him any more than I already have. George and I fought. He tried to strangle me. Then nothing. I'm more interested in Morgan's story. He came back from the mountains and walked in on George fighting with a big dog.

"Nobody knows where it came from or where it went," he says. "I shot at it. I think I even hit it, but it ran off. Animal control couldn't find the dog either."

A stomach cramp distracts me, and I double over, hoping I'm not going to throw up again.

He grins. "Anyway, that's one thing we can all be glad of. Since they couldn't find the dog, they have to assume it was rabid, and give George a bunch of painful shots through the gut."

Steph greets us at the door, holding Terry, and embraces both of us for a long time, all four of us together, a family. My relief is so extreme, it feels like every muscle in my body releases all at once, and I'm ready to melt into a puddle. I know they said the baby was all right, that George didn't have him, but until Terry was right in front of me, with me able to touch him, smell him, a part of me couldn't believe it.

"You should get to bed," Steph says. "We'll talk later."

Even though she hugged me with great affection, there is an edge to her voice, as if she's upset. With me? Why?

Because you abandoned the baby, of course.

No. No, that's not right. I didn't leave the baby until after —gunshots—no, it's gone.

I nod. "Good night."

And something else. I know Steph works in a bar, and might have spilled alcohol on her clothes. But I think I know the difference, I know that sour stink of partially digested alcohol on her breath. I'm almost certain that Steph has been drinking.

8

ABBY GOES TO A PARTY

I tumble onto my mattress still dressed, and sleep dreamless until nearly sunset. The fragrance of roasting meat wakes me, drifting in through the window and turning my thoughts bloody. I haven't been this hungry since being released from the Prayer Closet. It's as if I haven't eaten in days. I sit up, and realize that, somehow, in my sleep, I seem to have thrown off all my clothes. Why would I do that? Did I try to change into sleep clothes, without really waking up, and only make it halfway?

There's a stranger in the house, her unfamiliar scent prickling my nose like acid.

I locate one of the dresses Steph picked out for me at the thrift store: short, black, skirt edged with a design of bright red flames. I have never actually worn it. The fabric smells stale and rubbery, but it feels soft. I pull it on and run out.

"Abby." Steph, dressed for work, gives me a too-bright smile. "This is Celeste, from down the street? She's babysitting today. I thought you'd want a night off, after what you've been through."

Celeste smiles nervously at me. She's about my age, pale

without the freckles, taller and rounder. She looks like an over-
grown mouse. "Nice to meet you," she says.

What are they both so nervous about? There's something
going on here, but I don't want to have to figure out what it is.
Steph is right. I do want a night off. I do want to go out. I
want to—I want to—I want to have fun. That's what I want.
"All right. Thank you."

Steph nods. "Why don't you go have some fun with your
friends?" She hugs me, a bit stiffly. *Friends*, I think. *That's a good
one.* "Oh, you'll need money." She hands me a twenty. "Do
you think you'll be out late?"

"Oh, I don't know," I say, airily, grabbing my favorite
sweatshirt. "Probably not much past midnight."

Halfway down the block, I realize I left the house without
my shoes. Oh, well. I feel very light, almost euphoric. And
hungry. I close my eyes and concentrate on the smells around
me, ribbons through the air, textures and colors and patterns.
It seems like I could pick up a ribbon of scent and follow it
anywhere. Where should I go? If I can do anything I want,
that means I have to figure out what I want.

I decide to track down Smoking Girl, starting from the
corner where she and her friends usually hang out. This turns
out to be way too easy, when she's already there.

"Smoking girl," I call out, friendly.

"Gator girl," she responds with her usual cheerfulness. She
does a double take. "No wonder you always wear pants, your
legs are the most blinding shade of white I've ever seen. Don't
they wear shoes where you come from?"

"No, I'm a swamp girl, remember? A barefoot backwoods
hick from hicksville. What are you doing here on a Sunday?"

"Mom thinks I'm at youth group. What are you doing
here?"

"Looking for you."

She laughs. "Well, you found me."

I take the cigarette out of her hand and make a show of

puffing on it, even though all I do is take the smoke into my mouth and blow it out again.

"I thought you didn't smoke."

"I don't. I was just bored." I hand the cigarette back. "You know, that's even worse than I always imagined it would be."

She laughs. "Hey, I heard Lorinda has been picking on you."

"Yeah."

"That sucks. But don't let it get to you. She's a moron."

"No, it's good. Having my own personal bully makes me feel like the star of a teen drama."

She laughs again. "You know, I'm never sure if you're being funny, or just a weirdo."

"Both. What are you guys doing tonight?"

"Hanging out."

One of the other girls speaks up. "What about that party your brother told us about? Were we gonna go to that?"

Cigarette shrugs. "I dunno. It's kind of far. I'd have to drive and then I can't drink."

Another girl speaks up. "I heard Edison's band was going to play."

Cigarette shrugs, looks at me. "What about you? Do you want to go to my brother's friend's party?"

"Sure. My actual name is Abby, by the way."

"I'm Deena. Nice to meet you for real."

She introduces me to her friends, her pack. During the school week, when I see them in Saint Sebastian uniforms, they tend to blend together, but today in street clothes they seem more distinct. Nina, who wears plaid flannel and elaborately patched jeans. Claudia, an exotic neo-Victorian with clip-on purple streaks in her hair. Portia, who wears fresh jeans and a T-shirt that has something to do with, I think, video games.

By the time we walk to Deena's house and drive out to the party, the sun has set. We're near a big cemetery high on a hill, tall crosses and solemn stone angels stark against the bright moonlit sky.

"Full moon," Claudia says, admiring the view.

"Not quite. That was last night." I correct her, which isn't like me at all.

"It's full for three days," Deena says. "According to this werewolf movie I saw, anyway."

I give up. I could explain the difference between 95 percent full and 100 percent full, but it's not important. Is it?

We approach a house that borders the cemetery, a big white Craftsman-era like Steph and Morgan's house. Music thumps up from the ground, as if the dead are partying in the basement. We walk right in. Nobody seems to notice.

"This isn't a high school party," I observe, then feel ridiculous. Of course, what did I think it was going to be?

Deena grins. "Your first time? Here, let me get you a drink."

"No!" It comes out louder, more desperate than I intended, and the other girls give me a strange look. "I mean, I don't drink. My, uh, my aunt is an alcoholic. The one I live with. So I don't want to drink while I'm staying with her." The movies have prepared me for this moment to be a big deal, and instigate something called peer pressure. But Deena merely nods in understanding.

"You want a Coke or something anyway?" she offers.

"Maybe later."

We make our way down to the basement, where the music is too loud for any conversation, and people dance. I join the throng, hopping up and down, crammed in so close that we slam into each other without meaning to. People step on my feet a few times but the pain doesn't seem to bother me. Then, suddenly, an intense pain in my gut stops me up short. An intestinal cramp? I go back to dancing, but it hits me again. I start to worry that I'm going to throw up in front of all these people I don't even know. Or, equally embarrassing, I might fart. I leave the crowd and prop myself against the wall, hoping to feel better soon.

One of the guys comes over and looms, as if he's trying to impress me with his bigness, but I'm not impressed. I can see that he's soft, weak for his size, slow. He smells like lunch meat, but not in a good way. A cheap sandwich left out in the sun too long. I try to pretend I don't notice him.

"Hey," he says.

"Hey," I respond flatly and look away. Could my signaling be any plainer? But he ignores it.

"You wanna dance?"

"I'm tired, no."

"Yeah, you're sweaty. Your dress is sticking to your boobs."

Huh. This reminds me that I left the house not only without shoes, but also without a bra or any kind of breast binding. Why didn't I notice before? I wasn't thinking about it. But now I'm acutely aware of the way the damp fabric clings to my skin, outlining my shape. I have an impulse to hide, to fold my arms in front of me, but that impulse makes me angry. Why should this jerk make me want to hide? He shouldn't have that power over me. His lust stinks. How old is he, anyway? Not less than twenty, is my guess.

"I'm fifteen, you're not allowed to look at my boobs," I tell him. It's almost a joke, but I can hear the rising fury in my own voice. Any non-creep, any non-idiot, would take the hint and go.

Instead, he leans over me, exhaling his sour spent-alcohol breath. "That's okay, I won't tell if you won't," he whispers in a way that might be meant to be seductive. He grabs my arm. "Come on, you wanna get a drink, go somewhere private?"

I bat his arm away. "Touch me again and you die." I tell him this, calmly, as a matter of fact. It comes to me as I say it, and I realize I don't have an actual plan for making this death happen. Maybe that's why he laughs. But it makes me really mad, and I start to feel my body swarming with furious red bees.

He gropes my left breast, briefly, chuckling. "Okay, I'm ready to die now."

The flesh where he touched me tingles with the memory of insult and I let the bees fill me up, coiling around the middle of my churning gut, powering out to my arms, filled with a fiery power as the world slows down. Everything reveals itself. I know where to put my weight, where to land the blow, and—

Boom.

His jaw, my fist, bones tingling from the impact but otherwise fine. He reels backward, stepping, then falling, all the way down, until he's laid out flat on the floor like a defeated boxer.

Somebody shrieks and the music stops.

The DJ speaks through the sound system, disembodied voice amplified, like God in a cheesy Bible epic. "What the hell?"

A guy I don't know points at me. "Colin was coming onto that redhead over there and she socked him and he went down."

The DJ looks from me to the man on the floor. "Okay, dude is obviously too drunk to be here, somebody take him out." He makes eye contact with me, frowning thoughtfully. "You should leave too, Red. I don't want any trouble here."

For a moment I'm almost swallowed in outrage again. I am not the one who made trouble! That guy on the floor made trouble, I just responded. Appropriately! But I recognize that the DJ is the party host, his scent is all over the place, and this is his territory, so he does have the right to ask me to go. Unless I want to fight him, and I don't, I should leave. I look around for Deena and friends, find them watching from the corner.

"Good night, guys. Thanks. Sorry." I start trudging up the stairs. They follow.

"Are you kidding? That was awesome," Deena says.

"I've waited for years to see that guy get punched out," Nina says.

We make our way out through the party crowd, traveling slower than rumors of my exploits. Even though the party host is kicking me out, the uniform consensus is that Colin was a jerk who had it coming. We pause on the porch to collect Claudia, who is clustered with a black-clad knot of people, all of them smoking cigarettes perfumed with sweet cloves.

"Come on, we're leaving," Deena tells her.

She hands her half-finished cigarette to a girl, or possibly a boy, in pancake white makeup. "Is it true? I hear our little Abby utterly destroyed Colin Ambrose." She smiles at me affectionately.

"It's true. But now Troy wants us to leave. Because we're such troublemakers!" They all laugh.

One of the young men smoking on the front porch calls out, "Oh, hey, I hear that was some punch you laid on Colin."

It takes me half a second to realize he's talking to me, so Deena responds first. "Hi, Edison. I thought your band was supposed to play tonight?"

He shrugs, brushing a dangling curve of dark hair out of his eyes and blowing a cloud of smoke. Green, it smells green, that's not tobacco is it? "The drummer was late so we thought we'd let Troy stick with the canned music. That's what he likes anyway. He says it gets more people dancing."

"Well, I wanted to hear you guys play," Portia says, shy smile up through her brown bangs, nervously adjusting her glasses. Oh, she has a crush. When he turns his attention to me, I can feel her grimace in my direction.

"So, Red, how'd you do it?"

"What do you mean how did I do it? I punched him. He went down. It was a lucky punch. He was drunk."

"Yeah, but—I know I'm kinda stoned and my perspective might be off, but from here you look pretty small."

"I'm a ninja. I used secret ninja punching skills."

He laughs.

"Come on, guys, Troy wants us to leave." Portia starts to hustle me off the porch. "See you later, Edison! Are you guys playing the Howl?"

"Yeah. Invitations are out in a couple of weeks."

"The Howl?" I ask, feeling oddly disturbed, as though the word has reminded me of something I ought to remember, but can't put my finger on.

"It's another fine Troy tradition. First full moon in July, he hosts a party out in the woods. I'm sure I can get you an invitation."

"Doesn't Troy think I'm a troublemaker?"

"Not really. I mean, come on. It was Colin Ambrose. Troy's probably punched him on occasion. The dude is very punchable."

"Where to now?" Nina asks.

"It's getting late, it's a school night, I think we should go home." Portia shoots daggers at me again.

"Beth's Cafe," Claudia says. "I know, I know, eating actual food is so un-goth. But I've been swigging absinthe. Now I find myself in dire need of hash browns."

Deena bursts out laughing. "Claude, honey, nobody swigs absinthe. What the hell is wrong with you?"

At Beth's they don't want to let me in without shoes, but Deena has a pair of cheap rubber sandals, which she calls flip-flops, in the trunk of her car. They're barely shoes, but it seems to satisfy the cafe. Deena and her friends do most of the talking, easy banter referencing a shared history that both baffles and intrigues me. Meanwhile I devour a giant pile of hash browns smothered in eggs, vegetarian chili, and gooey cheese. I've been hungry for hours, I realize, and maybe that was the reason for the earlier cramping. I feel better now, anyway. I feel like I could curl up and go right to sleep. I start to droop inside the restaurant, where the wait staff seems to think it means I've had too much to drink, and Deena's friends seem to think this is hilarious. I doze off in the car, and stumble zombie-like when Deena drops me off.

"Keep the shoes," she says.

Inside the house, I find Celeste sitting on the couch, watching television, with Terry asleep in Steph's room. I plop down on the opposite side of the couch, smooth leather surface, dark leather odors poofing up around me. I'm used to the couch by now, but every once in a while I find the thought that it used to be the skin of an actual living animal to be distractingly macabre. Celeste smiles nervously at me.

"You're back."

"Yeah."

"Feeling better?"

"Sure." I stare at her and she glances down and away, flicking her eyes around in obvious unease. "Celeste? What are you so afraid of?"

"I'm not afraid."

"Yes you are. I can smell it on you." Why did I say that? Because I can. It's a prickly little scent, yellow and furtive. Spicy, like curry.

I tilt my head back, close my eyes, feel myself sinking back into a stupor of satiation. I start humming one of the songs from the dance: *bam bam bam-bam, bam-bam bam-bam, I wanna be sedated.*

Celeste glances at me with a nervous smile. "Did you, um. Uh. Did you have a nice—where did you go?"

"Out." I wave my hand, limp and vague, half asleep. I smile at her through half-closed lashes. "Are you afraid of me or are you afraid of George?"

"What? Oh, George."

"He's in prison."

"I'm still afraid."

"No you're not. You're afraid of me."

She clears her throat. "Why—uh, why would I be afraid of you?"

"I don't know. You tell me."

"I'm not afraid. It's just that Steph said you—"

"Steph?" I feel a flicker of anger. "You were talking about me? What did Steph tell you about me?"

"She was, uh, she was worried that you, uh, that you weren't feeling well. She said you had a lot of, uh, you know, trauma. That you came from an abusive home. She thinks you have, maybe, PTSD? Like soldiers get?"

"And that scares you? Sorry, worries you?"

"Well, I saw it on TV. Sometimes they snap, do things that —you know, things that aren't good."

"You're scared I'm going to snap? And hurt you?"

"Not—I mean, no—I don't think you're going to hurt me."

"Good. I'm not." Then an evil humor rises in me, and I add, "Unless you do something to really piss me off."

There, she's oozing yellow curry again.

I'm too tired to want to get off the couch and go to my bedroom, so I close my eyes and zone out for a while. Steph should know better than to have a little yellow mouse girl protecting her baby, I think, as Celeste drifts around me in lazy ochre ribbons. She needs a snarling, buzzing red thing like me. I fought George, I did. I stopped him. I did.

When Steph finally gets home, it's at least three in the morning, much later than usual. At first I think it must have been a rough night, but the sour bile of alcohol on her breath wafts in, preceding her, and her steps on the porch are uneven, lurching. I snap into alertness, feeling angry again. The food in my stomach sits in a heavy ball, like a rock.

"You're drunk." I stand up to accuse her, startling Celeste awake as well.

"I had a couple of drinks after work. With friends." Her words are slow and too careful, the words of a drunk trying not to slur. I fold my arms and frown at her. "I'm not pregnant anymore, I don't have to be a complete teetotaler," she insists.

"Did you drive home?"

"I told you I'm not drunk!"

"Yes you are! Don't lie to me! I can smell the booze on your breath!"

"I told you to not let me drink while I was pregnant, and you didn't, and that's great, but I'm not pregnant anymore and I need you to leave me alone!" Unsteady on her feet, she throws her purse into the corner with sudden violence. "And I was good the whole nine months and it didn't help! I ended up having a stupid baby who never stops crying anyway!"

The baby, who was actually sleeping peacefully until now, decides to wake up and start crying. Steph rushes into her room to gather him up, start patting him. "Terry, Terry, shh, shh, I'm so sorry, it's okay, Mommy's here." She glares at me. "Abby, can I trust you to pay Celeste with the cash from my purse and walk her home?"

"Of course."

Celeste and I walk through the dark streets, only a few blocks, but we go slow. She seems like a slow walker anyway, and my steps are burdened under the uncomfortable weight growing in my stomach.

"My dad and my mom always get into fights when he comes home drunk," she says. "They're exactly like that. He says he's not drunk, she says, did you drive home? I don't think he's really an alcoholic, though. He's never drunk in the morning or anything like that."

Is she trying to be comforting? "I don't know what to do. Steph really didn't drink the whole time she was pregnant. I mean, not once I was around. She was pregnant for a few months before I got involved. I guess I thought that meant she was going to be okay. Now I'm not sure." I realize I should probably talk to Morgan about it. He might know if this is really a problem for her, if she's really addicted, or if she's going through a bad patch, stressed out because of George and being a new mom.

We walk in silence the rest of the way, and I sense that Celeste isn't afraid of me anymore. She gives me a soft little hug when we get to her house. Then I walk home by myself, steps halting as my discomfort grows.

Outside the front door, my stomach lurches and I start to gag painfully, running back down the porch steps, barely making it out to the lawn before the chili starts to travel the wrong way. Nothing is more unpleasant. It goes on and on, feels like I might turn entirely inside out. Finally it's done and I catch my breath. Maybe George drugged me and that's why I keep throwing up. I decide to bury the vomit and stand up, trying to remember where we keep the shovel, when a silvery flash catches my eye. Metal. I threw up something metal. I don't have any idea how that happened. I swear, I was not so hungry I ate my fork.

(*wait doesn't that look like a smashed bullet*)

I bury it all without looking too closely at the metal object. Something that happened during the fight. Something George did to me. It has to be.

(*rifle Morgan shot the dog didn't he say that he shot the dog or was it a wolf*)

Inside, Steph and Terry are both passed out in the middle of nursing. I wonder if the alcohol is going to hurt him. I put him down in his crib and go to sleep in my own room. I'm disgusted and confused and utterly spent and, now that I lost my dinner, hungry again. But I'm too tired to do anything about any of that. I just go to sleep and hope everything works out in the morning.

9

ABBY GOES TO SCHOOL

In the morning Steph is silent, bleary-eyed. I'm groggy too. We don't speak. I help myself to some of the coffee and she doesn't tell me it will stunt my growth. It seems strange to think about going to school, like this is a normal Monday. After everything that's happened, I feel like years have passed since I last went to school.

I don't see Deena's crowd on the way there, but right before class a girl approaches me in the bathroom. "I heard you slugged Colin Ambrose. Did you really knock him out with one punch?"

"Well, he was drunk."

"That's cool. He's really a jerk. They just let him hang around the parties because he's old enough to buy beer."

All day long, people who I swear don't know me at all call me by name and ask about last night. Did you really slug Colin? Did you really put him on the floor? By the end of the day, the stories are growing: I knocked out two guys, three guys, four guys. I didn't knock them out, I put them in the hospital. He didn't grab my boob, it was attempted rape.

People offer me seats at lunch. They follow up their questions regarding the infamous punch with chitchat about upcoming finals and summer vacation plans. I don't know how I feel about this. Who knew that the secret to making friends in high school was to hit a guy? Am I getting all this attention because everyone thought he was a jerk who deserved it? Does it make a good ice breaker? Or are people really so impressed by violence?

My personal bully even weighs in, stepping in front of me to block my passage. "Hey, new girl," she says. She has never bothered to learn my name. "I heard you hit people now. Why don't you hit me? Hey?"

I fold my arms, look up at her, into her eyes for the first time, see them as muddy brown, bloodshot, tagged with dark circles that make her look older than a teenager. "Obviously you don't think I will, or you wouldn't be taunting me like that."

She makes a scoffing noise. "Of course not. Because you're scared."

"Scared?" I think about it. No, I'm really not. I look deep into my soul as far down as I can go and don't seem to touch any fear at all. That seems strange. Maybe I used up all my fear when George came. "Scared of what?"

"Duh. You're scared of me." She blusters, but I can tell that my refusal to play along with the usual script has thrown her off.

I continue to stare up at her steadily. "So, let me get this straight. You think the reason I don't hit you right now—here in the halls of the school, in the middle of the school day, with all the teachers watching—is because I'm scared of you?"

"Okay, you're scared of the teachers. You're scared of getting in trouble."

"Of course I don't want to get into trouble. Get real. You're not that important, Lorinda."

I put my hands into my pockets and keep on walking. I'm fascinated now by the place where my fear ought to be, and I keep poking at it, as if I'm exploring the empty socket of a lost tooth. Lorinda rushes down the hall to stand in front of me again. I inhale her desperation. She senses the situation spiraling out of her control.

"Hey, new girl!"

I stop. This is getting boring, but I'd like to put an end to it. I look up at her, straight into her eyes, make it a challenge. "Yeah?"

"You think you're so tough, why don't we meet after school? Someplace without adults around. Then you can prove how badass you are."

I consider that. I might enjoy the opportunity to get out our aggressions in a purely physical battle. I imagine myself tackling her, like I tackled George, punching her, like I punched Colin. When I imagine these things, she doesn't put up much of a fight in return. In my imagination she bats at me helplessly, like a tiny kitten, just practicing at being a tiger. "Okay." I shrug. "If it'll make you happy, Lorinda, we can have a little extra-curricular session of fisticuffs."

"Fisticuffs." She makes a scoffing noise. "You are such a freak."

"I suppose. When and where?"

"Shit, are you serious?" She scowls. "No way are you serious."

"I said I would." I continue to stare into her eyes, and she blinks and looks away. "Why do you think I'm not serious? Is it because you're not serious?"

She makes another scoffing noise, but it feels a little desperate now. "Of course I'm serious. But you're insane. I'd pound you into a jellyfish."

"Is that what you think would happen?" I continue staring into her eyes, and smile slightly.

Her scent changes, spike of yellow curry alarm, and she raises her arms in a gesture half of surrender and half of warding. "Whatever. Jeez, you are one crazy ass bitch." She walks away and leaves me in peace. For good, I hope. I wish I knew how to whistle a jaunty tune.

After school, I walk home alone as usual. Deena waves me over. "Gator! Wanna drag?" She holds up the cigarette.

"No, thanks. I didn't actually like it, remember?"

She laughs. "I thought you might be addicted already. So what's up?"

"Nothing's ever up with me. What's up with you?"

"Finals are coming. We should study," Portia says. She gives me another dirty look, which I have done nothing to deserve.

"Study?" Deena scoffs. "When have we ever done that?"

"I should study, but I don't think it's going to help," I say.

"You should join our gang. You can be the jock," Nina says.

"We're not a gang," Portia says.

"I don't play sports, I can't be the jock. But you're wearing plaid, aren't you the jock?"

She laughs. "No, plaid means I'm the lumberjack."

"Lumberjane," Deena says. "Claude is obviously the goth, and Portia's the nerd."

"I'm not any more nerdy than the rest of you."

"So, how do you guys know each other?" I ask.

Deena laughs. "Oh, that's a good one. We were all part of the same gifted program when we were ten. You know how they do those screenings for lice sometimes? We were all singled out because they thought we might have 'em. We didn't. Still, we formed a bond over the intense humiliation. Also, we had to wait in this boring room for hours until our parents could come pick us up. So we talked, and it turned out that we all had one thing in common." She pauses, as they exchange looks, then, in unison, all four of them say:

"VAMPIRES."

And burst out laughing.

"We were all big nerdy fans of this vampire teen romance

series. It's awful. I mean, I realize now that it's awful. But I was ten. Claude's the only one still into vampires."

She rolls her eyes. "Not those vampires. I like the classic stuff. Dracula."

"Sure you do, Claudie. Sure you do."

They all laugh again, as if this is a familiar joke cycle. But something else jumped out at me. "You were all in the same gifted class? Does that mean you're all good in school?"

Deena shrugs. "Yeah, pretty much. But I wouldn't make a big deal out of it."

My perspective flips all around. I assumed they were always hanging out so nonchalantly because they were indifferent to school, that they never studied because they got bad grades and were okay with that. Now I realize that they probably don't study because they don't have to. I feel unexpectedly crushed.

"Well, I have to get home and babysit, see you guys around." I smile, and leave, careful to not let my disappointment show. I'm not even sure if it's true, if I do have to get home and babysit. Steph and I didn't talk about it this morning. I don't know if she's getting Celeste again, or Mssrs. Singha and Davidson. I don't know if she expects me to be a co-babysitter, or what.

When I get home, I recognize the scent trace of Father Mulligan, the director of the school. I've spoken to him only a couple of times, but he always seemed nice. I find him in the living room chatting with Steph, and when I enter, they both stand up. They're nervous. Why?

"Abby," Father Mulligan says, with a fake-looking smile. "I'd like to talk to you, can we walk?"

I shrug. "Sure."

We're not far away from the house when he stops and turns to me with a serious look. "I hear you've been fighting."

I can't help it. I heave a big, disgusted sigh. "One time,

and it wasn't a fight. Jerk grabbed me, I punched him, and he went down. He was drunk and I got lucky."

He continues to wear his serious face. "You did get lucky, Abby. I want you to understand that. You can't solve your problems with violence."

Without warning, I'm white-hot furious. "So I should have let a strange guy fondle my boobs, is that what you're saying?"

Even under his dark skin, I can see him blushing. "I didn't mean—I wasn't trying to tell you it was wrong, only that it was dangerous. You're a petite young lady, Abby, not a—"

"Not a man?" I spit the words out, bitter. "Is that what you're trying to tell me? Men can fight back but little girls like me should roll over and take it?"

He stops. "Okay, this is not at all where I wanted this conversation to go. Fighting is dangerous. I don't care what sex you are or what size you are, violence can easily escalate completely out of control. It starts with one punch—and you're right, you got lucky, it was one guy and you knocked him right out, good job. But what if you hadn't? What if he'd been hopped up on something, some drug that left him feeling no pain? What if you punched him and all he did was punch you back, harder? What if he had a weapon? What if he had friends willing to fight on his side? You could very quickly find yourself in way over your head, no matter how tough or strong you think you are."

He inhales, sees he's not winning me over. I see the logic of it, almost, but my mind keeps going back to that moment where Colin grabbed me, acted like he owned my body, had the right to touch me wherever he wanted. I know in my heart I would do it again. I would do it every time. I don't care what happens.

"Okay, Abby, let's try this one more time. If you're alone and somebody attacks you, go ahead. Fight like a tiger, if that's what you want to do. That's completely your call. But when you're at a party like that, in a social situation, before you escalate the violence, think about the people around you. If you had started a brawl, innocent people could have gotten hurt."

Without warning, I imagine not any of the people who were there, but my sister Ash. I see Father Wisdom beating her with the rod. *This is your fault,* he says. *Your fault.*

"But there wasn't a brawl. Nobody else got hurt." My voice sounds small, timid. Father Mulligan gives me a little smile, knowing he's got me. He's good at this. Must go with being a priest.

"Not this time." He puts his arm around me and squeezes. "I know you have a lot of anger to deal with. Your aunt has told me about your history, the place you came from. But it's not always about how you feel. You have to use your head, too. Have you considered studying martial arts?"

"Sure. Yeah. That sounds like a good idea."

Back at the house, he gives my shoulder another squeeze and takes off. Steph waves goodbye, then asks me, "Did you have a nice conversation with Father Mulligan?" Her smile is stiff, brittle. It irritates me. She knows very well what we were talking about.

"It was lovely." I fling myself onto the couch, hard enough that it scoots backward a couple of inches. "Apparently I'm now a menace to society."

"He said you were fighting." Her voice is nervous, hesitant, reminding me of Meekness, and somehow it makes me angry. It all makes me angry.

"You know, here's the part I don't get. The whole time I've been here, you've been telling me that I'm too shy. That I don't speak up enough. That I should stand up for myself. And the instant I do, suddenly it's intervention time. What the hell do you expect from me?"

She looks hurt. "Abby. When I said you should stand up for yourself, I meant you should do it with words, not with fists. Honestly, what possessed you?"

"The guy groped me, Steph. He grabbed my breasts and I slugged him. That's what possessed me."

She grimaces. "All right, that was pretty bad behavior on his part, but you could have walked away. Charged him with assault."

"Really. I could have done that. Walked away." I stare at her, let the depth of my anger show. "Is that what you would do? Is that what Morgan would do?"

"Don't tell me you've been listening to my brother, okay? He seems to think you can solve every problem by pulling a gun on it." She pauses. "Mr. Singha is coming over to help with the baby. You can stick around and give him a hand, or take another night off. It's up to you."

"You don't trust me anymore, do you?"

"What? No, that's not—why do you say that? I thought you'd want some more time to recover. Something pretty serious happened to you on Saturday. If—George tried to strangle you. He could have killed you."

"If. You said if, then you changed your mind. What were you going to follow that up with? If I'm telling the truth?"

"No, that's not—"

"It is, isn't it? You know that one of us is lying about what happened, and you think it's me."

"Abby, no. I don't believe George. How could you say that? I'm concerned about you. You blacked out an awful lot of time, honey. There's got to be a reason for that."

"The reason is, I'm crazy. Right? That's what you're all thinking. You, and Father Mulligan, and—you."

"Honey, no. No, I don't think you're crazy."

Abruptly, I can't take it anymore. I stand up. "Okay. Fine. Have it your way. I am taking the night off." I stand up, grabbing my sweatshirt.

"Where are you going?"

"Out." I grimace. "Father Mulligan said I should take up martial arts. Gonna look for a class."

10

ABBY TURNS SIXTEEN

I don't end up looking for a martial arts class. I just go for a walk, sometimes a run, all over the Capitol Hill neighborhood and beyond, venturing farther away from Steph and Morgan's house than I've ever gone before. I find a huge, spectacular cemetery, much different from the above-ground crypts I've seen in southern Louisiana. I find parks, and bridges, and stunning older houses, their yards a riot of different flowering plants. I discover a kind of twisty red-barked tree I've never seen before. I find a boardwalk path laid through a cedar bog, a kind of northern swamp that makes me feel right at home. I watch a crew of muscular young men row a narrow boat through the channel that links the really big lake, Lake Washington, with the sort-of big lake, Lake Union. Across the water, that's the University of Washington. I could go to college there in a few years, and the prospect makes me unreasonably happy.

I find the top of the hill, and a water tower that gets me even higher, and look across Lake Washington all the way to another tall city—Bellevue, is it? Suddenly the scale of the urban area starts to get through to me. From my vantage point, there's city to the north and city to the south and city to the east and city to the west. And beyond what I can see, there's a city, Tacoma, nearly as big as Seattle. So many people. Thousands, maybe a million, maybe millions. I realize I have no idea, but I know it's vast, and it's mine. The hills, the water, the trees, the flowers, the buildings: all of this belongs to me.

At first, just mapping out all this territory seems like the most exciting thing I've ever done, and I can't believe I've never done it before. I've been here for months, can it really be true that I've trod the same well-worn pathways the whole time? Home, school, grocery store, the end? Seattle is beautiful, every square inch is full of amazing things

But over the next two weeks, the giddy energy drains out of my mood, leaving me bitter and morose. Even my newfound popularity starts to seem like more trouble than it's worth. I maintain politeness with an effort, but deep down I'm full of increasing spite for these people who couldn't be bothered with me until I punched a guy out. I hate them. I hate myself for hating them. Eventually I'm a seething ball of hate, slinking around the school getting ready to fail my final exams.

The confrontation with all those stark white sheets of paper really drives my ignorance home. Solve for X. Explain the role *Dred Scott v Sandford* played in the lead-up to the Civil War. True or false, the phases of the moon are caused by the shadow of the Earth? The final line of *Ozymandius* by Percy Bysse Shelley is "Look on my works Ye mighty, and despair." Please pick another single line or phrase from the approved reading list and compare and contrast.

By the end of the day, my brain feels like a fried egg. I walk home, eyes prickling with tears of frustration. I try to tell myself it doesn't matter. I'm still new to the outside world, even if this soggy messy spring feels like it's dragging on forever. These other kids have spent fifteen or sixteen years learning all this stuff. I've been at it only a few months. Of course I failed.

But what if I really am stupid?

At New Harmony I thought I was smart. I was good at sums, good at my letters. After my Humbling I was the one who taught the younger kids. I tried not to feel too pleased about this, because pride is a sin. But I guess, deep down, I did feel pride. And now I feel shame.

To make matters worse, after my dismal finals performance, I hope to find Deena and let her cheer me up. But instead only Portia is there, the one who doesn't seem to like me very much. Still, I try being friendly. "Hey, Portia."

"Hey," she responds.

"Is Deena around?"

"She had a thing." She folds her arms and glares at me, eyelids lowered. "Can I help you with something?"

Her hostility makes me feel angry in return. "Sorry I bothered you. I'll go."

She shrugs. "Fine with me."

I'm about to walk away, then I turn around. "No, wait. Why are you so mad at me? What did I do?"

She sighs, adjusts her glasses primly to stare at me through them. "Nothing. I'm not mad. I just don't happen to like you. You're Deena's friend, not mine."

Wow, that hurts. I stare at her, feeling my eyes go all wounded and prickly with tears. "Look, if I did something wrong, I'm sorry. I grew up in kind of a weird situation. Home-schooled and super religious and all that. So I don't always know how to act in the regular world. I probably screw up all the time without knowing it."

She is still hostile, but I sense a flicker of interest. "Really? Was it like the Duggers?"

"I'm sorry, I don't know what that is."

"They're, like, this super-religious family with a million kids. They have a reality show. Some people think they're great, but other people say they're a cult." Her eyes widen. "Oh, wow, did you grow up in a cult?"

Cult? I'm not entirely sure I know what that means. "Maybe. How do you know if something is a cult?"

"Huh, that's a good question. You should ask Deena. She's an expert on all that weirdo stuff. You know, serial killers and Bigfoot and UFOs and everything." She pauses. "Well, gotta go. See ya."

She walks away, leaving me feeling worse than before I tried talking to her. I'm not sure I can deal with this business of having a peer group.

My mood brightens a little when I walk into a house that smells wonderfully of baked chocolate. I follow the aroma into the kitchen, where Steph and Morgan sit at the table. In front of them rests a cake frosted deep crimson, HAPPY 16TH ABBY! scribbled in white frosting. Small red candles stick out of the top. Next to the cake sits a small pile of boxes, wrapped in bright red paper and black ribbons edged in gold. Steph and Morgan notice me and stand up. Morgan uses a lighter to set the candles aflame. Steph starts singing: "Happy birthday, to you" but Morgan doesn't join in.

She stops singing to glare at him. "Morgan!"

"I made the cake. I don't have to sing." He folds his arms, glaring at her in challenge.

"Jesus Christ, do you have to be a dick about everything?" She catches herself and gives me a nervous smile. "I'm sorry, Abby, I didn't mean—remember when you had to pick a birthday for your school paperwork? We picked June 16. That's today. It's your birthday."

I nod. I definitely managed to pick up on that, at least. But I'm still not entirely sure what's going on. "This is all because it's my birthday?"

Big smile. "That's right! You never had a birthday like this, did you? With presents and cake and all that?"

I shake my head. Nope. When I turned twelve, I partici-pated in a coming-of-age ritual called the Humbling, which involved solitary confinement, a shaved head, a beating with a

cane, and a sermon of epic length, which endured until I literally collapsed from the strain. In my whole life, nobody has
ever given me a present.

Steph continues, "Well, what you do now is, you make a
wish, then blow out the candles. There are sixteen of them.
That's one for every year of your life so far. If you blow them
all out with one breath, you get your wish. Then we eat cake.
Then you open the packages."

"Oh. Okay. Thank you." I contemplate the fiery candles
for a moment, picture myself blowing on them, calculate how
much breath I'll need to take in, how much force I'll have to
put behind it. I'm overwhelmed by the kindness of this
birthday custom, the obvious attempt to make me feel happy
and special. But I'm also struck by the morbid symbolism.
Every candle extinguished is a year of your life, snuffed out.
And each of us with only so many candles. What do they do
with the very old? Do the cakes get bigger and bigger?

The wish is a strange outsider custom. Steph is a not-
particularly-devout Catholic, and Morgan a fairly belligerent
atheist, but both of them speak casually about fate, wishes,
good luck, and other semi-magical concepts separate from the
notion of God or prayer. What power is supposed to grant my
wish? The universe itself? Any random creature that happens
to be listening? Something within me?

I inhale. I close my eyes. What do I wish? I wish—

I wish that I had taken Ash away from my father sooner.
But that's in the past, and there's no way that wish can come
true. I wish—

I wish that I could take all my siblings away from my
father. I don't have any idea how I would do that, but it's what
I want.

Throat closing in sorrow, I exhale. Sixteen years gone, as
burnt-out candles smolder with a faint odor of wax.

"I took the night off work," Steph says. "I figured after
you open your presents we could have a real girls' night out.

We'll get mochas and go to a movie. We could see something R-rated, what do you think?"

R-rated. That means naughty. "Okay." I smile. I don't know if I'm ready, but Steph seems so excited and I hate to disappoint her.

Morgan says, "And tomorrow afternoon we go to the gun range. At sixteen you're old enough to learn to shoot."

"Morgan!" Steph says. "I told you, you have to ask. Maybe she doesn't want to go to the gun range."

"Okay, Abby. Want to go to the gun range tomorrow?"

"Sure. Why not?"

The process of present-opening seems to have a well-defined ritual. Take up the package, smile for a picture. Open the package, slowly, giving time for a candid action shot to be taken. Remove the item. Try to look excited. Say thank you. Pose with the item for another picture, sometimes with the giver in the same shot.

Steph gives me several items of clothing adorned with skulls.

"You seem to like that old sweatshirt of mine so much, I figured you needed the whole set," she explains, smiling brightly. I get the message. Abby, stop wearing the same sweatshirt all the time. "Anyway, I figured you could go for kind of a punk look. That seems to be what your hair wants to do."

Morgan gives me a bright red pocket knife with a dozen different blades, including scissors and nail files and a little miniature saw. "Don't bring it to school. They don't like it when kids bring knives to school."

The final gift, from both of them jointly, is a small computer that they call a "netbook."

"Nothing fancy," Steph says. "But you can do your homework on it."

Final hugs all around. To my surprise, the process has left me feeling exhausted. I want to curl up in a corner and take a nap for a while, not go out to a movie. But, again, I don't want to disappoint Steph, so I dutifully go and put on my brand new skull-covered outfit, and join her in the car. It's a funny thing. I'm being coerced by sympathy, not the threat of pain, into an indulgent entertainment, not an unpleasant chore. But it still reminds me of New Harmony. This is how they do it on the outside. Kids who genuinely like their parents try to please them, because they don't want them to feel bad.

At the movie, we share a giant tub of popcorn, small nuggets of ice cream covered in chocolate, and a huge cola. "The junk food is part of the experience," Steph tells me with a smile. The popcorn smells delicious but tastes like packing material. Outsider chemical tricks give food bright colors, vivid odors, sweet tastes, but they don't mean ripeness or goodness. They mean somebody got busy in a laboratory.

"What's wrong?" Steph asks.

"Nothing. Still full from birthday cake." I smile and have another handful of popcorn. It gives me something to do, anyway, while we're waiting for the movie to start. The fat and salt render it barely palatable, and I suppose industrial food is better than starving. What am I so cranky about anyway? Steph is trying to make me happy.

The massive screen at the front of the theater starts showing commercials, like the ones we see on television, only with higher production values. Then the lights go down and we get commercials for other movies, obviously designed to make them look exciting, with stirring music and a breathless announcer. The sheer size of the image is impressive, but what I really like is the music. It emerges from speakers arrayed all the way along both walls, from in front and beside and behind us. I'm immersed in the sound, feel it vibrating in the core of my own body.

I'm getting better at making sense of movies, but this one —which seems to involve some vampires and werewolves who don't get along—still leaves me frequently baffled. People have conversations that don't seem to be about anything in particular, and fights just because, and the film goes to ultra-slow-motion sometimes to show us the intricate details of spattering blood and well-landed punches. The cast includes a fair number of attractive young males who take off their shirts and gleam majestically in the artificially blue moonlight. Then, some of them turn into badly animated wolves. Why? Who knows? Since I can't seem to follow the plot anyway, I find myself engaged in idle speculation: do the werewolves have to wax their chests in order to appear so smooth in human form like that? Do the vampires ever cut themselves on their own fangs? Are the two male leads going to kiss each other? Because sometimes it really feels like that's where this is going.

"So, what did you think?" Steph asks as we leave the theater.

"I liked it." My voice sounds unconvincing, even to me.

"Was it too scary for you?"

I stare at her, baffled, for a moment. Does she really not know how often Morgan and I watch horror movies together when she's at work? "No. Not too scary."

"You thought it was stupid, didn't you?"

"It was fine. I'm still not used to watching movies. I can't always seem to follow the plots."

She laughs. "No, hon, that was the movie, not you. But I told you right when we met, I got a thing for shirtless were-wolf boys. This had plenty of that, at least." She dumps the uneaten popcorn into an overstuffed garbage can.

THE NEXT DAY, MORGAN TAKES ME TO THE GUN RANGE AS promised.

"Imagine the target is your worst enemy. A test you failed, maybe. Or George. Picture George." Morgan tells me this as I aim. But when I try to picture my worst enemy, it's not George who comes to mind. It's my father. Father Wisdom.

I shoot. It goes wide.

"That's okay. You're new. Don't think about the gun, think about the target. The gun is an extension of your hand."

Abnegation, says the target. He takes off his broad-brimmed summer hat and smiles at me, the almost seductive smile he used when he felt the need to win a person over. He could be so charming when he wanted. *Child, you don't want to shoot me.*

Blam. Blam. Blam.

"You're getting closer. Think about holding the gun steady, not so much about the aim."

What if I did go back to New Harmony and kill my father?

No. Impossible. I can't believe I just thought that. I don't want to kill anybody. I don't.

Blam.

"Okay, that one went wide again. Is your arm getting tired? Remember, you want to use both arms, like this."

I want to help my siblings escape, like I did. And escape means more than just getting out of there in the body. I've spent months trying to get out of there in my head, and only now is it starting to seem like it's working. Only now is the outside world starting to seem truly real.

Suddenly I feel weirdly full of hope, as if I've turned a corner and things are sliding into place. My hand and the gun and the target are one, blam blam blam. I know what I have to do, now. This summer, when Steph takes the baby down to New Orleans to visit the grandparents, I'm going to go back to New Harmony and offer the way out to anybody who wants it. Steph will help me, I know she will.

"Wow. You really got it that time." Morgan claps me on the back encouragingly. "Why don't we quit while we're ahead?"

11

JUNEUARY

The final week of school is only three days long, displaced thanks to something called "snow days," school days missed during a storm in December, before I arrived in Seattle. I feel a little left out to have missed it. Apparently when Seattle gets more than an inch or two of snow, everything closes and people spend all day sledding down hills and making snowmen. I've never seen snow at all.

On Wednesday, the last day of school, I participate in a quaint outsider ritual that involves signing other people's yearbooks with vague pleasantries. I'm asked for my services in this regard at least a dozen times, which is probably not a lot for many people, but it's about a dozen more than I would have signed a couple of weeks ago. But at the end of the day I'm alone, trudging home in a chilly drizzle. The weather has turned so cold and rainy that people are calling this "Juneuary."

Deena calls out to me. "Hey, Gator girl! I got something that might cheer you up." She hands me a postcard, an invitation:

TROY'S FOURTH ANNUAL SUMMER HOWL
In the hundred acre wood,
aka Troy's parents' place in the middle of nowhere.
Food* and drink aplenty
Bring your own camping gear.
Party goes from noon July 3
to noon July 4
Ceremonial burning at dusk
Bring artifacts
*Yes, you hippies, we have vegetarian!

"Why do they call it a howl?" I feel a strangely familiar tingling at the back of my head, a sense of déjà-vu, like a memory that almost—almost—

No, it's gone. Like all those test answers I couldn't remember.

"Well, it's the full moon. Supposed to be perfect weather for the first time this year. Camping out, getting stoned. There'll be a keg and everything. It'll be a lot of the same crowd as the dance."

"I don't think that crowd wants to see me. Aren't they afraid I'll start a riot or something?"

She snickers. "You're kidding. Slugging Colin was a public service. Anyway, Edison is going to be there."

My heart thumps. "Edison. He seemed nice."

"Nice!" All of them dissolve into giggles.

"What? He did seem nice." I wince, feel myself turn hot and beet-colored, which causes them all to laugh again.

"You can ride out with us if you want."

"Okay. I'll talk to my aunt and see if I can go." I look down at the invitation. "What's this about burning and artifacts?"

"That's a thing they do with the bonfire—you know, toss in pictures of your ex and stuff like that. You could burn your grades."

Portia looks appalled. "She can't do that! Those are official documents!"

Deena shrugs. "Well, you get the idea. Let me know."

I take the invitation home, sure Steph will say yes without hesitation. But instead she glares at it suspiciously. "You want to go to an all-night party? With college boys? And drinking?"

"You should talk, sis," Morgan says. "Weren't you already well on the way to a lifetime of alcoholism and partying by the time you were Abby's age?"

"I'm not an alcoholic. I just—anyway, this is different. Abby was raised in a very sheltered environment. I don't know if she'll be able to handle herself at a party like this."

For a second I'm actually angry. She's thinking about telling me I can't go?

She seems to pick up on my mood, and sighs. "Fine. Go to the party. But I want you to memorize our phone numbers before you go, okay? You might drop your phone in the creek or something."

Or I might wake up somewhere, naked, with no idea how I got there. Right? She doesn't say it, but she's got to be thinking it.

"Thanks, Steph." I hug her, and hope that makes everything all right again.

For the next week or so I suffer from an almost unbearable rising excitement. Even when the dismal results of my final grades show up in the mail (oh, they're not so bad, Steph tells me), and Father Mulligan stops by to suggest, delicately, that I ought to think about attending summer school in a couple of subjects, the party is all I can think about.

I don't even know if I'll have a good time. In fact, I expect it to be awkward and sometimes lonely, as people who already know each other have conversations I can barely make sense of. Edison will be there, a boy who had kind words for me— well, any words at all—and who is rumored to play the guitar. A musician.

I decide to take the ceremonial burning seriously, and go back to the thrift store Steph and I visited, the one where I knocked over all the dishes. I rummage through the book section until I locate my father's books. Still there. Battered corners, spines broken. The thought that they don't have much resale value fills me with malicious satisfaction. I pick one up and stare into the eyes of the author photo on the back. When I was younger, when I didn't know any better, I thought my father's books were like the Bible, received wisdom from the ages, eternal truths written into the heart of the world. Even when I began to doubt him sometimes, after my mother died, I thought the problem was me, my own inherent wickedness, my beast. Right up to the moment I ran away, I thought I was the bad influence, the danger, and I was protecting my sisters and brothers by leaving.

But I wasn't protecting them. I was leaving them at his mercy, the mercy of Wisdom, and I'm not sure he has any.

"Oh, that's a fantastic book!" A woman's gushing voice commands my attention, and I turn to see the pink, smiling, fresh-scrubbed face of a woman who would be right at home in the outsider churches I remember from my youth. I look down at the book in my hands, the one she's referring to. It's *Perfect Obedience*, the one Wisdom wrote about how to raise children so that they behave. The one where he talks about how to break their wills with chastenings and corrections. The one where he quotes Proverbs 23:13: *Withhold not correction from the child; for if thou beatest him with the rod, he shall not die.*

"It is?" Until this moment, it had never occurred to me that, if John Wise published books, people in the outside world must have read them and heard of them. It makes me feel exposed, as if all my clothing has fallen away. If she's read this book, she knows things about me, about what I've been through, things even Steph doesn't know.

I stare at the front cover, with its stock photo of a blond child, four or five years old, clasping the hand of an otherwise unseen adult, looking up at him—the hand is obviously masculine—with a wide smile of adoration. That child is supposed to be me. It's supposed to be Sackcloth with Ashes (who did die, don't ever forget that). It's supposed to be Great Purpose, Chastity, Justice and Mercy, Righteousness, Unity of Faith, Steadfast, Diligence, Obedience, Humility, Repentance, Grieve Not, and... now I can't remember what Meekness named her youngest, still a babe in arms, though perhaps he has started to crawl by now. Promised, that's it. Promised is the baby. That plump, golden, happy child is supposed to be all of us.

Black rage fills me. I imagine myself tearing the book in two and throwing it in the face of the pinkly smiling woman.

"Our younger son was quite a trial. The techniques in there worked wonders." Her smile sags a tiny bit. "Are you buying it for your parents?"

I fight the rage for a moment, then give in to an entirely different evil impulse. "Oh, no, ma'am." I crank up the slight backwoods drawl in my accent. "This is for my own little ones. Got my curse at thirteen and started fulfilling the Lord's sacred duty right away. I'm sixteen. Already got three blessings and a fourth on the way." I pat my belly suggestively, using my stomach muscles to push it out a little bit, so that I look like I could be barely pregnant. She looks from me, to my stomach, to the book, with a look of dawning horror.

"But—does that mean you're already married, child?"

"In the eyes of the Lord, ma'am. My brother Japheth and I were joined in holy matrimony by our father on the first moon after my curse come upon me."

Her eyes are dinner plates. "Your brother?"

"Only half, ma'am. We share a father, not a mother. That's in the right, according to the good book. If we shared a mother it would be an abomination. Now, I'd best get back to my chores. You have a blessed day, now."

I start walking up to the counter with my stack of books.

She stares at me, deflated. In a small voice she says, "You have more than one copy of *Perfect Obedience.*"

"Thank you for pointing that out, ma'am. It's just that important of a book."

She leaves the store while I'm in line, her face so ashen that I start to feel slightly bad for her. The clerk raises his well-pierced eyebrows at me. "That's quite a stack of books you got there." I hear the suppressed laughter in his voice.

"Good kindling."

He nods. "Wish I'd gotten that little exchange on video."

12

THE HOWL

The day of the party finally dawns. Backpack and sleeping bag ready by the door, I pace around the house until Steph tells me to knock it off, she has a headache. I think she might have had a drink or two last night, hiding the smell from me by claiming a cold and going instantly to bed. But I can't worry about that too much. I can't.

The doorbell rings. Deena stands on the porch, grinning. "Ready to go? Oh, good, your bag is small. I'm afraid you're going to have to keep it on your lap, the rest of us kind of filled up the trunk space."

I hug Steph goodbye.She hugs back but I think she's deliberately avoiding breathing on me. It doesn't matter. I'm going anyway. "Have a good time," she says, with a smile that seems oddly sad. "You have our phone numbers memorized, right? And that emergency twenty-dollar bill?" I nod. "Okay, I guess you're ready."

Deena's car has seatbelts, but not exactly room, for five people. "Gator girl, you're smallest, so you have to ride in the middle of the back. You can operate the tunes."

Luckily for my pride, operating the tunes involves using a

phone like mine and Steph's, so I don't have to humiliate myself by asking what buttons to push. As my fingers slide over the glossy screen, I think of the many rants against rock music, television, movies, fiction books, consumer culture, and the feminist-homosexual agenda that I grew up hearing. Father never spoke of mobile phones or the Internet. Did he know about those things? They had them seventeen years ago, when he formed New Harmony, but it seems to me now that he was out of touch even before he sequestered himself there, looking backward to a social reality already twenty years out of date, where people worried about global thermonuclear war and not global warming.

"You're quiet," Deena says to me.

"Usually."

She laughs. "How did those finals work out? As bad as you thought?"

"Well... It looks like I might be going to summer school."

"Oh, that'll be fun. They offer cool classes during summer school that you can't get during the year. I had marine biology once. You mind if I smoke?"

"It's your car."

"I'll keep the window rolled down, I promise." Road noise roars in along with the rich warm air of a summer day, pungent evergreens and underlying stink of diesel, now joined by tobacco smoke. I close my eyes and sink into the music. Listening to the mix from Steph's dad has acquainted me with different styles of popular music, and I can now, sort of, tell punk from grunge, Brit pop from Motown, Nina Simone from Amy Winehouse, Led Zeppelin blues from Robert Johnson blues.

Have I made up my mind about the spirit in the music? I imagine Steph's father, smiling as he asks me that question. And I think I have made up my mind. The whole thing is a trick in human perception, because our brains work that way. A certain beat makes us want to dance, a progression of minor chords makes us feel sad. There is no spirit in the music or anywhere else, we just imagine there is.

Just like my father's demons, it's all in our heads.

We arrive at the location sooner than I expect. Deena's description made it sound to be in the middle of nowhere, but it's really only a couple of hours from Seattle. Several tents are already set up, and a huge fire is smoldering, the wood pleasantly aromatic. Luckily Deena and Portia seem to be able to get the tent set up without my assistance. I know a lot of things about nature survival, but I do not know how to put up a tent. The other girls grab beers, and I grab a soda, and we go out to mingle.

Everyone is friendly, but I can tell I'm not a good conversationalist today. I can't seem to focus on anything right in front of me. Instead, I keep getting distracted by things on the periphery. Flickering movement at the edge of my vision, transitory smells drifting through the air and begging me to follow, rustling in the brushes inviting me to run like a cat and pounce.

People offer me cups of beer and puffs of marijuana, but it's not difficult to turn them down. No thank you. No thank you. No thank you. I start to feel removed from everyone around me, as we occupy the same space but different worlds of thought.

The meat goes into the fire and I inhale an intoxicating aroma that makes me feel hungry. No, sick. It makes me feel sick. Aimlessly, I wander away from every conversation. I feel like I'm waiting for something. The sinking sun finds me alone on the edge of the party, staring out at the beckoning wilderness. The full moon rises and I want to go deep into the trees, away from everything, to run, to hunt—

Hunt? I didn't really just think that, did I?

"Whoo-hoo!" Behind me, a wordless shout of exultation. Out in the hills, a coyote lifts its voice in song.

"Dude, did you hear that? There's wolves out there."

Portia finds me. She's been drinking and her glasses are askew. She hangs her head. "I'm sorry I was mean to you before."

"That's okay."

"No. It's really not. I was a bitch."

"It's okay to be a bitch."

"Let me apologize, okay? I had this thing. When Deen first started talking to you, I was, like, wow, here's a girl who's even shyer and nerdier than I am. So I put you in that box, where I thought I was above you. Then when everybody started treating you like you were cool, it felt like a blow. Like I was back on the bottom of the totem pole again, and I treated you bad because of it. But it was my deal. I had to get over myself. You were right, you never did anything wrong."

"Sorry, Portia? I don't want to derail our touching reconciliation here, but nobody treats me like I'm cool. Where have you been hanging out?"

She laughs. "Okay, maybe not everybody. But my everybody. My best friend and the guy I have a crush on. But I think the punching out of Colin Ambrose and the scaring off of Lorinda actually did put you in the cool category. At Saint Sebastian, anyway."

"Ah. So my propensity for violence is the key to my social acceptability? That's a depressing thought."

"It's not the violence, dummy. It's the standing up for yourself."

I nod, find myself smiling. "Okay. That sounds a lot better."

"Anyway, friends?"

"Sure. Friends."

We hug, awkwardly, her half-full cup splashing beer on me. We pull apart and she gives me a perplexed look. "Oh, wow. Did the earth turn upside-down for a minute?"

"It seems unlikely."

She looks at her cup, now nearly empty, and giggles. "I must need more beer!" She totters back toward the keg.

"Woo-hoo!" There seems to be a lot of that going on. A shower of sparks rises from the center of the fire.

"It's burning time!"

Oh, shoot. I almost forgot about that. I run to the tent, grab the stack of my father's books, then hurry back out to the fire. Watching the flames crackle, feeling the heat on my face and the weight of the books in my arms, smelling them give off a faint dusty thrift store odor, the reality starts to sink in, and I realize I'm more keyed up than I thought I would be, excited, but also afraid. When I first thought about doing this, it seemed harmless and funny. But now I feel a weight to this act, a sense that I'm stepping through a one-way barrier into darkness. If anything my father said was true, if there is any kind of dark magic in the world, I'll find it here, in this pagan ritual. Bonfire at midsummer, dancing and singing under a full moon. Burning Wisdom's words, and his image, is like burning a piece of him. Nothing could signal more plainly my intent to say "screw you" to his spiritual covering. He would have me believe there is a beast waiting eagerly for that moment, waiting to pounce. But I decided I don't believe in this beast. This moment doesn't matter to anybody but me.

I guess we'll find out who's right.

I toss the first book into the fire, back cover upward, so I can watch his hated face crackle, blacken, disappear. *I reject you, Wisdom. I abjure you. I cast you out.*

The fire is intensely hot, and seems to grow hotter where the book is now flaming away merrily. Hell is supposed to be full of flames, isn't it? There, that's Father Wisdom in hell. Fragments of paper still aflame rise high into the air, drifting on the hot wind, catching in the spiny needles of a Douglas fir. I hold my breath, ready to stop a forest fire from spreading. But the tree is green and lush and the paper flickers harmlessly, turning into blackened ash that disappears into the darkness of the night.

The other books, I shove deeper into the fire, underneath the logs, so the flying paper sparks won't happen again. I want to watch my father burn, but I don't want to watch the forest burn.

Not long after, the music and dancing starts up. That keeps me entertained for a while. It doesn't matter that I can't seem to carry on a conversation, because when you're dancing and the music is loud, nobody expects you to talk.

When the band takes a break, Edison comes over to talk. "Nice dancing."

"Nice playing."

"Deena told me your name. Abby something?"

"Abby something, yeah." I giggle. Abby-negation. Negation of Abby. Oh, wow, that's what that means, isn't it? Negation of the self, I never really thought of it before—

"I'm sorry, I'm sober, but I think I'm getting a contact high."

He nods. "Could be. Or maybe it's the mountain air. It's got, like, more oxygen I think. Or less oxygen. You're not from around here, are you?"

"No. Louisiana."

"You a Cajun?"

I laugh. "No, not Cajun. They play music and dance and cook spicy food. My father hated all that stuff."

He nods. "Right. Deena told me that too. About you having a super religious background. Very sheltered."

"That's right." I think about Steph's Cajun grandmother and her stories about the rougarou—

Aroooooooooo

"Coyote," I observe.

"So. Uh. Is that hair color natural?"

I run my hand through it, where, in spite of being nearly six inches long now (six months, six inches, a lifetime, but not really so long, not really, the past is close enough to touch) it still has a tendency to stick out every which way.

"Pretty much," I say.

"Wow. Okay. Cool." He looks down at his plastic cup of beer. "I'm from around here. Business major. Pretty boring."

Business major? Oh. "You're in college."

"Yeah." Sheepish smile. "I know you're still in high school with Deena. It's funny, huh? I'm only a little bit older than her, but sometimes it's like we're in different worlds."

I don't really know what to say to that, so I nod. If beer smoothes over these awkward conversational pauses, maybe I get why people drink it at parties. I pop in with the question Steph's dad used to break the ice with me. "So, do you like jazz?"

He shrugs. "I don't really know jazz. I only learned to play rock. You know, the stuff I grew up listening to. Isn't that how everybody learns?"

"Oh, sure, sure. Everybody learns what they know." Ouch, did I really just say that? Well, he's stoned, he won't notice me sounding like an idiot.

He sips his beer and his eyes twinkle. "So, do you have a boyfriend?"

"What? No."

"Haha, you turned bright red. Match your hair." He sips again, looking up at me through his dark brows. "You ever had a boyfriend?"

I'm so uncomfortable now that all I can do is laugh. "No. No way. No."

"You ever want a boyfriend?" He grins, like he's offering.

I say, "Maybe," and I can feel the blush getting hotter and I look down, then look out again, moonlight on trees, beckoning, I could get out of this unspeakable awkwardness, this intolerable mating dance—

Mating? Did I really just think that?

"Ever been kissed?"

My heart pounds, thunder in my ears, and I answer, "What do you think?" and he leans down, I inhale his desire, like a spicy drug, but when his lips meet mine and his arm comes around my back I stiffen in shock. I didn't see it coming. I probably should have.

For a heartbeat, I have no idea what to do.

Maybe I want him to do that, kiss me, touch me. Maybe.

But this is too soon. He didn't wait for me to say yes. He's pushing it, setting the pace, trying to dominate me. I can't let him.

I can't let him be the boss.

In the next heartbeat, I use his weight and our height difference to flip him to the ground, onto his back, the surrender position, showing his belly, and a small noise escapes me, like a growl, and he says, whoa, and suddenly Deena is there saying what the hell, Abby.

A red veil falls from my perceptions, and I see the full impact of what I've done. Did I hurt him? Everyone gathers around us, asking if he's okay, kneeling down.

Deena rages. "Abby, what did you do? What did you do?"

Shame taints my thoughts, which swirl like a cloud of angry bees. How could I have done such a thing? How dare he challenge me? What if I hurt him? He should have known what he was doing. What's wrong with him? What's wrong with me? I can't take it. I want to disappear. I want to cease to exist. Abby goes away now, bye. Abby negates.

I run into the night, swifter than moonlight and fiercer than blood and the shame falls behind me, clothes fall away too, and I am nothing but the joy of the hunt as she catches the doe on the wind and gives voice in a full-throated howl and runs and runs—

13

WAKING UP NAKED IN THE WOODS

I wake up shivering.

Curled as small as I can go, arms and legs trying to warm my front, something else blocking the wind from my back. Meat, blood, death, smells so powerful and overwhelming they seem solid, as if I'm held inside of them. A prison of odor. My brain spits out the word: deer. Doe. Flash of memory, sensation of running at top speed, hands to the ground, teeth stretching out, tearing into the meat of her leg, one bite and she tumbles down. Like the wolves on a nature program I saw once. I remember.

Running on all fours. Biting into her flank with elongated jaw full of sharp—

No.

I stand up, back released to the air, damp with fluids that dry rapidly and chill me further. I glance down. I was nestled inside the partially-eaten carcass of a deer. Some animal killed it last night, maybe a bear, do they have bears around here? Do bears kill deer? What kills a deer?

(*Me*)

Wash myself, I have to wash off the blood and gore. Good thing I removed my clothes, unclean work, like when Father made me bury the dogs or my mother's bones. I don't think about this much—about why he did that. About what it felt like to put my own mother in the ground. I always forget, don't I, and then suddenly I remember. When she was dying, I ran to him and tried to get him to call an outsider doctor. We argued. I was so sure that he would see it my way, that he would believe Mother Blessed's life was more important than whatever taboo he had embraced against using outsider medicine. I imagined him using the special emergency radio to call for a doctor. I didn't imagine him just saying—

"If the Lord wills it, it must be so." I whisper, out loud. I was only nine. I didn't understand my father. I knew in my heart and was sure that he must know it too, that saving Mother's life was more important than any religious conviction. God was out there, sure—I hadn't yet begun to doubt that. But Mother was right in front of us, and she had to be more important, more real. Didn't she?

Not to him. *Bury your mother's bones. Wash thyself in cold water.*

I follow the crystalline scent of an icy river, half sure that this is a nightmare. But my feet prickle as my weight comes down on pine needles and small rocks, feet too accustomed to shoes now, and the pain seems to anchor me, making the world more real with every step. Plunging into the icy water of the creek shocks me to full alertness. No, not dreaming. Where did I leave my clothes? Why did I take them off? Did somebody drug me last night, slip something into my can of Coke? I've heard about such things happening at parties like this. That's why I don't remember removing them with my hands. Except that I do remember them coming off, on their own, as my—

Body—

Changed—

Shape—

No.

I inhale deeply, distant aromas of a human morning: fire

lit, coffee percolating, butter warming in a hot skillet. But the butter doesn't make me hungry. Instead, it reminds me that I feel overly full, bloated, as if my stomach is about to explode—

Kneeling, I vomit, flabby foulness in an alarming shade of bloody scarlet. Raw meat. Parts of a doe. Of course, what else would it be? I woke up in the middle of a partially eaten deer carcass.

I woke up. Naked. In the middle of a—

No.

Where are my clothes? Follow my own scent trail until I find them, mostly intact. Coyotes mauled everything, my sweatshirt and pants and shirt smelling distressingly strong of coyote musk. My shoes are shredded completely, as if I left them in the presence of a pet dog who felt neglected.

No longer naked, I hope I can get back to camp and collect my stuff before Deena wakes up. I run, impatient to get there, impatient to feel warmer. My feet seem to callus up rapidly, each step hurting less than the one before. Early morning hush, small handful of people huddled near the fire, fingers wrapped around mugs of steaming coffee. They don't seem to notice my approach, and I think it's best to avoid them. The enormity of what I've done to my fledgling social life hits me in the gut. Deena, the first person other than Steph to want to be my friend, Edison, the first boy to want to kiss me, both of them hating me forever now. The blow crushes me, but only for a second. I have bigger things to concern myself with. Because I'm—I seem to be—

No.

Quiet, I barely rustle the tent when I enter. Four girls snoring in a staccato rhythm covers up any noise I make while scooting out my sleeping bag and backpack. Outside, I stuff the bag into its carrier and shoulder my pack. Lighter, without my father's books.

No. I'm not going to think about my father.

Do I remember how to get back to the main highway? I try using my phone to get a map, but the signal is too weak. Instead I inhale deeply, try to pinpoint the direction of the diesel reek that signals a highway. There. I start walking.

Bare feet sink into springy, wet moss, as I walk down the side of a muddy gravel road. The gravel turns to pavement, then the pavement turns wider and straighter. Early, the day feels hushed and cool, rising sun hidden behind the hills. No cars. The quiet makes me think of the night I left New Harmony, fleeing to the distant and dimly remembered highway with no clear destination in mind. Running and running, a doe chased by hunting dogs. But now I'm the hunt—

No.

Yes.

I have to face this thing.

Because, no matter how ridiculous, how impossible it seems, Steph was right about the rougarou. She was right about me.

I am something almost exactly like a werewolf.

14

THE ROUGAROU

I'm so preoccupied that I forget to start checking for phone signal, and the sound of its ring shatters my thoughts like a scream. It's Steph. "Abby? Abby, what the hell is going on? Where are you?"

"I'm here, Steph," I say, then realize that "here" has no meaning for either of us. I'm walking down the side of a highway, somewhere in Washington State, cool summer morning smelling of dust and evergreens. "Sorry, I mean, I'm okay. I'm trying to get back to civilization."

"Damn it!" Her anger is driven by worry, I can hear it in her voice, and I start to feel guilty, I didn't mean for her to be afraid for me. "How could you just walk away like that?"

"Deena and I had a fight." I don't want to talk about it, but I might as well confess now, if only to explain to Steph why I acted so strangely.

"She told me about that. But you shouldn't have—you're out in the middle of the woods! You could've been eaten by a bear!"

I fight back a giggle of hysterical giddiness. *Oh, Steph, don't be silly, I was a wolf last night. How often do wolves get eaten by bears?* I try to picture it. Did I look like a normal wolf? In the movies, werewolves are often hideous mutant creatures, but I think that's because they're played by human actors in costumes. Real werewolf legends—well, I only know the one Steph told me, a half-remembered fairy tale learned at her grandmother's knee.

With some effort, I rip my racing thoughts back to the conversation. "I'm sorry, Steph. Deena was really mad at me. I thought I should leave. I was going to text her and call you as soon as I had signal, really, I was."

"God! Okay. Deep breath." She takes one. "Tell me where you are and I'll come get you. And never, ever, ever do anything like that again. Ever. You don't just walk away without telling anyone."

But Steph, that's how we met. I walked away without telling anyone. "I'll call you as soon as I figure out where I am, okay?"

"Find a safe place to wait for me. Somewhere with people around. A gas station or a coffee shop or something, can you do that? Do you still have that twenty I gave you?"

"I do." Coyotes did not eat my money.

A couple of miles later, I find a gas station with a small convenience store, new and slick, contrasting with its rustic surroundings. On entering I sneeze a few times, irritated by smells of plastic and cheap coffee and the young male clerk's extremely powerful cologne. He glances at me, bored, then goes back to watching a small television behind the counter. It takes him forever to respond to my presence. On the screen, I notice that he seems to be watching race cars drive around and around in circles.

"What?" He sighs, heavily, so put-upon. He's probably only a little older than I am, seventeen or eighteen. Acne erupts across his cheeks and his beard is patchy.

"My aunt is picking me up here. I need to give her the address. What is it?"

With more sighs, and much in the way of eye-rolling, he retrieves the address from cash register receipts. Then he says,

"You can't just hang out here forever. You have to buy something."

"All right, I'll have a hot chocolate."

The biggest sigh yet, heaved at me with a tangible weight, like a sack of potatoes. "You get it over there. Then you bring it up here and pay for it." His eyes flick briefly to indicate where "over there" is. Hot water sitting on a burner, next to a vacuum pot of coffee, a terraced plastic structure supporting packets of powdered hot chocolate and sugar and non-dairy creamer, white capsules of half-n-half, pink plastic coffee stir-rers, clear display case of ancient donuts and other sad pastries. I saw this setup a dozen times on the road with Steph, and have a sense of déjà-vu, feeling again the stunned wonder of the first time I beheld such a sight. My voice, timid and lost: *but there's so much food.*

My father's voice, thundering: *Abnegation, thou art marked by the beast that waits to devour thee, shouldst thou ever leave mine own spiritual protection.*

Well.

Crap.

It's like Father Wisdom always said, isn't it? The beast did devour me—in a manner of speaking. He could have been more specific. He could have mentioned that the beast was a literal wolf, and "devour" was poetic preacher talk for "turn into." But he must have known what I was. Why else would he tell me all those stories?

At the last minute I decide that hot chocolate sounds too thick and sweet, and select a foil packet of herbal mint tea instead.

The clerk says, "Two dollars."

Drop the bag into the paper cup full of hot water, let the fragrant steam bathe my face. When I take a sip, it tastes faintly of old coffee. I blame the sullen clerk. He seems like the kind of person who wouldn't clean out the pot thoroughly when it goes from holding coffee to holding plain hot water.

The liquid churns in my unsettled gut, still messed up from
—*gorging on raw deer meat, Abby. If you can do it, you should be able to
think it.* Still—although the sensations of being in wolf form
and bringing down the deer are still frighteningly vivid—it
doesn't feel like something the real me really did. It's more like
remembering a dream. Sick with dread, I recall some of the
other things I've done in dreams, in my most horrifying nightmares. Would the wolf do any of those things? Would she kill
a person? Eat a person?

I close my eyes and swallow hard over rising nausea. I
can't throw up again, not here in a convenience store.
Although it does amuse me a little to imagine the clerk forced
to mop up my vomit.

"Hey, Red! Are you barefoot? You can't be in here with
bare feet."

It takes me a moment to realize the clerk is addressing me.
"A coyote ate my shoes," I tell him, flouncing outside in high
outrage.

I think about continuing down the road until I come to
another gas station with a friendlier clerk, but I have no idea
how long that would take on foot and it seems like too much
trouble. I lean against the outer wall and call Steph to give her
the address, which she accepts, curtly. Then I wait, pacing
around, sipping my tea. It cools rapidly in the outdoor air.
Finally, the sun rises high enough that I can warm myself in a
clear beam of it. I close my eyes and try to relax, thoughts
drifting freely until they slam up against a memory, the exact
flavor and texture of hot deer blood bursting into my mouth.
Disturbed by its vividness, I try to shut it out, but it won't go.
It's not only the physical sensations that disturb me, it's
recalling how much she—I—she enjoyed it. How badly she
wanted it. How ferociously hungry she was, for the meat and
the blood and the kill. Predator, prey, law of the jungle, law of
the fallen world. But she doesn't think about laws.

I'm lucky, I realize suddenly. She made a big kill and she

made it early, gorging herself to satiation and then curling up to sleep for the rest of the night. It could easily have gone very differently. What if she—I swallow, gorge rising again—what if she had found one of the campers before she found the deer? What if one of them had followed me into the forest? Worried about me? What if somebody—Deena—Edison— had gotten eaten in exchange for their concern?

Cars start to pull into the station, for gas and snack foods and packs of beer. The eyes of the people glance lightly over me without stopping, almost as if I don't exist, but I'm okay with that. I'm not sure I want to exist right now, not with all these broken and twisty barbed-wire thoughts.

A low, blocky brown car pulls up and a couple gets out, the man in a navy suit too small through the gut, the woman in a pinkish flowered dress with a dropped waist. Church people, I think. That sunny, wholesome, but somehow desperate look is a dead giveaway. I wonder if they're on their way to church right now. Is it Sunday? Without school to measure things by, I've lost track again. The woman smiles in my direction, the vague unfocused smile that church people wear as a matter of habit, then her gaze focuses as she seems to really see me for the first time. She veers in my direction, presses some paper into my hand. A dollar bill and a religious tract. "There you go, sweetie," she says.

I stare down at the items in my hands. She gave me a dollar. Why did she do that? Do I look that bad? Like a beggar? Maybe that's why the clerk was so bitchy at me. The tract is a cartoon style I've seen before, in some of the outsider churches. This particular tract is called *The Beast*. Of course it is. Not sure whether to be angry or amused, I decide amused is easier to deal with and read through it, marking the familiar text, the familiar ideas, all of them bizarre and hilarious in this context, like a low-budget horror film. Humanity is corrupt. Great tribulation, seas turning to blood. Demonic forces running amok on the earth—goat-headed priests, horned demons, hollow-eyed vampires. All our favorite monsters. Where's me? Ah, yes, right in the corner there, a wolf standing up on its hind legs, ready to eat a woman in a hood. That's the werewolf. Is the woman supposed to be a witch? Or Little Red Riding Hood as an old woman?

NOBODY ELSE CAN SAVE YOU. TRUST JESUS TODAY.

I shut the pamphlet, feeling ill. My father said he was the only one who could save me from the beast. It's ridiculous. I know he was lying, just making things up. The demons he talked about weren't real. But the beast was real. And it did come upon me after I left him.

Damn him all to hell, but he was right.

Steph's car pulls up. The door opens, familiar smells wafting out, stale but welcoming. "Get in." She pulls onto the highway impatiently, tires spitting gravel. "You are okay, aren't you?"

"I'm fine."

"You picked the worst possible time to take off like that. George is free. He's out there somewhere. There was some kind of prison riot last night—they're still sorting out exactly what happened, but it was pretty bad. Several people are dead. When they rounded everybody up, they didn't find George or his body."

"What? But how could he get out?"

"Nobody knows." She pauses. "There might be details of the investigation that they're not sharing. I'm going by what Officer Lou told me. They put some police around our place in case he shows up, but so far he hasn't. It's possible he is dead and they just haven't found the body yet." She glances at me. "You see why we were all so worried about you?"

"I know. I'm sorry. I wasn't thinking."

"I know. I know you're a teenager. I can't expect you to be thinking all the time." Slight smile, and I feel forgiven.

We don't talk for a while, then I work up the courage to ask her, "Steph, remember the night you picked me up and you told me about the rougarou?"

She glances at me with a perplexed look. "Yeah. Why do you ask?"

"Oh, we were telling ghost stories around the campfire. This was before the big fight. It was the full moon so I thought of your story and kind of wanted to tell it, but I couldn't remember enough details to make it interesting."

Her mood brightens. "Well, okay. This story works best on the night of a full moon if you can hear something howling out there—coyotes usually. I don't think you'll find any proper wolves coming that close to your campsite. So if you see a wolf, why, it's not likely to be a natural wolf, no ma'am. That's the secret with a campfire story, is to make the people around the campfire start looking out into the dark mysterious woods and being kind of afraid.

"Granny always said that one way you could spot a rougarou was that they would have red hair and freckles, when everybody around them was dark." She grins. "I guess that makes it a good story for you to tell. Otherwise it works if there's another redhead you can pick on. Their eyes are green or blue or yellow, never an honest brown. Sorry, that's how Granny phrased it. 'An honest brown.' You can also spot the rougarou because they don't want to go into the church."

"Are they supposed to be afraid of crosses and holy water, like vampires?"

"Well, the rougarou isn't quite like that. You can't burn them with holy objects. They don't want to go into the church because they have no power when they're inside it and you can kill them like they're a regular person. Other times you can't kill them unless you chop off the head. Bullets go right through 'em."

"What about silver bullets?"

"Granny never mentioned silver. I think that silver bullet thing is from the movies. She did say they were scared of frogs."

"Frogs? You've got to be kidding me."

She laughs. "It's Granny's story. She said you could get a rougarou to leave you alone by throwing a frog at him. And you could keep 'em out of your house by scattering rice on the threshold and the windowsill, because they feel compelled to stop and count every grain before they enter."

"So they're supposed to have severe frog-phobia and crippling obsessive-compulsive disorder? That doesn't sound very scary."

Her eyes twinkle with mischief. "Oh, that's because you don't know their true power. It's the power of seduction. Because in human form that rougarou is going to be the nicest, prettiest, most polite person you ever did meet. He's going to come up to you looking like everything in the world you ever dreamed about. A snappy dresser, a free spender. He'll show you the best time you ever had. Until that full moon comes along, and he reveals his true self and eats you all up. Or bites you, makes you one of them. Then you're a lost soul. Can't ever find heaven, then."

Bites you. I have a twinge of anxiety, thinking of George. When I changed a month ago I bit him, didn't I? Morgan said something about rabies shots. I must have bitten him. Does it work like it does in the movies? Is he a rougarou now?

"So is that the only place the rougarou comes from? When one of them bites you?"

"Well, some are born and some are made, that's what Granny said. Some are under a voodoo spell, can't help themselves. But some of them voodoo themselves on purpose, because they want to go out and do bad things."

Swallow hard, tinny memory of deer blood at the back of my throat. "What kind of bad things?"

"Eating people, mostly. Apparently unbaptized babies are a favorite rougarou snack."

Unbaptized babies. Is that Terry? Steph has not taken him to be baptized yet, I don't think, in spite of her sometimes-Catholicism. "Steph, is Morgan the one babysitting? Is he the one taking care of Terry?"

"Of course. Abby, it's okay, these are just folk tales."

I take a deep breath, my head spinning. "But what if they were real? That dog Morgan saw, he said it looked like a wolf, didn't he? And wasn't it the night of the full moon? And didn't it bite George? What if George is one of them now?"

"Oh, honey, please, don't let yourself get freaked out. There's no such thing. Vampires, werewolves, all of that stuff, none of that is real. It's stories people like to tell. Campfire stories, remember?"

"I know, but—"

"But nothing. George might be out there, but we've got the police helping us, and we can handle it. He's not some supernatural monster, okay? He's just a bad guy."

A bad guy. But I have a sinking feeling that now, he's a monster, too. And I made him that way. If he comes after us again, any power that I had to fight him off before—now he's going to have it too.

INDEPENDENCE DAY

B ack home, we find Morgan's sitting in the living room watching the local news broadcast. He holds Terry out in front of him with both hands.

"Oh, hey," Morgan says, when we enter. He rises and hands Terry to Steph, creating a fresh whiff of dirty diaper. "You're just in time."

Steph groans. "Morgan, you know how to change a diaper."

"Yeah, and if it had taken you another ten, fifteen minutes to get back, I would've done it."

She shakes her head, and takes Terry off to the changing table.

I get sucked into the images on the television. Yellow POLICE LINE DO NOT CROSS tape spans the trees, like enormous spider webs. Police officers and other investigators mill around at the muddy bottom of a deep ravine, which the text indicates is Ravenna Park, a few miles from here. WOMAN'S BODY FOUND says the text. APPEARS MAULED BY ANIMAL says the text. "Have you been watching this?" I ask.

"Yeah. Big scary news."

"Do they think it's the same dog that attacked George?"

He frowns. "No, they didn't say anything about George. Or, dogs really. This animal is big. They're saying it might even be a bear."

"A bear? How could a bear get all the way into the middle of the city?"

"I don't know. That is an interesting question, huh?"

So it's even worse than I thought. There is no doubt in my mind that this is George's doing, that he's a rougarou now, and a killer. I need to track him down, but Steph doesn't want me to leave the house.

"You want to go for a walk?" She folds her arms and gives me an I-can't-believe-your-bullshit look. "Didn't you get enough walking this morning?"

"You never objected to me going for a walk before."

"Well, you never took off into the woods without telling anyone before."

"Come on, Steph, please. It's not like anything bad actually happened to me, is it? Everybody was upset for a while, and I'm sorry about that. But I promise I'll be back at whatever time you say."

"Why do you want to get out there so bad? Are you meeting someone?"

"What? No, of course not. I don't even know anybody except Deena, who's mad at me. Who would I meet?"

"I don't know." She shakes her head and folds her arms tighter. "The restaurant is closed tonight for the holiday. I don't want to hang around this house thinking that every firecracker going off is George breaking in, so we're all going down, as a family, to the Lake Union show, and then we're spending the night in a motel. I'm serious about this. Until they find George, I don't want you out there alone."

From her perspective, I understand. But I hate the sense that she doesn't trust me. Our relationship has changed. It feels almost broken. That hurts to think about. But what can I expect? I really am a monster, right? I don't trust me. I'm afraid of me. Why should it be so painful coming from Steph?

Anyway, if all she wanted to do was keep me from investigating at Ravenna Park, she's doing a great job. The fireworks show, my first, is fun, if distractingly noisy and brimstone-scented. It seems like half of Seattle is crowded along the shores of Lake Union, and there's no chance to get away. We spend the night in a cheap motel along Aurora Avenue, what used to be the main highway before they built the Interstate. I'm sharing a bed with Steph. When I get up in the middle of the night to head out to the balcony, she notices.

"What are you doing?" she says.

"Getting some fresh air. Although I think there's a fire somewhere, do you smell it?"

She sighs. "Abby, we've been through a lot together. And I know I helped you out, took you in, but you helped me a lot too. We've been good for each other, I think. So I want you to be straight with me. Tell me the truth. I think we owe each other that. Are you using drugs?"

"What? Of course not."

"If you're really not, this might seem like it's coming out of nowhere. But about a month ago everything about you seemed to change. You had new friends, you kept different hours. you started dressing different, acting more aggressive and moody—look, I used to run with that wild crowd myself, the drug crowd. I know what it's like. I know the signs."

I don't want to, but I feel a sludgy resentful anger. "Do you see any tattoos? Obviously it's not the same crowd."

"Please don't try to make this about me, okay? I did smell the marijuana and beer on you when I picked you up after that party."

"The smoke was in my hair and the beer got spilled on my sweatshirt. Just like the smell of the campfire, did you notice that? I think I got some hot dog mustard on me too. It doesn't mean I ate a hot dog. Steph, if you think my problem is drugs, you are seriously barking up the wrong tree." Barking. Ha-ha.

She shrugs. "Okay. So what is your problem?"

"I don't know." I fold my arms tightly. "I'm a teenager. That's my problem."

She smiles a little. "There's more to it than that, kiddo. Everything seemed to change after the first time George showed up. Does that fit?"

"Maybe."

"That's what I thought. I talked to Father Mulligan and we both think the confrontation with George triggered something called PTSD—post-traumatic stress disorder. You know, like what combat soldiers get? Because of your childhood in a. you know, in a cult."

Cult. There's that word again. I don't know why, but it makes me feel deeply upset. "You've been talking to Father Mulligan about me? Behind my back?"

"Abby, calm down. This isn't gossip. We're trying to help you. Get you appropriate treatment."

"You mean like a psychiatrist?"

"That's exactly what I mean, and don't look at me like that. Don't you want help? Do you like having nightmares all the time? Blacking out, waking up someplace with no idea how you got there?"

Insane laughter burbles up. *No, Steph, I know exactly how I got to be naked in the middle of a deer carcass.* Pressure grows at the back of my head. *Tell her, tell her.* She won't believe it. *Tell her anyway.* But I can't bring myself to say anything out loud. "Fine. I'll see a psychiatrist if you want."

She nods. "All right. Now come back to bed. If there's a fire out there, you can let the firemen deal with it."

We have breakfast at Beth's Cafe, the place I went with Deena and her friends. I had no idea we were anywhere near it, and I realize that my conception of Seattle geography is still extremely vague. I think back to that night, the one night it seemed like everything in my life might be going right for a change. But now I know it was a lie. It was all because of the wolf. She was the only reason anybody noticed me or thought I was interesting. Her aggression got people's attention. But she had already bitten George by then. She had already created her murderous progeny. She was already dangerous. I should never—

"Aren't you hungry?" Morgan asks. I'm poking dispiritedly at a plate of hash browns with vegetarian chili, same thing I got last time.

"Not really." With some effort, I smile. Did I explain that two nights ago I ate about half a deer? I think I'm still digesting it.

"Abby, you need to eat something," Steph says. "That's the last thing I need, is for you to go all anorexic on me."

I shake my head, answer honestly. "Sometimes at New Harmony we were genuinely starving, I don't have the patience to starve for vanity. I'm just not feeling well today."

"It's nerves," Morgan says. "You're worried about George. Right?"

Steph is staring at me with concern. "Genuinely starving?"

"Well, my father thought that God called upon every man to be a farmer, but he was kind of bad at farming. I think he assumed that because farming was natural and Godly, therefore, he would have some kind of innate God-given knowledge of how to do it?"

Morgan laughs. "I've known guys who get into hunting like that. They assume that because people did it with Stone Age technology, it must be easy to do."

I nod. "Yeah. Wisdom preached that the only things anyone needs to know are all right there in the Bible, so he tried to live that way. And mostly he failed." I don't mention the additional starvation that happened, as discipline, or the more regular fasting that we all were expected to engage in. Thinking back, regularly depriving your children of food doesn't actually seem like the best way to ensure they'll grow up smart and healthy.

But, what if that was why the wolf never appeared before a month ago? What if limited food is what kept her at bay? It almost makes sense, if I think about the transformation taking extra energy, which I wouldn't have had until recently. And once again, I come back to the horrible idea that he did know something about controlling this.

"See, this is why religion is stupid," Morgan says. "You're a father, right? Your most important job is to take care of your family. Even wolves do that. But you add religion, and suddenly some idiot thinks pleasing a God he's never seen is more important than feeding his own kids." Steph frowns at him, and Morgan glances at me. "Uh, no offense."

"No, it's fair. My father is an idiot." But is he an idiot who happened to be right?

When we get back home, Steph still doesn't think I should go out for a walk by myself. Chafing, I retreat to my room and engage in werewolf research. If I'm going to stop George, I need to know more about how we work. The Internet reveals a plethora of information, much of it contradictory. Silver hurts them, or it doesn't. Garlic hurts them, or it doesn't. There's something called wolfsbane, which might be toxic to werewolves, but only because it's toxic to everybody.

I also decide to look up information on cults. This bears more substantial fruit, revealing not fiction and contradictory folklore, but nightmarish real histories of abuse and mass suicide. Did I really grow up in a cult? Some of the brain-washing techniques, the torture and solitary confinement, sound awfully familiar.

On the werewolf front, I try a little experimentation on myself. Pictures of frogs do not cause any noticeable reaction. In the dining room, I locate the silverware, a legacy from their grandmother, tarnished but genuine. Holding a silver fork does not feel any different from holding a stainless steel fork.

Licking the silver does not appear to do anything. Biting into a bulb of garlic is a little spicy, but nothing else happens. I take a handful of rice and scatter it across the threshold of the kitchen. Any impulse to count individual grains before I step across? Not that I notice.

Steph catches me. "Abby, what are you doing?"

"Sorry, I spilled some rice. Just cleaning it up."

She frowns, perplexed. "Were you making rice? I thought you weren't hungry."

"No, I was, uh, looking for the herbal tea. I knocked the bag of rice over. It was an accident."

"Oh. The herbal tea is here." She indicates the correct cabinet. "I thought you knew where it was. Aren't you the one who put it there?"

"I'm sorry. I forgot."

Retreating to my room with a silver-plated knife, I engage in more serious research. A butter knife, it won't break the skin no matter how much I saw back and forth. I pull out the pocket knife, Morgan's gift, make a shallow cut. It hurts, but I have a high tolerance for pain. Thank my father's corrections for that, I suppose.

Inserting the silver knife into the cut does nothing, other than get blood on the knife. The cut heals right away, barely having time to bleed before it closes up again. I test this, making a number of cuts, daring to get deeper as I accustom myself to the pain, and become more certain of my rapid healing. The cuts do leave very small, fine, white scars behind. Rapid healing doesn't include lack of scarring, apparently. Still, the bullet holes when Morgan shot wolf-me didn't leave any marks behind. Maybe all the scars disappear when I change shape? I guess I'll find out in another month.

"Abby! Come out and have some lunch!" Steph calls, and I come out to the dining room to pick at a peanut butter sandwich.

We stare at each other silently for a long time, then

Morgan says, "I got a call today. The Paramount Theater needs some emergency repair work done before a big Broadway show that's supposed to open tomorrow. It could keep me there pretty late. It's really lucrative, but I'll turn it down if you want."

"No problem," Steph says. "Abby can take Terry next door tonight. Mr. Singha and Mr. Davidson will take care of them."

Morgan looks skeptical. "Those—guys? Really? You think they can protect the kids if George comes around?"

Steph glares in response. "Sorry, brother, your bigotry is showing. You remember how after you shot at the dog and got George subdued, the cops arrived outside and they already had Terry with them? Did you think about why that was? Did you think about who called the cops?"

He looks taken aback. "I had a lot on my mind at the time."

"It was our neighbors. They heard screaming and called the police right away, and then went over to investigate. Mr. Singha ran right in there while George was fighting with the dog. He rescued the baby, took him outside."

"Really?" He nods. "Okay, that did take a lot of guts. It was a pretty scary looking dog."

Screaming. So maybe my screaming did some good after all. I never thought about it. But now a sick feeling starts to bubble up. What if—what if the only reason the wolf never hurt Terry is that Mr. Singha got him out before she had the chance? What if I can't trust her around him? The more I think about it the worse it gets. Even if she didn't attack him deliberately—

(*unbaptized babies are a favorite rougarou snack*)

(*shut up shut up shut up*)

After lunch, Morgan and I clean up the kitchen. I'm stacking dishes in an upper cabinet when Morgan's gaze zeroes in on my left arm.

"What are those marks on your skin?"

"Oh." I follow his gaze to the white scars. "Those are from the party. Blackberry vines."

"Uh-huh." He looks skeptical. "Those aren't fresh, kiddo. And they're not random. Don't lie to me."

"Okay. I don't know where they came from."

He shakes his head. "So you're a cutter, too. The long sleeves in July should have clued me in."

"I wear long sleeves because it's still kinda cold and rainy around here, in case you hadn't noticed. What's a cutter?"

He folds his arms. "Look it up. You can talk to the counselor about it if you want. And don't do it again. Don't make me regret I gave you that knife for your birthday."

16

NEIGHBORS

Not long after lunch, Deena and Edison show up at the front door unannounced. Steph is out back, so I open the door.

"Jeez, Abby, don't you answer your phone?" Deena says, her smile acid. Edison stands behind her, tall, dark-haired, utterly gorgeous and depressing.

"What are you guys doing here?"

"We were worried about you, dummy."

"But didn't Steph tell you—I mean, she told you I didn't get eaten by a bear or anything, didn't she?"

She rolls her eyes and looks at Edison. "You see the extreme weirdness that we have to deal with here?" Her expression turns to a frown. "Seriously, what is up with you, Abs? You look all haggard and stuff. Did you start doing heroin?"

"It's my guilty conscience," I say, as if it's a joke. But of course it's not. "When did you start calling me Abs?"

"It's a thing I'm trying. I don't think I like it though." She smiles. "I know I flipped out when you flipped Ed over here, but I didn't know that he kissed you without waiting for a yes."

He smiles down at me. "And it was a clean throw. Like in

martial arts. Look, I play football for the Huskies, right? I've been tackled by guys three times your size. You weren't trying to hurt me."

"No! No, I wasn't. It was just…" I trail off, unable to explain. It was just the wolf. The wolf reacting. "I don't want to hurt you."

"And I don't want to hurt you." He steps up to the porch, putting us close together, emphasizing the difference in our heights, but also putting us inside each other's space, inside the sphere of warmth and subtle smells that tell you another person is very near. His voice takes on an intimate low murmur. "I think I can handle whatever you're ready to dish out."

I laugh, nervous. But he doesn't have the faintest clue what the wolf can dish out. "That's a pretty bold claim, Edison." We meet each other's eyes, and I notice that his are large and long-lashed and a deep, deep brown. An honest brown, did Steph say?

Deena speaks up. "Okay, my work here is done. I'll leave you guys alone to—whatever. See ya!" She blows a kiss and saunters back down to her car. Edison stays right where he is.

"Don't you have to go?" I ask.

"I'm meeting a friend around here a bit later." He grins. Devilishly, it seems to me, and now my entire body is tingling with awareness of him. No, this isn't good. Is it?

"So. Do you want to kiss me? Notice I'm asking permission this time."

I want to say no. I should say no. "Yes." Whisper like a hiss.

Powerful arms actually lift me off the porch by a foot. His lips are warm and his sweat is spicy, almost edible, reminding me fleetingly of the marinade on the lamb skewers Mr. Singha was cooking. His tongue startles me by thrusting past the barrier of my own lips, a buzzing electric feeling, a bright pulsing excitement bubbles up, stronger and stronger, as I wrap my legs around his waist, my arms around his shoulders, and I'm ready...

Morgan. His scent approaches and I hop off with guilty suddenness, backing away. Breathlessly we look at each other.

"Wow," he says, his voice low, more an exhalation than a word.

"I, uh—" I can't find words.

Morgan walks up onto the porch and looks at us, eyebrows raised. He's carrying a sledgehammer. "Oh, hey, don't you kids stop making out on my account."

"It's okay. I was just, uh, leaving." Edison looks a little faint and turns away, hunched over as if somebody punched him in the gut. "See you later, Abby?"

"Yeah. I'll, uh, I'll call you." I know that's a lie. It makes me feel like a bad person, but it's hardly the worst thing I've ever done. Or the worst thing I'm going to do.

Edison lurches awkwardly out of sight. Morgan shakes his head. "Poor kid. I remember when I used to get boners like that." He glances at me. "Sorry. That was probably, uh, inappropriate language."

I'm still trying to catch my breath. What just happened? I mean, I know it was a kiss, but—it inspired a lot more—feelings—than I was expecting. I've see people kissing on movies and TV and it never looks like such a full body experience. "It's all right. I know what a boner is."

He shrugs. "Well, yeah. If you're causing 'em, you ought to be able to talk about 'em." He continues walking into the house, then stops to glance back over his shoulder. "You know, this might not be the right time to tell you this, but until now I kinda thought you might be gay."

Disturbed, I pace a circuit through the yard, front to back, dazed perceptions sinking into the July mud. I was almost ready to do something crazy, throw Edison to the ground again only this time with me on top, throw off all my clothes. It's the wolf, I think. She's a slut. It's hardly her worst quality, I suppose. But still it disturbs me, the power of it, the sense that my decisions were not entirely my own. As if she was ready to take over. What if I let her? What if she hurt him for real, broke his back or something? She wasn't thinking about that. She—she assumes she's dealing with another werewolf.

That's it, isn't it? Among my own kind, I wouldn't have to hesitate before tossing a guy on his back, because I could break every bone he's got and it wouldn't slow him down much. Morgan shot me and I healed right up. And now I don't know. My own kind? That assumes I have a kind. But George became like me after I attacked him. Does that make him my kind?

It doesn't matter. It makes him my problem.

"Abby! What are you doing?" Steph calls from the back porch.

"Getting some fresh air!" I call back.

"Well, get back inside. I thought I told you not to leave the house?"

I join her on the back porch. "I was in our yard. I thought that would be okay?"

"Well, it's time for you to watch the baby while I get ready for work."

Steph hustles me and Terry and a bag of diapers and other supplies next door. "I might be back as late as two thirty, is that still all right?" she says.

"Of course, of course. Let me have the baby!" Mr. Singha holds out his hands and I deliver Terry, a lump unexpectedly in my throat. Mr. Singha saved him. From George. From me.

"Hon, are you okay?" Mr. Davidson leans down, to put us at eye level. "What's wrong?"

"I have a lot on my mind. George, and everything."

"She had a fight with her best friend," Steph says.

"Oh, hon, that's terrible. Do you need some chocolate? A selection of mournful breakup songs?"

In spite of myself I laugh a little bit. "No, I'm all right.

Actually, I think we made up already." A fight with my best friend. That would mean I have a best friend. Like a regular girl.

"Have fun!" Steph leaves.

"This way." Mr. Davidson touches my shoulder to steer me inside, and I become freshly conscious of his cologne: subtle, pleasant, probably expensive. Still it makes my eyes water and my nose prickle. Cologne hits my sense of smell like a too-bright light hitting my eyes, and for a moment the cologne is all I can think about.

Suddenly something strikes me. The house reeks of their little dog, but she's nowhere to be seen.

"Where's Emily?"

"She's in her carrier," Mr. Davidson says. "Since she can't seem to behave herself around you."

I think back to the jogging woman in the park. "I think I have an idea. Is she closer to you, or Mr. Singha?"

"Oh, she's Paul's little doggie, without question."

"Let me wear an article of clothing that belongs to him, then let her out of the cage."

"Well, that's an interesting idea." He looks skeptical, but does it, draping me with a lovely shawl of painted silk. I don't even have to ask if it was imported from India, because it still carries the smells of unfamiliar plants, Indian spices, incense. It also smells strongly of Mr. Singha. It seems to work. Emily is never going to be my bestest friend, but she stops trying to bark me away.

"Well, that was a good idea, wasn't it?" Mr. Davidson says.

Their house is almost identical to Steph's in layout and age, but seems nicer, probably because they've been living here longer. It has a settled look. That rug goes there, that picture is here, this wall is painted deep mahogany. At our house, they've cleared out most of their grandmother's things, but they haven't been putting up things of their own. No art, no bookshelves, no extra furniture. Maybe that's because they don't intend to stay forever. They intend to modernize and sell it for a million dollars. And then go where?

Which reminds me—where am I going to go? When the full moon comes, if I don't have any better ideas, I have to just go away, don't I? Into the wilderness, well away from people. And if Steph doesn't want me to go, I have to go anyway. I'm pretty sure the only way to make her believe I'm really going to change into a wolf is for her to see it with her own eyes, and that seems far too risky. I don't want to think the other me would hurt Steph. But I can't know she wouldn't.

"What do you want for dinner?" Mr. Davidson asks me. Mr. Singha is wrapped up with the baby, bouncing him around and singing songs in a foreign language and cooing. Just like Steph's mom. It hits me: he wants a baby of his own. Two men can't really have a baby of their own, can they? Well, I guess they can adopt.

"I'm a vegetarian," I say, although the thought of food is still remote and a little unpleasant. Most of the deer meat still seems to be there inside me, working its slow way through my intestines. I feel heavy, bloated. If my clothes were tighter you could probably see the bulge, and I would look like one of those starving children, with skinny limbs and a weird round belly. Grotesque and sad.

"How about pizza?"

I grimace. "No pizza. Unpleasant memories."

He gives me a look of understanding. "Of course. The last time you had pizza it didn't go well, did it? Well, how about Indian food, do you like Indian food?"

"I don't think I've ever had Indian food."

He grins. "How do you feel about mushy, heavily spiced vegetables?"

Mr. Singha hands over the baby to Mr. Davidson (a touch reluctantly) and makes it a class in how to cook Indian food for myself. "All vegetarians should know how to make Indian food!"

While we cook, we listen to Mr. Singha's music: beat-heavy, overlaid with a strange wailing style of vocal, but very catchy. When I'm the one holding the baby, I dance around the house with him, which seems to please Mr. Singha. "You like the Bollywood?" he says.

"Is that what this is? What does that mean?"

"Like Hollywood, only in Bombay. Only it's Mumbai now. Hollywood in India. Hindi language. A lot of musicals, very colorful, big dance numbers." He grins. "No plot."

As the sun sets and the still nearly-full moon rises, my appetite comes back, and the dishes like saag paneer (spinach and some kind of cheese) and daal (lentils) are delicious.

I help clean up while Mr. Singha puts the baby to sleep. They have a machine that washes dishes, and when I exclaim over it, Mr. Davidson frowns at me. "You've never seen a dishwasher before?"

"In restaurants. I didn't know people had them in their houses."

"Well, they probably haven't finished modernizing the kitchen over there." He thinks, seems to do a double take. "But seriously. You have never previously been in a private home with a dishwasher? Not once in your life? Aren't you fourteen or fifteen?"

"Sixteen. But is that really so weird?" I ask, but of course it must be or he wouldn't be stuck on it. "I grew up on a farm. My family was kind of, um, old-fashioned? Like the Amish?"

"You're Amish?" He goggles at me.

"No, not really. Just kinda like that. Isolated, religious? That's how I grew up."

"So." He studies my face. "It's probably a little strange for you to encounter two married gentlemen such as ourselves, isn't it?" I nod. "Do you think we're sinners?"

"Everyone's a sinner. Except I don't think I believe in all that stuff anymore." But Wisdom was right about the beast, does that make him right about other things?

No. Shut up, brain.

"But it still affects you, doesn't it? You don't want to think bad thoughts about us, but you find yourself thinking them anyway?"

Wow, that's a little on the nose. I nod again. "Yeah. Okay. You're right. I don't think I believe any of those words, but they come back to me anyway. Like having a song stuck in your head."

"I want you to know something, Abby. Most gay people grew up with at least a little of that ourselves. In churches or families or cultures that told us we were wicked because of who we fall in love with. We tried to make the feelings go away, but they didn't. We tried to pretend to be normal, but sometimes we were found out anyway. Then we'd get bullied, beat up, kicked out of the house. A lot of us ended up hating ourselves, when we were around your age. Sometimes we hated ourselves enough to want to die."

"That's awful." I'm sincerely shocked. I never tried to imagine what it was like to be a person who was gay, who had a childhood and a family and a church. In my father's fevered imaginings, "Sodomites" sprang as fully-formed adults from the mind of Satan, like wicked Athenas.

"I'm sorry if I ever acted weird toward you guys. I didn't mean to."

"I know you didn't. I just wanted to clear the air a little bit. Hugs?" We hug. "Now, you're a guest, why don't you let me finish cleaning up? You go keep Paul company now that the baby's asleep. I think he's dying to show you some Bollywood dance numbers on video."

Later, toward the end of the night, after Mr. Davidson is snoring in the recliner, I talk to Mr. Singha. "A month ago, when George came—you rescued the baby from the wolf, right? I mean the dog."

"It did look very much like a wolf, now that you mention it. But wolves and dogs are not so far removed, are they?"

"But when you were there did it threaten you at all? Did it threaten the baby?"

"The animal was very focused on its fight with the man George. But I was there only briefly. Why do you ask?"

"Well. They never found it. And now there's another animal attack. I was wondering how many things out there we have to be worried about."

He hugs me. "Oh, Abby, there's nothing to worry about. We will take care of you."

"You will, won't you? You'll help Steph take care of the baby. If I can't."

He looks concerned. "And why would you not be able to?"

I shrug. "I don't know. Things happen. You never know, right?"

"Kismet," he says. "As the Muslims say. All things only as God is willing."

"Yeah. That's it. Whatever God wants." I don't share my growing opinion that God is a sadistic bastard, and for that reason, perhaps my father really does speak for him.

17

ABBY MAKES A DECISION

Steph collects us right at two a.m. I'm relieved that she doesn't smell as if she's been drinking. Terry remains peacefully asleep while we carry him back home, where we find Morgan sitting up at the kitchen table, smelling of guns and paranoia.

"What are you doing?" Steph asks.

"I finished the job a couple of hours ago. Now I'm waiting in case George comes by." He shows us his pistol.

Steph exhales, long and weary. "You don't even have the safety on, do you?"

"I'm at the ready. I'm on guard. That's exactly when you have the safety off."

"Well, now the baby's here, so put the safety back on, please."

He obeys, with obvious reluctance, and we all go to bed. But I can't sleep. In front of the Bollywood marathon I was dozing off, but alone in the dark I can't stop my racing thoughts. I find myself strangely envious of all the gay teenagers out there. If only my big hairy deal was getting to sixteen and suddenly realizing that I had a big crush on Deena instead of Edison.

I have to find out if George killed that girl, and where he's gone. His trail is already a couple of days old, and the longer I wait, the worse it gets. No matter what Steph says, I need to go to that park.

And then what?

Okay, I have to think this through. If I'm wrong, and George isn't a werewolf, and he didn't kill that girl, I'll be back before morning and Steph none the wiser. Or, she'll know I went out, and I'll get in trouble, but we'll deal. I'll go see a counselor. I'll talk about my pain. I'll have nearly a month to figure out what to do about my own transformation at the next full moon.

That's the best-case scenario, but I don't have much hope it's the right one. If George is a werewolf, and he did kill that girl, then I'm the only one who will know, and I'm the only one who can stop him from killing again. And how, exactly, am I going to do that?

Well, if I found him, I could probably get him arrested.

Right, and then what happens? The next full moon there's another inexplicable prison riot, more people dead, George free once more. So that's no good.

Okay, what if I make a bargain with him? I won't turn him into the cops, on the condition that he stays away from us forever. He goes somewhere far away, and whoever he kills at the next full moon, it won't be someone I know. I shudder. That scenario is almost tempting, but I can't trust it. How could I be sure he would keep such a bargain? He wouldn't. I'd be right back where I am now, with even more deaths on my head.

All right, another bargain. I don't turn him in on the condition that we both go away, right now, into the wilderness, possibly forever. Maybe he'll want that. He's not a good guy, but maybe he doesn't want to be a killer. Or, maybe he's pragmatic enough, he knows that if wolf-him makes enough trouble, eventually somebody will succeed in killing the wolf, like at the end of a werewolf movie. Self-interest will get him to see my side.

But if he won't do it? If he won't go away with me?

I'll have to make him.

And how will I do that, exactly? Any power I have, he has it too. And he's a lot bigger. Could I drug him? Chain him up and carry him out into the wilderness with me? I've barely started learning how to drive, I don't think I can get us safely all the way out to the Cascade Mountains. I'm not even sure the chains would hold him. And if I did get him out there, what's my plan then? Keep him chained up permanently?

My thoughts keep circling around, coming back to this. I don't want to be here, but I can't seem to go anywhere else. There is no other conclusion. If he won't listen to me, if he won't willingly set himself apart from people, then I have to kill him.

Do I even know how to do that? If he's like me? Morgan shot me, when I was in wolf form, and it hardly slowed me down. I have a feeling—possibly an instinct—that sufficient damage to his head or heart would disable him for a while even if it doesn't kill him. That would give me a chance to do something like—

Go on, think it, Abby. You could remove his head. That'll kill anything. Right?

No, that can't be it. That can't be the only solution. But nothing else comes to mind. Nothing. Not one little thing. Dread pours through my body like tar, dark and sticky and foul-smelling. It's a disease, I'm sick with it, and somewhere back in Louisiana my father is laughing, bitterly, knowingly. *Told you so. You see what it all comes down to? You left my protection, and now you're going to become a murderer.*

I take a deep breath. All right. It doesn't matter how I got here. The past cannot be undone. I have to think like a cop, like a soldier. Officer Lou probably doesn't want to kill anyone, but she would shoot a man if she had to. She would shoot

George if she had to. And if I have to, I have to do it right. I still have the gun Morgan lent me, when we went to the gun range. If my concentration is good, I can even hit what I'm aiming at. And I have a knife, maybe a little small for the task. I hope it doesn't come to that. Please don't let it come to that. I feel like I'm praying, but have no idea what I'm praying to.

I pull out Steph's rosary and finger it for a while, just in case, but no other answers come.

Then I think of the small coiled braid of Ash's hair. I run it through my fingers, shocked by the ghost it summons of her presence. It feels like her. It smells like her. I can imagine that I feel her, like a warm breath stirring the air. Ash, are you an angel now? A saint? Can I pray to you? Will you help me?

My petition to Ash brings no fresh insight, but still I tie her braid loosely around my neck for luck, and to remind myself of why I'm doing this. I'm trying to save innocent people.

I dress up like a ninja and ready my backpack: extra layers of warmth, in case we take off to the mountains right away; energy bars, in case it becomes hard to find food; Deena's flip-flops. Then at the top I put the gun. It seems to double the weight of my pack. Now I have to wait until everybody is deeply asleep, maybe an hour? But if I lie here waiting in the dark I might fall asleep myself. So I decide to write Steph a letter. If things go the way I hope they will, I'm leaving for good. And if I do have to kill him? I don't know. I guess I'm a coward. I'll try to cover up my crime, try to come back here and live normally until the next full moon. The thought of doing that makes me feel guilty. You're not really a criminal until you plan how you're going to get away with it, are you? Imagine yourself throwing the gun into Lake Washington, removing your fingerprints from the scene?

If that happens, I'll be back before dawn and I can destroy the letter.

Dear Steph,

I'm sorry you have to find out like this. But if I disappear, you deserve to know the truth. Remember when you asked me if I was a rougarou? You were joking. You didn't think it was possible. But you were right. I am a werewolf. A month ago, during the fight with George, I changed for the first time. In wolf form I bit him. Now I think he's one too. I think he killed that girl in the park. And I think that means I have to stop him. But I don't know if I'll succeed in that. If I fail, you know he'll come after you. Please remember what you're really dealing with. You might not be able to hurt him with bullets, and I don't think silver will do anything either.

How can you stop him, if I fail? I don't know. I think he won't survive having his head removed. Could be Morgan needs to learn how to use an ax instead of a gun.

You won't want to believe any of this. I don't blame you. I don't want to believe it myself. I would like to pretend it's not true, do what you tell me, stay at home, be a good girl, let George go where he will. But that kind of denial is going to get innocent people killed. Next time it could be people I care about, like you or Terry.

Thank you for everything. You've done more for me than you'll ever know. I hope you and all your family have a good life.

Love, Abby

I STARE AT THE LETTER FOR A WHILE, WONDERING IF THERE'S more I need to say. My eyes are starting to fill up with tears, landing in splotches on the page. Love. Love, Abby. Abby was the name she gave me and I took it. My father named me Self-Abnegation. The other me doesn't have a name.

I fold the letter and seal it into an envelope. I write on the outside: *For Steph*. I weigh it down with the rosary.

Then I wait.

18

ABBY HUNTS GEORGE

The park is quiet, but not empty. Homeless humans nestle in for the night among their bags and shopping carts, reeking of cheap alcohol and ground-in sweat. Almost they make me think of dogs, and I wonder if all humans would smell like that if we didn't bathe regularly. It's easy to locate the place where the girl's body was found, because of the riot of smells there: guns and chemicals and sandwiches and so many different people. I start to despair of being able to pick out any one person-scent. Maybe this isn't going to work after all.

Blood, like a slap. It soaked into the ground here, and I think the bulk of the crowd was kept away from this exact location, so I can still make out the dead woman clearly against the olfactory din. Young, but homeless herself I think. Here at last is a clear whiff of George. He marked a tree with urine, trying to claim this territory as his own. I feel a primitive surge of anger. My territory. Not his. Mine. Within me, the wolf snarls in irritation.

It occurs to me that I'm doing this wrong. Human perception defaults to the domination of sight, and as long as I can see, vision fills my head and crowds out smell. If I want to use my nose properly, I need to stop looking at things.

I steady myself against a tree, and close my eyes.

Darkness for a moment, then the world begins to sketch itself in scent. Color, shape, texture: all of these, somehow, conveyed in smell. I raise my fingers to stop my ears and eliminate another distraction. Hollow nothing roars in my ears, while I concentrate on inhaling, exhaling, lungs filling deeper with each breath. The scent map of my surroundings grows stronger, more solid. Almost, it seems that I can see, hear, and feel with only my nose.

There. The fizzing brownish stain of my enemy. I follow his trail, getting a vivid picture of his activities. In wolf form, he walks this way, at his leisure, with nothing in pursuit. In his mouth he carries flesh from the body, maybe a hand or a foot. He stops to mark territory again. In those bushes he curls up to sleep and stays there for some time, probably until morning brings his return to human form. In human form he stands up and begins moving faster, not stopping to sniff or mark, and his trail becomes harder to follow. Then it disappears entirely.

Frustrated, I look around for other clues. The act of opening my eyes is when I realize I had them closed the entire time. Disoriented, I prop myself against a tree as smell and sight fight for dominance, eventually reach a truce. Smell: fuel, rubber, George again. Sight: glittering pebbles of broken glass, black tire marks. George stole a car. I try to follow the car's trail, but lose it in just a few blocks, as the car pulls onto a busy street. I have nothing.

My frustration is so great that I want to sit back and howl.

All right. I have to think. The wolf part has done everything she can do, now the human part has to do what she's good at. What I'm good at. Reasoning things out. Thinking it through. Getting into the head of the enemy and anticipating what he's going to do.

So, I'm George. I just woke up after my first night as a

werewolf. I don't remember exactly what happened. I was in prison, and now I'm naked, in a park, with no idea how I got here. I steal the first car I see, and take it where? What's my first priority? Clothes? Probably clothes. Do I call somebody? But I don't really know anybody in Seattle, and I'm a wanted fugitive. I won't want anybody to figure out where I am. So where do I take the car?

Theory one: I want to escape, and take the car as far away as possible. I could be anywhere.

Theory two: I pick up where I left off.

George went to the house.

Panicked at the thought of our house without my protection, I run, bare feet pounding the pavement. But when I get near, I notice the scent trace of the cops who have been patrolling, Officer Lou and others. Of course. Even if he came back here right away, first thing in the morning, they already had the cops stationed all around our house hoping to catch him. They didn't catch him. So, he must have gone somewhere else.

Where? Not down the hill, toward the greater crowd of people. Up the hill, maybe to a park or abandoned building, somewhere he could hide. I start to comb the area block by block, fanning out slowly. Sometimes I crouch down for a clearer sniff at the sidewalk, which I imagine must look ridiculous. It's late enough at night that not many people are around to see me do this. The people who do notice me keep a wide berth, probably assuming I'm drunk and about to vomit.

Nothing. Okay. This could take all night, and what happens if it does? If Steph finds me gone tomorrow morning, whether or not she reads the letter, she's probably going to start the cops searching for me, isn't she? And if I'm still in town, nosing painstakingly after George, they'll probably find me before I find him.

I go back to the start and fan out in a different direction. Jackpot. Clear as sunlight, his dirty-yellow-brown urine scent against one tree, and then another. He marked his territory, at a height that indicates he did it in human form. That's odd. I follow the trail, like breadcrumbs through a forest, until I find a row of three houses, set apart by a chain link fence, windows and doors boarded up, every surface covered with graffiti. A dejected white sign, also covered with graffiti, seems to announce that this was once going to be the site of some new thing, a building or a train station. Now the project has been neglected, perhaps abandoned entirely.

His trail leads to the back of the house, where lush blackberry vines with killer thorns hide the structure from the street. I spot some boards that hinge easily, obviously rigged to move out of the way. Unwashed humans live here, like animals making a den, leaving behind smells of sweat and food and defecation and sex. Spent alcohol, old tobacco, marijuana, a tense chemical reek that might indicate stronger drugs, meth or crack. Dust and mold and the detritus of nested pigeons and squirrels hover in the air. But all of that is memory, residue, ghosts. The person alive and present is George. He sits in the far corner from the entrance I used, cross-legged, nested in a pile of dirty blankets, covered in blood and filth.

He is naked. His eyes are closed. In his lap, he cradles a large hunk of meat, not fresh, almost-rotting in the summer heat. It takes me a moment to identify it as a human foot and lower leg. It belonged to the dead girl. Right, he carried it away—in his mouth—

I swallow, fighting back an urge to vomit. He's still gnawing at it, after several days in human form. But no longer perfectly human. His face has been distorted, as if someone began the process of morphing it with the face of a wolf: nose and jaw elongated, ears swept back. His hands are human hands, mostly, but the fingers seem shorter and more rounded than I remember, and his nails at least partly hardened and sharpened into claws. I feel the squeeze of guilt, not just for what I did to the dead girl, through him, but for what I did to him. He was a bad guy, sure, but I turned him into a monster, a hideous thing.

He glances up at me with a curiously emotionless expression. "You came. Good." His voice is flat, with a hint of a growl.

"George. I came to help you."

He snorts laughter, sounding more human. "Help me what? You already helped, little sweet thing. When you bit me." He holds up his arm, where the tiniest bit of scar tissue announces the past presence of her—my—teeth. "See that? Looked like hell when they first brought me in. They thought I might lose the arm. Then it healed right up."

"You were in prison."

His eyes lower, and he gurgles rage deep in his throat. "Dirty rotten fuckers thought they could put me in a cage." Then he brightens. "But your gift got me out a month later. Gotta thank you for that. Hurts like hell, but the power is incredible."

"It hurts? You mean when I bit you?"

He laughs, a huff-huff chuckle through his nose. "Hurts to change, darlin'. Ha, guess that's always the way, isn't it?"

"It doesn't hurt me. George, I think something went wrong when I bit you. I think you need help."

He laughs, a barking hyena yip, inhuman. "Something went wrong! Something went right. Change hurts, but nothing hurts now. Not even cold. Before this, cold the whole time here, Seattle, nasty damp clammy gray town, waiting for the bitch to spawn, waiting for my son, my son, next moon gonna go on and take him back, eat that bitch all up, give him the gift. Give it young. He'll always be a wolf."

Is that what happened to me? A bite in infancy, dormant until now? Until I was fully grown, perhaps? Huh, this could be my full adult height. That's a depressing thought.

"No. George, it doesn't work that way. We have to get

away from people. Don't you understand that? If we're here in the city at the next full moon—they'll find us."

"And then what? Shoot us with ordinary bullets?" More laughter.

Bullets. Shit. My gun is still in my backpack. That was a colossally stupid move, if it turns out I do need to shoot him. What am I supposed to do now? Hey, George, mind holding still while I get a deadly weapon out of my bag and point it at you? My heart begins to pound, and he senses it, stretching his deformed face into a big, toothy grin.

"You. Smell like prey."

The wolf rises in anger. We can't let him talk to us like that. Challenge, challenge for territory. She thinks she could take him in a fight. She's a moron. A furry, toothy moron.

Shut up. I'm still driving this body. "George, you've seen the movies, right? You know how they end. They wouldn't end that way if the wolf just had the sense to get away from people."

He raises the foot and takes a big bite of the aged flesh, making a big show of chewing, relishing. He's trying to needle me. He can tell I'm disturbed. Knowing he's doing it on purpose doesn't make me feel any less upset by his—cannibalism. Go ahead and think it. He's holding her flesh with his mostly human hands. He's not even hungry. He's eating the girl's body because he likes it. Because he wants to.

I shudder. Weakness, I know, but I do it anyway. He thinks it's the funniest thing in the world.

"Never tried human before." He takes another bite, eyes glittering in challenge. "Best flavor in the world, for a while. Now it's just dead meat. But it's good. Tender. Fatty." Behind the gray of his eyes, a red flash, as if caught in the beam of a headlight. "Bet that bitch Steph'll taste—"

Provoked beyond reason, the wolf takes over for a moment. My head pounds with a ruddy darkness, and I'm growling and ready to launch my still-human self right at him, use my still-human teeth to rip out his throat.

Several things happen very quickly. I hesitate in my attack, as the human thinks about how to get the gun out of the back-pack and the wolf is confused by the shape of her own paws. George smiles, a small, nasty, human smile. He says, "You got my invitation, didn't you?" This sparks an *oh shit* moment cascading through my brain, as I realize that his urine trail was not him marking his territory like a wolf. It was him leading me into a trap, like a human. Breadcrumbs through the forest. He wanted me here. And that means—

A rifle pointing at my guts. "Shotgun full of silver," he says, smug as he fires.

19

WAKING UP NAKED ON THE HILL

I wake up. Under a bridge, in some muddy bushes. Dreamlike, I remember trotting here on four legs. Remember the sensation of enemy flesh shredding under teeth, savage joy in triumph, the hot blood when... she... I... she...

Feasted on his entrails.

Vomit now, some of those very same entrails, gray and bitter tissues that disgust me so much I gag again, then spend several moments having painful dry heaves. I touch my stomach where I remember the pain of the silver bullets going in. I see no wound or scar, but I feel heavy and uncomfortable there, as if the shot is still in my tissues. The pellets will work their way out again. Or they won't. Maybe I'll have to wander around for the rest of my life with silver embedded in my flesh.

One question answered for sure: no, a silver bullet will not kill me.

A man is nearby and I glance over, see his dull-eyed shock. He notices me looking and smiles nervously. "Need some whiskey, kid?"

"No, thank you. What I need are clothes."

"Yeah, I can help with that! I can, just a minute, here." He rummages through the plastic bags in his shopping cart. He finds a long, shiny dress, muddy. Looks like it might be somebody's prom dress. "This don't fit me, here."

"Uh—thank you."

He turns aside as I wriggle into it. It smells like the girl who wore it, her perfume, her boyfriend, the cheap beer they were drinking. The fabric is stiff and strange, like wearing plastic.

He takes a swig from his bottle. "So, how long have you been a werewolf?"

Another question answered: he did see me transform.

"I don't know. Maybe my whole life. What did you see?"

He nods, with a smile and an exhale of whiskey breath. "Well, at first I thought you were just a big dog. You get stray dogs around here sometimes, and they're good company, keep you warm at night, so I tried to make friends. But you didn't want any of my whiskey. You growled and I got a little scared. That growl was when I started thinking you might be a wolf. What big teeth you have!" He chuckles to himself for a while. "So I backed off. I figured you escaped from the zoo or something, but a wolf is really just a kind of mean dog, and you didn't seem like you wanted to hurt me if I left you alone. You curled up and went right to sleep. I looked away, and then when I looked back you were a girl." He chuckles again. "Funny, huh? You seemed like a big dog, but you're a little person."

Conservation of mass, I think. My wolf form is about the same size as my human form, distributed differently. More of her is teeth. "But you didn't see it happen?"

"No. Felt a little funny maybe. Like the back of my neck was tingling. And there was a smell or something, all sharp in my nose, like I wanted to sneeze." He pauses, looking thoughtful. "Of course, you could be the DTs. Sure you don't want some whiskey?"

"Don't the DTs happen when you stop drinking?"

"Oh, yeah." He grins, swigs some more from his bottle.

Awkward pause. "Well. Okay. I'd better go. Thanks."

"Yeah, good luck, werewolf girl! Unless you're not real!"

Barefoot, in a prom dress, I go back to the abandoned house for my things. Feeling like a criminal, I collect my clothes and backpack, trying not to look at George's eviscerated corpse. When the cops find him, will they know I was here? Will they be looking for me as a murderer?

No. She did it. The wolf. Not me. Don't say it was me.

But I would have killed him, as the weight of the gun in my backpack reminds me. I wanted to be ready to kill him. The only reason I didn't kill him is because I screwed everything up. She did what I was too incompetent to do, not what I was too moral to do.

I shoulder the backpack and head outside, where the moon is invisible behind thick clouds turned lurid orange with city lights. George is dead. I killed him. And when I did it, I was a wolf. Even now, I only half believe it. I walk down the hill, the weight of the gun, the weight of memory both tugging at me, nagging at me. I should be able to go home, right? It's all over. The bad guy is dead, because the monster killed him. But nobody knows I'm the monster, so it'll be fine. Won't it? I can just go home and go to sleep. The guilt will stop troubling me in a while. Why should I feel guilty, anyway? George tried to kill me. I tried to kill him back. I succeeded. And it wasn't really me anyway. Was it? It was the wolf.

The clouds part briefly, giving me a glimpse of the moon. The waning, gibbous moon.

That's it. That's the problem. The moon isn't full, and I changed shape anyway. Because I got shot? Because the bullets were silver? Because I was already hyped up to fight my enemy? I don't know. But I need to know. If I can change shape at any time, it means I'm never safe to be around, ever. Unless I can learn to control this.

I finally turn to face the idea that has been gibbering at the edge of my brain since I woke up naked in the middle of a deer carcass and knew what I was. I touch my neck, where the braid of Ash's hair remains, even after going to my wolf self. I'm sorry, beloved. I need to go back to New Harmony, but not the way I planned. Not in triumph, as a rescuer. I need to go back humbled, as a penitent, to find out everything Wisdom knows about controlling the beast.

20

ABBY LEAVES TOWN

The first step of my journey is easy: hang out near the Capitol Hill entrance to I-5 southbound until a band with a van full of musical equipment gives me a ride to Portland. When we hit the city, they make a stop and give me a coffee and my pick of extraordinary donuts from a pink box labeled "Voodoo." In the early morning light I help them move their equipment into a lovely historic performance space, and they give me a T-shirt.

Summer finally seems to have arrived here in the northwest, and Portland gets hot before the day is out. I head south, into hotter and hotter weather. I use Officer Lou's T-shirt-as-skirt trick many times, as fresh T-shirts have a way of coming to me at random, but other clean clothes are harder to get. California I know is a populous state with plenty to see and do, yet I-5 south of Redding and north of Los Angeles seems to be nothing but one long brown scrubby desert of rolling hills. I can smell the sea sometimes, or the dark organic rot of agriculture, but from I-5 these things are invisible. Sometimes it feels like I'm getting nowhere, trapped in a nightmare where I run and run and stay in one spot.

Everyone asks the same set of questions. What's your

name? How old are you? Where do you come from? Where
are you going? Why are you going there? Why are you hitchhiking? Don't you know that's dangerous? Do you know the
Lord?

Sometimes I'm a college student, eighteen, but of course
I look really young, and I'm hitchhiking as research for my
anthropology class. I'm sixteen, and going back home to my
family after running away two years ago. I'm twelve,
heading to stay with my aunt while my mom is in rehab.
The car broke down. My dad was giving me a ride and we
had a fight and I ran off and now I don't know how else to
get home. I have no fear, because I know the Lord will
protect me. My fundamentalist parents found out I'm gay,
and kicked me out of the house. I tailor my story in light of
the people who pick me up, and how I happen to be dressed
—are my T-shirts for a church camp, or a heavy metal
band?

None of my Seattle exploits seem to have made a splash in
the national news. I've been checking the headlines on news-
paper boxes that sell *USA Today* or *The New York Times*, pausing
to watch snippets of CNN or FOX on television. Nothing like
STALKER EX HUSBAND KILLED BY BIG DOG. If
there's a hunt going on for me, or for George's killer, I don't
know about it.

Most of the people who give me rides want to talk about
themselves, which comes as a great relief. They tell tales of
unfaithful spouses and ungrateful children, failed businesses
and lost hope. They talk about all their marvelous plans, and
how things are surely going to be different in the future. They
extol the wonders of God and Alcoholics Anonymous and the
Paleolithic Diet and juice made from wheat grass. They rant
about the conspiracy to cover up the aliens who landed at
Roswell, and how forces within the federal government
secretly engineered 9/11 and the Kennedy assassination. They
share stories about their psychic abilities and premonitions

and higher spiritual awareness and that one time they saw a ghost.

They like to tell me that they picked me up to make sure I'd be safe, because they don't know about the other drivers out there.

They give me T-shirts, and paperback books they've finished reading, and food. Sometimes they get weirdly insistent about the food, even going so far as to sit me down in a roadside diner and buy me a whole meal all to myself. Maybe I give off a perpetual aura of being about to expire from hunger. Or maybe it's something worse, maybe they sense the wolf, a veiled threat on some dim subliminal level, and have an instinct to feed her to keep her quiet. Whatever it is, it makes what I thought was going to be the hardest thing about my trip into one of the easiest, and I almost never have to resort to dumpster-diving.

When you operate on the margins of society, you run into other people on the margins of society. Most of them are kindly, if drug-addled, like that homeless man in the park who offered me whiskey and a prom dress. But some people are mean, and some are desperate, and some drugs turn people mean. So I see ugliness too. Some boys try to steal my backpack right out from under me, as I'm sleeping on it in a little park near Sacramento. Of course I wake right up. I tell them to go away, but for some reason—maybe because I'm only half-conscious still—the warning comes out not in words, but in a low, rumbling growl. I feel ridiculous, but it works. Their eyes go wide and they run, leaving me to puzzle out what just happened and what it means.

A couple of days later, in the evening, I'm hiking along a lonely Nevada highway from my "aunt's house" back to a freeway entrance. My flip-flops dangle from my fingers—I'm worried about wearing them out, unlike my self-repairing feet, and they're not suitable for long walks anyway. The air is hot and dry, with a dusty, used-up smell about it. The landscape to either side of me is a dreary emptiness that fading, graffiti-covered signs announce was going to be some kind of exciting future development. Now it's a lot of hard-baked dirt. To entertain myself I sing along loudly with the music player Steph's dad gave me, grateful that it still hasn't run out of charge yet. The feel of singing gives me a weird kind of hope. It's all going to work out. I'm going to tame the wolf, and go back to live with Steph, and her dad is going to give me more music, and we'll all be happy forever.

Then I become aware that a car is right beside me, and has been for some time. At first I took no notice, but now it seems improbable that any car would have kept to my walking pace for so long. Also, a person smell is drifting from the open windows: a musky smell of sex, but old and foul, curdled, somehow.

My heart pounds. Anger? Fear? Both? Anyway, I'm all stressed out now and the wolf is alert, stretching and flexing her claws. I march right up to the driver's side window. "Why are you following me?"

He answers in a language I don't know, his voice husky and low, almost a groan. Then I notice that he's got his penis out—okay, that's it. The wolf is ready to tear him apart. I glare straight into his eyes and he stares back, face going slack as if hypnotized. "You! Go to the police and tell them what you've been doing!" My voice comes out sounding strange, with a weird rumble layered on top of it, and I can feel some-thing in my stare, a kind of a flash, as if my will is lightning, striking his heart. "GO!"

I release his gaze and he shakes himself, sweat spiking with yellow terror. He shouts a single foreign word, "Strigoi!" which strikes me as a little familiar, and speeds off in the car. I continue on my way, laughing now. I hope he really does go to the cops. But the longer I think about it, the more troubled I am. Using the power of the wolf to make him afraid—I liked it, but now I don't know if I like that I liked it. Anyway, I can't get too attached to the wolf. I'm heading back to New Harmony to make her go away for good, right?

At the eastern edge of Texas, with New Orleans or Baton Rouge the next logical destination, I give up.

I wake with the dawn to another sticky, used-up day. It takes a moment to remember where I am, why I'm not indoors, and my first thought is that the wolf took over again. But then I realize that I'm still wearing my minimalist outfit of two T-shirts and a floppy hat, and still curled around my backpack as a kind of pillow. My eyes are still closed when a strange person scent comes near and an officious male voice intones, "You can't sleep here."

"It's a rest area, isn't it? I'm resting." I'm already smoldering with anger when I open my eyes to look at him. He wears a uniform of some kind, but I don't think he's a cop.

"It's for people in cars. You have to be in a car. You can't just sleep on the bench like that."

I sit up and peer into his face: an ugly heavy-jawed white guy somewhere in middle age, his mind dim and predictable, but self-importance puffing him up like a balloon.

"That's the most ridiculous thing I ever heard." I catch and hold his eyes, ready to growl at him, make him be afraid, but the wolf doesn't want to come up. I feel her, sleeping like a coiled-up snake. But she won't wake, not for this guy. Instead I drop his eyes, grab my backpack, and flip him off. It's the first time I've done that to anyone. I start walking back to the highway, heading vaguely east.

"How old are you, anyway?" he calls after me angrily. "I bet you're underage. I'm calling your parents!"

"Good luck, asshole!"

Everything I can see is brown and moldering. Backpack, brown with dirt. Black T-shirts, fading to brown under the relentless sun. The summer sky of dirty blue turns to brown at the edges. Even my arms are brown, freckles growing together and darkening, although the skin on the underside remains as pale as the squirming flesh of a dug-up worm. I flip my fore-arms over, up and down, both fascinated and repulsed by the abrupt change from mottled pinkish brown to pallid blue-veined white. My skin is ugly. The wolf, with her thick red coat, is prettier.

There's no point to this, is there? This is all for nothing. Wisdom has no cure for the wolf. There is no cure. How could there be? I should stay out in the wilderness forever, learn to kill squirrels with my bare hands and eat them raw. Why not? Maybe the only real solution is to give in completely, go to animal form and never come back. I'll terrorize the country-side, until sheep farmers tell ghost stories about the crimson wolf that can't be killed with bullets.

The sun rises, growing warmer and stronger, until it's hammering down like a solid thing. My stupid little hat offers so little shade that it's like a bad joke. I veer off the highway toward a worn-out gray-brown building, hoping for shelter during the hottest part of the day. It seems to be an aban-doned store. Other homeless creatures have holed up here in the past, coyotes and humans and birds, but right now I'm alone except for a handful of nervous rats.

Almost hungry enough to eat the rats, I have an energy bar instead, and wash it down with stale tap water from my plastic water bottle. Still hungry, I have another energy bar, then curse myself for gluttony. It's a deadly sin, and I don't care about that, but it's stupid. I'm running low on energy bars and don't know how long it's going to take to get the rest of the way to New Harmony.

What are the deadly sins again? Lust, gluttony, envy, greed, wrath—obviously wrath is my favorite. But what are the last two? Sloth, that's it. And... despair? Boredom? I take out my iPod, remember that it finally ran out of charge yesterday, and kick it to death. Slam, bang, until the case cracks and its electronic guts are strewn all about the dusty wooden floor. The sight of them makes me want to cry. Why did I do that? It seems so cruel now. The iPod never hurt me.

I take out a tattered paperback that I picked up in a free bin, back when the fact that it was about werewolf love struck me as incredibly amusing. But today the obvious romance tropes fill me with a sullen, resentful anger. I start ripping pages out of the book, one at a time, until they are littered around my feet like autumn leaves. Fragments of words and sentences form dada poetry, all meaning turned to gibberish. I shred the pages into smaller and smaller pieces, as if I'm a loathsome giant rat, building a filthy nest out of old paper.

If I want to travel later, I should sleep now, but my brain won't shut up. Instead I pace the room like a tiger in a cage that's too small, until I stub my toe on a disused ice machine. Then I kick at the ice machine for a while until the rest of my foot hurts too. Maybe I should try to exhaust myself to sleep. I lift the ice machine and toss it across the room. It crashes through some rotten boards in a satisfying manner, but something in my back tears with a searing flash of pain.

Well, pain is distracting at least. I lie on the floor, waiting to heal with my usual rapidity, but it doesn't happen. The pain shrieks at me like a banshee, even as I sit up and crawl to my backpack for some water. How strange. I take out my pocket knife and make an experimental cut on my left forearm. It doesn't heal right away. Instead, it bleeds and aches for what seems like a normal amount of time. Another cut, same thing. And another.

The wolf is gone. That's what this is. But not gone for good, no, I can feel that. She's left, but she'll be right back when the next full moon comes. She took a chunk of my soul along with her, left me staring at the dark empty place it used to be. A part of me has always been her, hasn't it? Without her, I'll never be more than half a person. And with her I'm a danger to everyone around me.

Everything I've ever done swirls around in my head like a

swarm of stinging wasps. If there's a Hell, I probably belong there. Not the wolf, me. I'm the one who got Ash killed, by talking back to my father. I'm the one who bit George and got that girl in the park killed. I don't even know her name. I should know it. I've barely thought about that girl. I'm horrible. I remember the moment at Ash's funeral, when I noticed her body smelled like roasting meat and it made me hungry. That was me too. It's always just me. The wolf wouldn't even come to me if I weren't ready for her, if I weren't the right sort of person, if I didn't have that evil in my heart already.

I move the backpack, and notice how heavy it is. Because of Morgan's gun. I've lugged it all this way, not knowing what else to do with it. It's still loaded with bullets. Maybe there's an easier solution, what if—

No.

A head wound?

No.

But what about—

I take out the gun and empty it into the far wall, BANG BANG BANG BANG BANG BANG. There. Now it's just a paperweight. I throw the gun to follow the bullets, and wait for the sound of police sirens. But I guess you can shoot a gun out in rural Texas and nobody cares.

Weeping, I fall eventually into bad, empty dreams. When night comes I head outside to look for the moon, and can't find her.

21

BACK TO NEW HARMONY

This morning I feel normal.

Normal for me, anyway. The wolf is there as usual, alert, ready to step up if she thinks I need her help. All my despair and worry and confusion and self-hatred are still there too. But it's different. Yesterday I was drowning, trapped in a jar with my emotions closing over my head and no way to get out. Today they're just a part of me, like the wolf is. When the clerk at the gas station gives me a worried smile, I smile back and it feels totally natural.

"Hon, do you need me to call somebody? Come out and pick you up or something?"

I study the map on the wall for a moment, then tell her, "I'm headed to Baton Rouge. My family is there."

She brightens a little. "You're going back home to your family? That's nice."

Nice? I stifle an ironic giggle. Nice, sure. "They'll be glad to see me, I think."

"Oh, I think they will. Say, are you looking for a ride?"

"I am."

"Lemme talk to my friend Arty. He's got a rig, makes that run a lot. Hold on."

While she pulls out a phone, I study the calendar on the wall. When did I leave Seattle, exactly? July 6, I think. A couple of days after the Howl, anyway, July 3, the full moon clearly marked as a white circle. Today is the nineteenth of July, judging by the days crossed off the calendar. About two weeks. It feels like I've been gone forever. Yesterday has a little black circle, the new moon, the exact opposite point in the lunar cycle from full.

Huh. Is that why I felt so bad yesterday? Maybe I have moon-related bipolar disorder. It's kind of hilarious, really. I wish there were somebody I could tell. I can tell my father about it, I suppose, when I get there, but he won't think it's funny. My father doesn't think anything is funny.

The nice clerk gets me an uneventful ride to Baton Rouge, and from there I easily find a ride from Baton Rouge to New Orleans. He wants to talk to me about God, but I know I'm going to get plenty of that from my father, so I pretend to be asleep most of the time.

I snap to attention when we start drawing near New Harmony. I watch the side of the road attentively for the signs I remember, the little towns that pepper Highway 61 between the two incredibly different cities. There, Wallace, that's the place. "Thank you, sir. This is my stop." I smile, and gesture at the side of the road. I imagine I can still see the black marks from Steph's tires, where she screeched to a halt to avoid hitting me and a couple of dogs.

"But, child, there's nothing here." The man frowns at me, and doesn't slow down.

"It's beyond the trees. You can't see it from the highway, but it's not far."

"Oh, child, please. I can't put you off in the middle of nowhere. You must've made some mistake. I thought I was taking you home."

Inwardly, I groan. Of course. Two weeks, three thousand miles, more than a dozen rides, and the first person to give me any trouble is the one taking me to New Harmony, the man who had to move a Bible out of the passenger seat before I could sit down, the man with his radio tuned to a country preacher ranting in tones that remind me of my childhood. "Sir, please. I do know my own home. This is where I need to get off, although we've gone past it now."

"Nonsense," he says.

Now I'm getting mad. "You know, if you don't stop the car and let me out when I ask, this whole thing turns pretty quickly from you giving me a ride into a kidnapping."

It doesn't penetrate. He shakes his head. "Child, please. When you entered my car I became responsible for your welfare."

I can't take it any more. I let the wolf come up, the growl work its way into my voice, the green fire flash behind my eyes. "Stop. The car. Now."

Shocked, he screeches to a halt. "What? What?"

"Thank you, mister." I grab my backpack, all sunny smiles as I slip out of the car. "You have a blessed day now!"

Still confused, he nods distractedly and drives away again. Damn, I wish I didn't like using that little trick so much. I take stock of my surroundings. We're not more than five miles from where I wanted to stop, and walking five miles is nothing to me now. I take off the flip-flops I wear for show and start hoofing barefoot up the road, warm pavement at first soothing under my thick calluses. I blink at the sun, hanging familiar in the thick air of a Louisiana summer. It won't be long now. I'm almost glad of the extra walking. I've had the last two weeks with almost nothing to do but think about what's going to happen when I get to New Harmony, and still I don't feel ready for it.

I stop. Well, here I am. I have to get back across that canal, which looks higher and wider than it was in the winter. No help for it. I take off my T-shirt skirt and pile it on my head, wade through stinking swamp water that reaches mid-thigh. I walk half-naked through the trees, lush with their summer foliage, letting my legs dry before putting my skirt back on. Somebody could see me, half-naked as I am. I literally do not care.

Much as I came to hate New Harmony, the landscape here feels so familiar, it is almost like coming home. The thick riot of smells on the moist air, from sweet to foul, as a heavenly fog of flowers and cypress leaves gives way suddenly to the poisonous reek from a nearby refinery. The feel of the uncertain terrain, completely flat and more than half water. The smooth, rounded nubbins of cypress knees poking up through still water. The burbling cascade of birds, singing unseen in the dense growth. I feel so good right now, once again I'm tempted to stay in this moment. I don't have to keep going, find New Harmony. I could stay out here in the swampy wilderness. Plenty to eat, plenty of places to hide. Maybe there are other rougarou out here, like in the tales. I can find that fais-do-do with the naked werewolf boys, the one Steph was giggling about.

But thinking of Steph reminds me of my purpose. If it is at all possible, I have to figure out how to control this thing. If that fails, then I can think about disappearing into the wilderness forever.

My throat tightens. I don't want it to fail. I want to see Steph and Terry again. I want to go to school. I want to hang out with Deena and her friends. I want to maybe kiss Edison.

Okay. None of that is going to happen if I don't do this thing.

The trees thin as I approach New Harmony. My thumping heart doesn't prepare me for things to seem so peaceful and familiar. I inhale cooking, growing plants, fertilizer, familiar people-smells of my brothers and sisters. I walk past fields of high, sweet corn. It looks like this turned out to be a good year after all. I even—yes, I even smell sheep. And young dogs, puppies. How is this possible? Is everything restored? A rustling in the corn, and a part of my brain starts to fantasize that my sister Ash will run out laughing and tell me that Jesus came again and made every bad thing untrue, the glorious Millennial Kingdom come at last.

But no. Scent doesn't lie. Long before I see him, I know the rustling is my eldest brother Great Purpose. He steps out, covered in sweat and dust, carrying a hoe. "Self-Abnegation," he says, with a smile and without any apparent surprise. "Welcome home."

"Great Purpose." I smile and nod. "How are—things?"

"Good, good. Fertile, as you see. A good year. Father says I might seek a wife soon." He positively beams at that, at the idea of being allowed to seek a wife. He must be close to eighteen by now.

"Uh. Good for you. I—were you expecting me?"

"Father Wisdom said you would return. The Lord gifted him a vision."

"Really. Okay, that's... Okay. What else did this vision tell him? Did it tell him why I would return?"

"The Lord said, you needed help to tame the beast. And only Wisdom in the Service of the Lord knows how."

22

FATHER WISDOM

Father Wisdom seems to have got word of my coming. He stands on the front porch of the main house with a benevolent smile, arms open in a pose of welcome. The sight of him causes my entire body to stiffen, tremble with suppressed rage. For a moment I am tempted to simply let the wolf loose and maul him to death.

But I need to find out what he knows.

"Self-Abnegation. The return of a prodigal is always a most welcome event."

Anger aside, I slip into practiced behavior and smile brightly, a masked mechanical expression that doesn't reach my eyes. He can't tell the difference. When he smiles, it never reaches his eyes either. I dip my head, a gesture of submission that irritates the wolf. *Not to him, we don't dip our head to him.* Shush, I tell her. "Father. I come seeking your wisdom."

He nods. Of course, isn't that what everyone comes to him for? He named himself Wisdom for a reason. "Come this way." He turns around and begins to head down the hallway, his footsteps creaking, the odors of dampness and neglected carpet overwhelming me with a dreadful sense of familiarity. All of Seattle might have been a dim, gray dream. Now I follow my father through the main house, anticipating his counsel, his wrath, his chastisement. I might never have left.

Wait. Something is different. We pass rooms full of cardboard boxes, pungent with newly pressed paper, printing ink, binding glue. Books. A promotional poster shows my father's face, smiling, and text identifying him as THE BEST-SELLING AUTHOR OF PERFECT OBEDIENCE who has a new book called *Twenty Years Living God's Plan: The New Harmony Story*.

If I thought I was enraged before, I had no idea. I squeeze my hands into fists. Oh. Oh, the dirty rotten filthy liar, that's why things are going well finally, you have the money from a new book, and it's full of lies, you're going to tell them how wonderful this place is, how holy, how blessed—

"New book, Father Wisdom?" I say. My voice trembles just a bit.

"That's no concern of yours," he says.

My hands curl tighter, fingernails threatening to draw blood from my palms. Stigmata, right? A miracle. Except we're not Catholic. But Steph is. I'm here for her. I'm doing this for Steph, for Terry. I have to keep reminding myself of that. If the wolf eats Wisdom now, it's all over.

Father's study is a forbidden space, to be entered only in his company, and he always spent much of his time there. Inside, the air is heavy with his sweat, a kind of luncheon-meat odor that I have never liked. It seems strange, now that I consider it. Shouldn't my own father's scent be a source of comfort? I start to feel nervous. This situation is slipping out of my control. He closes the door, locking it, another note of disquiet. Nobody will disturb us in here without his leave, why does he feel the need to lock the door? My eyes stray, unwilling, to the aged latch, and I swallow back a sense of unease. No, it's okay, it's all right, I have nothing to be afraid of.

"You want to know about the beast." It's not a question, but I nod in response. "Very well. We raised you as our own and tried to claim you for God Almighty. But you rebelled, driven by the taint inside you. And when you left my protection, the beast claimed you instead. Is that not what I foretold?"

"I didn't believe you." I swallow hard, my throat suddenly constricting in reluctance. I don't want to tell him this. I don't want to say these words. "But you were right."

"Of course." His smile broadens for a moment and then settles into his neutral benevolent look, eyes somewhat glassy, unfocused. "You were led astray by the evil spirit inside you. It comes from your father."

Comes from my father? But—

Oh. *OH.*

"Then you are not my father?"

He closes his eyes, nods, bows his head as if in a moment of prayer. Then he takes one of his diaries from the shelf and flips through it, as if refreshing his memory, but I can tell he already knows what he's going to tell me. He does this in his sermons, with the Bible. It's a prop. *Listen to my authority*, it says. *I looked it up, I must be right.*

"She came to me in New Orleans," he says, in the pleasant rolling tones he uses when preaching, words closing over my head like warm water, washing me away. "My first angel had been taken up to Heaven, and I had three little ones to care for on my own. We walked the street named after vice, and we ministered to the adulterers and fornicators and idolaters and Sodomites—do you know the Sodomites, Abnegation? In the outside world, did you meet them? The men who burn with unnatural passion for one another?"

They were my next-door neighbors, I think. They taught me to make Indian food. The thought brings a surge of protective anger on their behalf. You don't even know them, how dare you condemn them? But I need to hear what he has to tell me. So I nod, feeling cowardly and disloyal. "I did."

"Bourbon Street, Bourbon Street, ah, no man has ever

seen such a sewer. A river of piss and vomit, all the filth and foulness of the continent gathered there before it empties to the sea. But we accustom ourselves to the stink, Abnegation. To sickness we acquaint ourselves, to degradation we grow numb. They mocked me when I walked the filthy streets holding the cross aloft. They mocked and heard not a word and continued to follow their stinking path to Hell. Down the river of mud and sorrow they continued, unbowed and unashamed."

Is he going to go on like that all day? No longer used to his rhetorical excesses, I fight the urge to fidget and roll my eyes. He might be one of those ragged men who rants about God on the corner of Pike and 4th, who merit from passers-by not much more than a pitying glance and maybe pocket change. But if I display my impatience, he's likely to clam up and not say another word. I unfocus my eyes and hold my mouth in a slight smile, my head cocked in a pose of attention, a look I have practiced since I was a small child.

"She came to me in the early evening, when the street was quiet and a full moon rose in the sky. She wore a white dress, and her skin was pale as milk, her hair like gold. She looked almost an angel as she came to me, and I felt my faith strengthen at the sight of her. She begged my help. Her family had forsaken her, on account of the child in her belly. Was I a Godly man? she asked me. Was I a faithful man? God welcomes all sinners, I told her, glad in my heart to be able to speak this truth. But she told me the child was not born of her sin. She told me that on a night like tonight, when the moon was swollen and round, a terrible beast had come upon her, and taken her by force. Her family did not believe this tale. Modern, corrupt, they did not believe in demons, and thought her a liar. I knew her to be holy, a visionary."

"What? Are you telling me that my real father—that he raped my mother—in wolf form?" Horror-struck, the words seem to rip themselves out of my throat. Wisdom's stern glance tells me I should have remained silent. Hold your tongue girl. Hold your tongue. But—

"Demons take many beastlike forms." His voice is hard, metal grinding against rocks. "The one that attacked her was something like a wolf, yes. She told me that even her pregnancy seemed monstrous, for yes, she had been pregnant before. That was another cause for her family's scorn, because in their eyes she had already sinned in that way, that first child given up for adoption. But this pregnancy was different, bringing with it strange feelings, cravings for raw meat, rages without cause, as if she nurtured Lucifer himself. And on nights when the moon was full, the baby inside her would not rest, kicking and churning all night as if it wanted escape, although she was several months from her due date still."

He stares at me, dark eyes penetrating. "Even in the womb, the beast called out to you. We prayed together, and knew what we had to do. God Almighty brought us together, and her devil child might be the Antichrist, signal the true end times at last. I purchased land and took my sons and my daughter and my new wife to live as the Lord intended, off the land. I went to prepare the way, to be ready to welcome our Lord Jesus when he comes again, Of all the nations, we here at least would be ready for the Millennial Kingdom."

"So it's my fault. You started New Harmony because of me."

He slams his hand down on his wooden desk, sharply, rebuking. "Abnegation! Do not aggrandize yourself with evil or virtue beyond your power! You were at most a catalyst, proof from Almighty Lord that we followed the correct path. Now listen to what I say. You were born in the new world and appeared an ordinary babe. Noisy, and willful, true, but you took well enough to the chastisements. I thought the Lord had given us power to tame your demon in truth. But I found at the last, when it all failed, and you defied me, and left us, that the fiend was merely biding its time."

His eyes stray to the bookshelf and I follow his gaze, see that he is looking at a row of perhaps a dozen identical books: *Perfect Obedience.*

I swallow, heart fluttering in my ears, everything too hot. "Please," I say, careful not to look at him. "Did you ever discover anything more about the one who spawned me? Did you see him? Talk to him?"

"Of course not." He leans in close, his breath foul, his sweat stinking. Not my father. How many nights did I pray, when I still had the faith to pray, that this day would come? When I would find out that it was all a mistake, that my real father was someone else, that I could go to him instead? And now it's true. I have a real father, somewhere, and he's worse than Wisdom.

The full realization sinks in with a physical nausea, dragging me to the floor, to my knees, to a little ball of self-hatred. My father is a monster. My other father is a monster. And I see no hope, no way to be other than a monster myself. My new-moon despair returns, and with it, an urge to just stop, to cease, to annihilate myself. That's what he wanted, isn't it? He named me after what I needed to do. Give up myself, because my self is such an irredeemably horrible thing. And perhaps, somehow, in not-self, I can find salvation. I can find peace.

"Abnegation," he says. He lays a hand on my head. "I instructed you with the truth. I told you never to leave my protection, my covering, but you did, and the beast devoured you. But you can be clean again. It can be as it was before. The wolf can be made again to lie down with the lamb."

 I swallow. My throat barely works. "How." My voice cracks. "How can this be done?"

"You must surrender your self, your authority to the Lord Almighty through me, as you did before. When you entered the threshold of adulthood, of accountability, and were Humbled. That can be done again. Like baptism itself, if you have strayed from the path, the Lord will welcome you back. You have only to go to him in the proper spirit."

Humbling. Three days in the Prayer Closet, three hours on the Mercy Seat. Then I will stand before the congregation while Wisdom preaches. His sermon will endure for as long as I do, until I collapse, able to stand no longer. Torture, yes. But it might have been torture in a good cause. It could be that New Harmony practices really are what kept the wolf at bay for so long.

Liar. Betrayer. Murderer.

My hand reaches to my throat, instinctively, to feel the silken lock of hair. Ash, I'm sorry, I'm so sorry. I didn't want it to be this way. But I have to try.

I bow my head. "Father Wisdom, I will do this thing."

He rests a heavy hand on my head. "Thou art a child of the Lord."

23

THE PRAYER CLOSET

The Prayer Closet is an outbuilding of gray concrete industrial brick, roughly the size of a small prison cell. Dirt floor, bucket in the corner for waste. The bucket stinks to high heaven during the summer months, like now. Plastic jugs of water, measured out for the number of days of confinement, sit in a neat row. Enough to keep me alive but none to waste, none for bathing. Bathing happens at the end of the ceremony, after the collapse. My thin white rags, filthy by then, will be stripped off, my hair will be freshly shorn, and I will be baptized in warm water and emerge clean and whole into a bright new world.

Or, so the story goes.

I'm already starting to doubt my course. As we approach the gray building, my father (but not my father) before me, my older brothers (but not my brothers) each taking an arm, I start to want to bolt. I can't go in there, don't make me go in there.

"Don't struggle," Justice tells me. "You wanted this."

"I asked for it. I'm still not sure I want it."

"No talking from the penitent," my father says. But not my father. I have to keep telling myself that. It seems to change everything, yet it also changes nothing. My brothers and sisters, half-siblings only. Even little Ash, not fully my sister. My older brothers and sister, and the younger ones, from Meekness, they aren't genetically related to me at all. But what difference does that make? I was raised here. I never knew a different life.

(*Until Seattle. Until Steph.*)

For a moment, facing the open door like a mouth ready to swallow me, I'm ready to flee, run into the wilderness and never mind what happens after that. *You already know it's not going to work,* suggests a familiar snarky inner voice. *You just want to punish yourself because you feel guilty.*

I breathe steadily and keep walking. So what if I feel guilty? I have good reason to feel guilty. Anyway, Wisdom was right about the wolf, so maybe he's right about this. How else can I know? I have to try, right? Don't I have to try everything?

Now I'm inside. I know the smells of this place, the dust of despair, the stink of open sewage. Wisdom takes my shoulders and turns me around to face him. His expression hardens, and he rips the lock of Ash's hair from my neck.

"Ye shall not make any baldness for the dead. Did you think I wouldn't notice?"

The door slams shut, bolted from the outside, trapping me inside, while I clutch my suddenly bare neck in shock, then anger. I want to kill him. I'm going to kill him. No, I can't. Not before I know if this will work to control the wolf. Wait, not ever, what am I thinking? I can't kill my own father. But he isn't my father. No, I can't. It was one thing to plan to kill George—he was a danger to everyone, a real-life werewolf with no conscience and a taste for human flesh. But my father is just—

A cult leader.

No, shut up.

Why? You know it's true. And maybe he didn't murder

Ash, not with intent, but he killed her. You know he did. He beat her, and she died. You know that getting beaten badly enough can kill a person. You saw it on that news program—

No. No, no, no. I can't. I have to do this. I have to submit, I have to—

I smash myself against the rough concrete walls: kicking, punching, slamming, until I'm bleeding, and I'm pretty sure I broke a few small bones. It doesn't matter. I heal right up. Eventually the fight burns out of me and I sink down to the dirt floor. Silence, nothing but buzzing flies and my own breathing. But if it rains, the cheap tin roof will rattle ferociously. I could get out through that roof, I think. If I really had to. This thought quiets the wolf a little.

There's nothing in here except the water, the bucket, and a little podium, a lectern with a Bible and some John Wise books on it. When we sleep, we sleep on the dirt floor. This is why we come out so filthy. I'm not tall, and even I can't stretch out fully unless I lay diagonally. I wonder what my brothers did, when they were Humbled. Sleep curled up in fetal position?

"Abnegation." Father's voice, coming through one of the air vents. A Prayer Closet bonus, he'll lecture me until he gets bored. "Listen to my words. There is no self in the Lord. Give up thy self to his purpose. Only the self experiences torment. Only the self feels pain, humiliation. Only the self hungers. Only the self fears. Thy self is a prison smaller and more oppressive than the walls of this small room. The self is a burden greater than the weight of all these bricks. The self is your beast. Give everything up to the Lord, even your self, and he will bless you for it. He will take your burdens away."

We'll see about that, I think.

He murmurs at me for a while, then goes away, leaving me to my own devices. Leaving me to the deepest of deep boredom, almost unimaginable if you've never experienced it. Of course, nobody ever enjoyed the Prayer Closet. It wasn't meant to be enjoyed. But now that I've been in the outside world, seen a few movies, read some history unfiltered by the New Harmony agenda, I recognize it as a classic technique for torture and brainwashing. Solitary confinement in an over-heated swamp. This can't be right. Can it?

But I don't know. If torture and brainwashing are how we get the wolf to lie still, I have to find out. I don't know any other way to be certain.

I wait. A day, a hundred days, a night, a hundred nights. Time loses all definition, stretching and contracting extrava-gantly, like the universe breathing. With nothing else to read, I read the Bible, and it seems both familiar and unutterably strange. Did these words once have meaning to me? If they did, I can't seem to touch it again. But is that part of this experience? If I can find that meaning again, is that what keeps the other me away?

Hunger starts to gnaw at me from the inside. I pace my confines while my stomach growls. The wolf growls. She wants to get us out of here, climb the walls, go through the roof. No prison can hold us, she says. We are invincible, inde-structible.

I tell her to quiet down.

Three days alone with the wolf, the Bible, and his books. Everything seems less real the more hungry I get. I dreamed the outside world, Seattle, my family and friends there. I'm dreaming this, too. All that we see and all we seem, are but a dream within a dream. That's not from the Bible, where is that from? I can't remember. It doesn't matter. Here I am in the gray space, protected. Nothing will ever happen again. In time, that troubling sense of self will disappear. The self is where the beast comes from, right? That's what my Wisdom says.

Lie still. Lie down with the lamb.

Lie.

THREE DAYS BEFORE THE FULL MOON, THEY COME TO RELEASE me from the Prayer Closet. I'm thirsty and starving and twitchy, the wolf pacing around inside, ready to pounce on something and eat it raw. I'm seriously doubting this course of action is the right way to tame her. It seems to be having the opposite of the intended effect. As my human self droops, weakened, my other self begins to dominate. Now I think I understand what happened when George shot me. She has a powerful, all-encompassing will to live. She shares this body with me, and will take the damn thing over if that's the only way to keep us both alive. It's almost sweet, in a way. She protects me, the way I once tried to protect Ash. Will her failure be as great?

"Father Wisdom, I am no longer sure of my course. The beast inside feels stronger, not weaker."

"Trust me, child," he says. "The wolf will lie down with the lamb as foretold. Drink this, it is my blood." He hands me a small bottle of—grape juice? I don't remember being given grape juice before. No, it's not really juice, it's one of those fortified electrolyte drinks. Grape-flavored. Maybe he wants to make sure I don't collapse too soon, so that my suffering is maximized. Still, I'm very thirsty, and drink it in one gulp. The flavor of artificial sweeteners is more delicious than I ever imagined.

My older brothers hold my arms, and I have a visceral memory of being led in this way when I was twelve. Then, I was so weak that they had to half-carry me to the Mercy Seat. Now I walk under my own power. If I'm sure this is wrong, I can easily break away from them. But I'm not sure. Why can't I be sure? Is this really the only way?

We walk. I try to make my mind a blank. One foot, then another. I stumble. I'm weaker than I thought. Purpose helps me right myself. Dizziness overwhelms me for a moment and my knees buckle. My limbs, my eyelids, heavy, as if my body has turned to lead. This isn't hunger. It's something else, something—

With effort, I crane my head around to see our father where he walks behind us. "You drugged that grape drink, didn't you?"

He smiles benevolently. "The devil will be subdued."

24

THE BEAST

The drug never renders me fully unconscious, but it seems to sap my will to move. I comply, as my brothers make me lie face down on cold granite, spread out my arms and legs in a wide X, shackle my wrists and ankles. Even with eyes closed I can sense my family, hear the rustling as they breathe, smell their familiar sweat wafting out as they seat themselves in the pews. The Mercy Seat is at the front of the chapel, like a shrine. I am on display for the benefit of the congregation.

As a child, I thought of this place only in terms of pain and humiliation. But now that I have spent some time on the outside, I notice how strangely perverted it all seems. Morgan has watched nearly-pornographic horror movies much like this, half-naked young woman chained to the black altar, awaiting sexual abuse at the improbable limbs of demons. In this horror movie, I will be caned, hard but carefully, so as not to leave permanent marks. But like everything else, this sometimes failed, and permanent marks I do have.

The abuse will not be sexual. Not intentionally, anyway. But the older I get, the older my brothers get, the more naughty it all seems. I'm still not much of a woman, not at first glance, but more than when I left. And my older brothers have always been rather handsome, lean, clean-living farm-boys that they are. They're not even technically related to me.

A dark, cynical giggle wells up in my throat, which I suppress and it comes out in a choked gurgle.

"She's awake!" Justice calls out.

"Then you should begin." My father's voice.

How could you go back to him? It's Ash's voice, but I think I'm imagining it.

I didn't go back to him. I wanted him to help me.

He has no help to give. He only wants to make you hurt one last time.

Burning, I see her on the altar, skin blackening and peel-ing. Still on fire she stands up and raises out a hand, pointing at me, her eyes aflame. I jerk awake, and only then realize that I must have passed out. For a moment Ash's accusing ghost remains, lingering against the hot sunlit reality of the chapel. Brilliant colored light dances in through the stained glass Jesus, fragmenting the horrific phantom into purple and gold, Jesus coming in all his glory, raised from the dead.

THWACK

Justice lowers the cane. Heavy, stinging pain across my buttocks.

THWACK

Purpose brings his own cane down from the other side. When I was younger, Wisdom would do the caning himself, but of course by the time of my beating six months ago, he had Justice and Purpose do it. When I was very young, we didn't have the Mercy Seat at all. Wisdom was strict in those days, harsh and sometimes unloving, but not insane. He founded New Harmony for my sake, to get me and my beast away from the corrupting influence of the world, but it took him many years to turn this place into the hell on earth I ran away from. That happened after my mother died. That was when the punishments first started to become more extreme and frequent.

THWACK. THWACK. THWACK. THWACK. THWACK. THWACK.

My mother grew sick not long after Ash was born. It seemed that she never recovered from childbirth, she just grew sicker and sicker. We prayed over her, certain in our faith that the Lord would heal her. Then, when she wasn't healed, when she died, that was the Lord's will too. He wanted all the angels in heaven with him. I almost believed it all, when I was nine. The Lord works in mysterious ways, which just happen to coincide exactly with whatever Wisdom says.

THWACK.
THWACK.
THWACK.

My thoughts start to feel as if they're leaving my body, going out into the brilliant stained glass Jesus. The pain seems far away. I remember this, the distant golden floaty sensation that comes with a particularly painful correction. Wisdom told us it was God's grace coming upon us. Now I know it's endorphins, natural opiates made by the body to help us survive pain and injury. And if that's God's grace, then it's meted out equally to everyone in pain, to injured soldiers and women giving birth, to cancer patients and people who run marathons for the fun of it. It succors atheists and Hindus, Catholics and Quakers, all of us alike.

My father's face comes into my field of vision. He's smiling. He looks as happy, as pleasant, as he ever does. "Let Jesus take the pain. Let it go. Let everything go. Let yourself be consumed by Jesus, and he will shield you from all diabolical powers."

This is what I came for. His wisdom, whatever it brings. I try. I try to let go.

THWACK

"Everything will be all right if you just give up yourself. Deny yourself. Abnegate yourself. Lay your *self* down and become one with Him, with the Almighty. Give up. Lay yourself down. The self is a prison. Give Him your Self."

I try. Again. I try, I relax, I send my thoughts out and away—

THWACK

The wolf shakes off the lingering influence of the drug and yawns, irritated.

THWACK

She growls, a warning. *Stop that or I'll eat you.* The noise comes out of my own human throat, but doesn't sound human at all.

"It's the beast!" Justice calls out, alarm in his voice, in his spicy yellow curry sweat.

Slam! Returned fully to my body, to all its pain and sweat and thirst and hunger. When I drifted, she was right there, ready to take over. Not Jesus. The wolf is what waits for me if I give up my self. Not salvation, but its opposite. I need all my human self, right here, fully present, to keep my animal self in line.

In an instant my view flips, and I feel like I see everything clearly for the first time. He knew the beast spawned me, but that was all he knew. If I didn't change until after leaving New

Harmony, it was nothing he did, no power he had. It was coincidence. Or, two results, same cause. The rising wolf making me defy him openly for the first time, and giving me the courage to leave. Either way, now I know. Wisdom's approach is the wrong approach, and it will never work.

But I'm still chained to the Mercy Seat and being caned, so that could be a problem.

"Keep going! Bring out the fiend to exorcise it!"

"Father, no!" I shout, and I can feel the collective gasp as everyone in this room is equally shocked to hear me give Wisdom an order.

He comes into my field of vision, scowling. "Self-Abnegation in the Service of the Lord, that defiance is the beast in you. This is the devil emergent! Come out of her, I say! Fiend, I order you hence!" He picks up his rod, the length of black PVC pipe no more than one inch in diameter, the one he talks about in the book. The one he used to beat Ash. He begins to strike my shoulders and arms, not as hard as the cane on my lower body, but it hurts more intensely, especially where he hits bone. "Justice and Mercy in the Service of the Lord, strike harder! Great Purpose in the Service of the Lord, strike harder!"

They obey him without hesitation.

THWACK THWACK THWACK.

It's getting more difficult to think, more difficult to focus.

"You don't understand! When the beast emerges, I'm going to turn into a real wolf."

"The wolf is just another form of demon. Bring it out. Let it out."

Rage begins to build inside me, frustrated rage, the rage of a lifetime. He never would listen to anyone else, certainly not a child, not a girl. "Wisdom! You're an idiot!"

More gasps. Enraged himself, he comes into my field of

vision once more, seizes my head as if he's going to rip it off my body. "The spirit in you is foul and blasphemous," he says, spitting out each word, his saliva spraying my face. We lock eyes.

I say to him, "You really don't seem to understand. When my mother told you about my father being a wolf, did you think that was metaphor?"

"Of course not. Demons are as real as angels, as real as Heaven, and they do walk among us."

I want to laugh now. Of course. Demons to him are as real as angels are—to him. But not the kind of real you can touch, not real like this table. Not the kind of real where anybody would see it, believers and unbelievers alike. Not the kind of real that bites, and leaves blood and teeth marks behind.

Our eyes remain locked. He's trying to out-stare me. It's not going to work. I let the rage boil up again, and my voice comes out in a resonant half-growl. "It's true, John Wise. My demon is real. Literal. If you succeed in bringing her out, I will change shape. My teeth will be fangs like swords. My nails will be razor claws. And when that change comes, in the form of the beast, I will slip right out of these shackles. The monster will be free. And she will be very, very upset with you." In his eyes, do I see the tiniest flicker of doubt? "Stop this now. Stop before the hellbeast comes."

For a moment he hesitates, a blank look on his face, and I hope I've done it, finally gotten through to him. But then he shakes himself and moves quickly out of my line of sight. He calls out, "The devil has a silver tongue! The infernal power is wily! It tries to protect itself! We must thresh it out, like the tares from the grain!" He picks up something new to use, a leather whip or a flail, some other medieval torture device. He rarely used whips because they sometimes cut us, leaving scars. It was a whip that gave me the scars on my shoulder. But now he's beyond everything, seeking an ultimate end. Do or die. He knows this. I know this.

It's such a challenge, now, to stay anchored in my body. When will he stop this? When I pass out? When I yield? Is that what I have to do, surrender, pretend to have my demon exorcised? I'm nearly certain now that he won't know the difference between real surrender and fake surrender. Everything he told me about his spiritual power to conquer the beast, that was stuff he made up. He believed my mother's story, but he didn't understand it. He never grasped the difference between his "real" demons and a literal, actual, physical monster.

I think about yielding, about playing submissive, and it galls the wolf. She wants to kill him.

It might be too late anyway. I can feel that things aren't right in my body, beyond the pain which I barely feel anymore, I sense that they are damaging me, so badly that without the wolf's power, it might well kill me. (*Ash that's what he did to Ash you know that's what he did to her*) Anger surges through me, a moment of pure hatred and desire for revenge, my impulses and hers entwining, both of us ready to rip out his throat and drink his blood—

No.

The voice, my sister Ash? Not real. In my head. But my eyes are drawn to the glowing Jesus, and I never noticed before, that he looks like my sister. She smiles, loving, not the terrifying apparition from earlier. She steps down and puts her hand on the back of my neck, a warm breath, a hand of light, and she says, *Do not slaughter him.*

I won't. Tears running down my face. The physical pain could not make me weep, but the pain of love, that hurts more than anything. Ash are you really here? Is it really you?

You must avenge me in a different way. A more lasting way. Expose him. Discredit his works. Make sure that no child is ever again treated according to the words in his books. Make sure the world knows him for what he is. Make sure they know what he really did to me.

Yes. Certain, at last, of something, I close my eyes, and surrender. My thoughts fly away. My body relaxes.

"The Beast!" My father calls out, dark triumph in his voice. "The Beast emerges!"

Damn right she does.

She bounds straight toward the chest of her enemy, bowling him over, about to snap his neck, but inside the word of command: *NO.*

The voice is her master. She knows this even as she squirms under its authority.

But he's right there underneath claws oldest enemy time to break kill eat his guts howl in triumph—

No. He must live. Sweeter meat in the forest.

Frustrated, she snarls her fiercest at everyone in the room. Her teeth snap inches from her enemy's neck, to prove how easily she could have killed him. She runs into the forest where, as promised, there is sweeter meat in great abundance.

25

WAKING UP NAKED IN THE SWAMP

In human form I wake up. Naked, of course. In a mud puddle. The wolf was thirsty, came here to lap water, then settled herself down in the mud to cool off. I remember vividly the peculiar sensation of panting like a dog, tongue dangling against my enormous lower fangs. This weather is too hot for her, all covered in thick fur. But bare-skinned human me is glad of the warm, humid weather.

I uncurl, remembering the moment when I told the wolf not to kill my father. She obeyed me. She accepted me as dominant over her, which is encouraging. But I had to be very focused. And why was I so sure that she needed to leave him alive? Because I didn't want his blood on my hands? Or, technically, my mouth?

Was it for the sake of my family? Because I didn't want them to watch it happen?

No, there was something else.

Ash. That's it. I saw a vision of Ash. She didn't want me to kill him because—

Gut-punched now I think of her fully, a crushing misery of loss and guilt that makes my body shake. I weep, possessed by sorrow much as I am possessed by the wolf, helpless. I could tell the wolf no but I can't tell my tears no. Grief threatens to drown me.

Then, finally, the tears abate, and I can think again, make plans. Ash didn't want me to kill Wisdom because she wanted his spirit killed instead. If John Wise dies in an animal attack, then he remains a best-selling author, one whose star will fade perhaps, but who continues to be highly regarded in some circles. His reputation needs to be destroyed. He needs to be exposed as the monster that he is.

Police. I need to get the police there. They need to see what goes on, before he has a chance to clean it all up. They need to find her bones.

Self-conscious even though I'm alone, I kneel down and sniff the ground, picking up the now-familiar scent of two eager dogs, the ones who chased me when I first left New Harmony. They must live nearby. The man, their master, seemed willing to help me once. I can probably go there for help, although I'm not sure what he's going to think when I show up at his door stark naked. I look down at myself, surprised to see my skin discolored by ugly bruises. It's almost reassuring. I didn't imagine it. I really was chained up and beaten severely, although with my rapid healing, it looks like I was beaten badly a few days ago, rather than almost to death a couple of hours ago. Still, I think I have my story.

At the edge of the cabin's property, the two dogs come tearing out toward me, barking and snarling. We regard each other for a moment, staring into each other's eyes, me calm, the dogs worked into a fury that gradually drains away. I wonder what they think of me. Am I human or wolf to them? Maybe it doesn't matter. They would react the same way to either kind of intruder.

"Daisy. Buttercup." I don't know which is which. They react in confusion to the sound of their names coming from a stranger. I step forward, put my hands on the back of their necks, force them down to the ground. Dog body language, a crude trick, but it works. They recognize me as dominant and stop barking, rolling over onto their backs and releasing a small amount of urine. I kneel down, patting them and speaking soothingly. I stay kneeling as a woman comes out of the cabin.

"Daisy? Buttercup? Who's there? Is someone there?"

She's got a rifle cocked. It seems to take her a moment to notice I'm there, possibly because I'm the same color as the dirt.

"Just me, ma'am." I raise my arms in surrender.

She jumps, startled, but she knows what she's doing and the barrel of the gun goes up into the air right away. "A girl. What are you doing here?"

"My father. I finally ran away from him."

"Your father?" She seems to reevaluate me, take a second look at what she's seeing. "Child, are you naked under all that dirt?"

"Please, ma'am." I huddle tighter into myself. "He took my clothes so I wouldn't leave. But after my sister died I couldn't take it anymore. I ran anyway."

Her jaw drops, eyes wide. She's buying the story, I can tell. "Oh my God. I—just a minute, stay right there." She runs into the house and comes back with a bathrobe, pink terrycloth emblazoned with Disney princesses. "Here, put this on."

"Thank you, ma'am." It smells like a young female, probably a daughter. Bathrobe on, I follow her into the house and tell her my story, the one designed to bring the cops. My father beats me. He beats all of us. He beat my little sister and she died. There are things I leave out, like the fact that she died six months ago. But it's a true story.

The woman—Mrs. Debord—calls the cops and I listen vaguely as she gives directions and information. Then I hear the word, "cult."

"Child, are there a lot of weapons there at New Harmony?"

I try to remember. "I don't think so. There's a rifle, but I've never seen any other weapons."

Now that I'm thinking about cults, I'm thinking about the stories I read. Jonestown. Those saucer people in California. David Koresh at Waco. Cults where the leader kills everybody when the police come. Wisdom doesn't have a lot of weapons. Just the one rifle. But would he start using it on his people if he thought his empire was crumbling? If he thought he was about to get arrested?

Did I make a huge mistake telling the wolf to let him live?

Shit. I have to go back there right now. Before the police get near. Before he knows. Shit shit shit maybe he already knows. Maybe he's already guessed what I would do.

I stand up, make eye contact with Mrs. Debord. I mouth the words, *I'm sorry, I have to go.*

Then I run, still wearing a borrowed pink bathrobe covered with Disney princesses.

26

JOHN WISE

I run at top speed and the thought crosses my mind that I could run faster on four legs. But I have no idea how to make myself change shape purely at will, and anyway, I don't trust her. So I run on two feet, and it seems to take forever.

I don't have much of a plan, except to go straight to my father and prevent whatever he's planning. It's easy enough to track him, to the chapel with everyone else. I burst in, panting, on what appears to be a normal service, everyone sitting quietly in the pews, Wisdom lecturing at the front. Is it Sunday? I try to recall the gas station calendar, decide it doesn't matter.

"Abnegation, welcome back." He smiles benevolently. Isn't he ever surprised by anything? He takes a rifle from behind the lectern and points it right at me. "This rifle is filled with silver, which I believe is the correct remedy for demons of your kind."

Silver? I almost want to laugh. I didn't think he watched those kinds of movies. But where did he lay his hands on enough silver in such a short time? Has he had it prepared and secreted away for my whole life, knowing this day might come?

I raise my hands in surrender and try to look scared. Actually, I am scared. But not for myself. I take a single step forward. "Father, forgive me. I knew not what I did."

He begins walking down the aisle, gun steady. I inhale the tension in the room. Everyone in here is scared of us. They're scared Wisdom will shoot me. They're scared he'll punish them. They're scared I'll turn into the wolf again. We can hardly breathe, as the tension in the air seems to thicken it, make it like walking through gelatin.

"I do forgive you." He smiles, a creepy wide-eyed smile. "You cannot help what you are. I see that now. There is nothing that will drive out the fiend inside you, not even my spiritual remedies."

"Please don't shoot me." I take a step forward. We're close now, almost close enough for me to be sure of grabbing the gun before he can fire. I wish I knew how fast I really am. Faster than a normal human, but how much faster? I've hardly been tested. I have no idea.

"But what else can I do? I tried to drive out the devil, but it's too late. When you are chastised, it takes over, to protect itself. I see no way for you to be free, save your death. The cleansing fire."

"We can try something else. Not the Mercy Seat, not physical pain. More of an exorcism?"

"Papist nonsense." He cocks the gun, aiming at my heart, and I do feel a quiver of doubt. We're so close, the gun would destroy my heart. Would that kill me? "Pray with me, Abnegation, before the beast takes you over again. Pray with me so that your place in Heaven will be assured. Our father, who art in Heaven—"

There. I see the moment when his attention wavers a little from the gun, as he slips into the familiar rhythms of the prayer. I close the gap between us, wrenching the gun out of his hands, kneeing him in the groin, kicking my heel into one of his kneecaps. Surprised at last, he reels backwards. I throw my weight into him, toppling him to the floor with me on top. He's a tall man and I can feel that I don't have the mass to hold him long by sitting on him. I need to knock him unconscious. The movies make this look easy, but I hit his head with the butt of the gun a few times and he's still awake and struggling. I use both hands to press the gun down on his neck. Maybe that will knock him out.

"Thy beast..." His voice is a strangled whisper, but his eyes are fierce. "Thou art become thy beast... Abnegation, thou art lost to Heaven forever..."

I want to say his words have no effect on me, but that would be a lie, and I'm done lying. They resonate. They even scare me a little. I lean down harder on the gun, putting my face close to his, locking my eyes with his eyes. Yes, I am afraid. But that won't stop me. "John Wise, you're an evil man. A murderer. If there's a God out there who thinks that you're the good guy in all this, that God is a monster and I'll have no part of Him. Do you understand me? I reject your teachings. I reject you."

"You reject wisdom's path," he says, but his voice is so weak I can barely hear it. His eyes flutter shut and his body relaxes. I raise the gun, cautiously, in case his surrender is a trick. Nothing. I check his pulse. He lives. Good.

I look up, at a roomful of shocked, still faces. I forgot that we were being observed.

Well, they're used to being given orders. Maybe they'll take orders from me. "Justice. Purpose. Help me drag him to the Prayer Closet." They nod, rise, and lift him up, draping his arms over their shoulders. They both have plenty of experience carting unconscious or semi-conscious people around. Not usually Wisdom, though. He's the only one of us taller than they are, and his feet drag the ground. I march behind them, gun pressed into our father's back. Silver bullets won't kill me, but they will kill him.

We don't talk on the way. I wonder if they're plotting how to get the gun away from me, and I'm nervous when we get to the door. Either I have to go in front of them and open it myself, or one of them has to stop holding our father to do it. I decide it will go smoothest if I open the door, which I do quickly and warily, stepping aside in case they try to shove me in. "Put him on the floor." They do, still without speaking, "Shut and latch the door," I tell them, and they do that too. They don't seem to be plotting at all. Could be I've watched too many outsider movies.

They stand, blank, like robots awaiting further instructions. It's starting to give me the creeps.

"Let's go back to the chapel," I tell them. And we do. Still blank. Still nothing. Are they in shock? Finally I can't stand it any longer. "Justice, Purpose, what are you thinking?"

They blink at me in surprise. "Thinking, Sister?" Purpose says, slowly, carefully. "What do you suppose we are thinking?"

I blow out my breath, exasperated. "I don't know, that's why I asked you! I mean, your prodigal sister comes home and turns into a wolf—you did see that, right? The part where I turned into a wolf? Then your father tries to kill her, then she takes his gun away and orders you to put him in the Prayer Closet—are you doing what I ask because I have the gun? Because you were waiting for the chance to get rid of him? Because you're scared of me? Why are you all staring at me like that? Why isn't anyone saying anything?"

"Silence is a blessing," Justice says.

"Sister, it seems that your time in the outside has changed you more than you realize. Here at New Harmony we do what needs to be done and say what needs to be said. Wasted talk is seed spilled upon the ground."

We enter the chapel, still in mid-argument. "Yes, but do you agree with me that locking Wisdom in the Prayer Closet was a thing that needed doing? That's what I'm trying to figure out here. Whose side are you on? Whose authority do you answer to?"

"God's authority, of course," Justice says.

"*ARRRRRGH!*" I let loose a gutteral scream of frustration and it affects the New Harmony people like a gunshot, leaving a shocked ringing silence in its wake, everyone staring at me with wide eyes. "Look, I'm trying to help you. Wisdom is going to jail. That's a thing that's going to happen. But after that, what do the rest of you want?" I point at Meekness, who sits quietly in the pew with Grieve Not snuggled close and the infant Promised in her lap. "You. Meekness. Do you have family you can go to? Friends? Any kind of life you left behind when you came here to marry my father?" Listen to me, still calling him my father. Well, genetics isn't everything.

She clears her throat and answers in a small voice. "I do have family, yes. In Tennessee." She casts her eyes down and leaves them there for a long moment. Then she raises them sternly. "Abnegation, what are you doing? I am the eldest female here. Purpose is the eldest male. Authority belongs to one of us, not to thee."

I shrug. "Look, if you or Purpose want to stand up here and talk to everybody, go right ahead. It's open mic night. Everybody gets a say. I'm keeping the gun, though."

Meekness stands up. "Abnegation! Go and release thy father from the Prayer Closet!"

I'm about to answer with a simple no, but to my surprise Chastity stands up, hands on hips and a look blazing in her eyes that I've never seen before. "Oh, Meekness, pipe down. You saw what he did. He was ready to shoot 'Gashun—ready to kill his own daughter! That's not a thing a good father does, or a good man, either."

"But you saw yourself that she's a wolf demon! A real demon! He was protecting the rest of us from her!"

"Oh really? 'Gashun, are you planning to hurt us?" She

turns to me, eyes still blazing.

I drop the bullets out of the back of the gun, silver sparkling as it falls to the floor. "Of course not."

"There, see! Anyway, you're barely older than I am. It was practically criminal when he married you."

"How dare you suggest that our union is anything less than holy and blessed by the Lord!"

Some of the younger children, Grieve Not and Humility, begin to cry, loud sobs that would never be allowed to continue with Wisdom in the room, although the rest of us ignore it. The older boys, Righteousness and Unity, seem fascinated by all the yelling. They watch as raptly as if they stared at a television set.

"Sisters!" Now Justice is the one looking upset, glaring from Chastity to me. "It is not your place to speak up now!" He strides toward me, hand out as if he would take the gun. I step back, cradling it closer, and he hesitates. "Abnegation, I was wrong to listen to you. Wrong to put our father in bondage. It was the voice of the demon."

"Justice!" Purpose booms out. "If you truly believe in Wisdom's plan for authority, from God the father to the earthly father to the rest of the congregation, then I am the senior male in this congregation here right now, and so you listen to me."

Justice folds his arms and glares at his older brother, but he keeps quiet.

Purpose continues, "Now, I've known our father longer than any of the rest of you. Meekness, you are his third wife, but I am his first child. And I can tell you this: when his first wife died, Mother Patience, I was just a little boy, but I remember how the light went right out of him. He got that light back when he married Mother Blessed. But when she died it left again. No offense to you, Mother Meekness, but it did not come back when he married you. He stayed dark. He has been dark now for some time."

Justice scowls. "You would betray our father to these heathens!"

"Brother, you know I'm not a heathen." Purpose glances at me as if to ask, *are you a heathen?* I shrug. He turns back to Justice. "You speak out of anger."

"I speak out of duty. Listen, my family, this is our father we speak of! I go now to release him."

"You will not!" I interrupt. I try to catch him and hold him with my eyes, but he won't look. Instead I walk down the aisle and position myself at the doors, gun out. "Nobody leaves until the police get here."

Justice barks out a bitter laugh, and starts walking toward me with confidence. "Sister, I saw you drop the bullets out of that gun."

"Oh yeah." I reposition it to hold it like a baseball bat. "Wisdom is going to answer to the outsider authorities." The little kids begin to whimper again, but the older boys have turned around in their seats, watching us eagerly, perhaps hoping for more violence.

"And what of answering to God, Sister?"

Did I hear a car? The law might be parking at a distance, arriving here on foot in order not to panic anybody. "If there is a God, he'll answer to God."

Justice makes a sour face. "So you are a heathen after all. Just listen to you. 'If' there's a God." He turns to the congregation. "You see where it goes when you reject Wisdom's path? Darkness and Hell." He drops his voice to a menacing whisper. "I always knew your beast would swallow you whole someday." He lunges toward the door, but he telegraphs his intent so nakedly that I barely have to exert any effort or speed to block him.

At last, I hear footsteps outside. I inhale deeply, trying to get information about the new arrivals. Strangers, yes, with guns. But one scent is very familiar: Steph is here.

27

THE END OF NEW HARMONY

The happiness that wells up inside of me at a whiff of her presence is a surprise. I didn't know I missed her that much. I find myself running outside, running toward her with my arms open, and we embrace, and I feel that she's wearing something weird, like a thick heavy apron—

"Bulletproof vest," she explains.

"Steph, what are you doing here?"

"The, uh, the Debords were alarmed when you disappeared. They didn't know what was happening."

"Oh, I'm sorry. I didn't mean to do that. To scare them, I mean. Once it occurred to me that my father might try to take everybody else in the cult with him, I panicked. My only thought was to get back here as quickly as possible. But that still doesn't tell me why you're here."

She smiles. "I was in the neighborhood, kiddo." Then she laughs. "Oh, don't look at me like that. It wasn't hard to figure out where you'd gone. I was already talking to the cops about finding this place, then we got your phone call, and here we are." She looks around cautiously. "So what's going on? Is anybody here currently trying to kill anybody else?"

"No. No, I think everything is fine. My father is locked up and everyone else is in the chapel." Then I realize that I'm still holding the gun. "Uh, I took this away from him. What should I—"

"Put it on the ground."

I do, kneeling, and suddenly I'm surrounded by a dozen cops. I keep my hands up. I don't think they want to shoot me, but it still makes me feel awfully tense to have so many guns pointed my way. I wonder what would happen if they all shot me at the same time. Would I change shape right now, in front of all these people? Or would such a profusion of bullets simply kill me?

"It's okay," Steph calls out, to the cops. She inclines her head to speak toward her collar, must be a microphone. "It's okay. Everything is all right."

Two cops come up and put my hands behind my back. "You have the right to remain silent—" one of them begins, but Steph interrupts.

"What the hell? You're arresting her? For what?"

"Those were our orders, ma'am."

"Well, get new orders!"

They converse with their radios, briefly, and then nod. They step away. "All right, ma'am. We were told to make arrests as necessary to prevent violence. We saw only one person with a gun and judged accordingly."

"She had the gun because she already took it away from the bad guy. Okay? Is everyone clear on that? Now, could somebody help me get out of this ridiculous vest thing? It's about a hundred degrees out here." She smiles at me. "I can't believe how quickly I got used to the weather in Seattle. Was Louisiana always this hot?"

"In July, yeah, I think it was." I smile, in spite of myself. It makes me so happy that Steph is here and trying to take care of me. But I can't bear the thought of leaving her again. A female officer comes up to help her take off the bullet-proof vest. Underneath, her clothes drip with sweat.

Purpose now comes out of the chapel, followed by Chastity. "Abnegation, what's going on out here? Did the police come?" His eyes widen in alarm when he sees that the answer to that question is "yes" and they all have guns pointed at him.

"Hands up and behind your head, both of you."

They comply, but as the cops frisk them they turn looks to me of confusion and betrayal. I feel unexpected guilt, as I realize that I've just set up my whole family to be treated as criminals. "Chastity, Purpose, it's okay. They're just trying to make sure you don't have any weapons. They aren't going to arrest you." I try to catch the eye of the cops. "You're not going to arrest them, are you?"

"No, Miss. Not unless they make trouble."

"You see? Now, you just left the chapel, what's happening in there?"

"Nothing." Purpose shakes his head. "Justice and I argued a bit, then I announced my intention to leave. Chastity followed me. He called us heathens, but he let us go." Frisked and clean, the cops let them go too.

"Abby, are these your siblings?" Steph asks. "Do you want to introduce us?"

I inhale, about to answer, when something odd tickles my nose. Distant, perhaps back in the chapel, a sudden release of sweetness: chocolate... and almonds?

!!!!ALMONDS!!!!SHIT!!!

I take off running at top speed toward the chapel. Behind me, I sense consternation as the officers aren't sure whether or not to fire. I think I'm moving fast enough that they would have trouble hitting me either way.

The chapel doors are locked from the inside. Battering them down would take a while, although I'm pretty sure the wolf could do it eventually. It's easier to take a running leap through the stained glass window, through Jesus. I have a moment of regret, to be destroying the one beautiful thing we ever had here at New Harmony, but I know it doesn't matter now. Jesus explodes into a million tiny fragments of beautiful color that rain down as I land on the floor. Tiny pinpricks of glass all over my body cause an annoying, itchy little pain, too small to worry me now. Where is the almond coming from? THERE.

I tackle Justice and his thermos goes flying, warm chocolate and (I assume) cyanide flinging everywhere. His skull cracks hard against the wooden floor and he looks up at me, bewildered. "Abnegation? Is that you? I thought you'd gone."

I raise my head and look over the chapel. Everyone is seated obediently in the pews, staring at this new altercation with wide eyes. Nobody looks obviously poisoned. "Did any of you have any of the chocolate?"

"No, Justice was still preparing the final sacrament," Meekness says. She bounces baby Promised on her lap. "Didn't it smell good, precious?" She glares at me. "Abnegation, there is no end to the trouble you've caused."

"Trouble? Meekness, that chocolate was poison! He was preparing to kill you all."

Justice continues to look perplexed. I let him up. Since the poison is spilled, I don't know what more harm he can do. I also realize that my ridiculous princess bathrobe has become indecent, and tuck it back into shape.

Justice sits up, rubbing his head. "Abnegation, you don't understand. To you it might have seemed a poison, because you've become a heathen. But to us it was the body and blood of our savior. Wisdom explained it all."

"It was poison, Justice. Cyanide, just like at Jonestown. It was going to be poison for everyone. That's how poison works."

"Jonestown? Cyanide? I don't understand."

Then it clicks. He really doesn't understand, does he? Did I know about Jonestown before leaving here? No, I did not. I didn't know about mass suicide and cults. I didn't know we were a cult. I didn't know about cyanide. I didn't even know about chocolate.

Wisdom, you're a bigger monster than I realized.

"All right, look, brothers and sisters, Mother Meekness. The police are outside and they're here to help you. Seriously. They've got the place surrounded. Any minute now, they'll be ordering us out with our hands up. Let's get ready, okay?"

I hold up my hands in the proper manner, and people respond, almost in spite of themselves.

From outside, Steph's voice, amplified through a megaphone. "Abby? Abby are you in there? The police want to know what the hell is going on."

I shout out, "We're fine, Steph. I had to do more to manage the situation than I anticipated. I've got everyone in a cooperative mood now. What should we do?"

A few moments of conversation outside dimly heard, then Steph says, "Okay, everyone should come out of the chapel one at a time, so the cops can search each person for weapons. They will not harm you. Understood?"

"Understood. Okay, everybody, slow march out the front door."

I stay at the rear, alert for any further trouble. It seems to take forever for the whole line of us to get outside. They're even searching the little kids.

When I finally get out the door, it's worse than I thought. The media found out about this somehow, and our march of shame is documented by three local news outlets and two cable stations. At least they aren't getting in our faces with microphones. The police probably ordered them to stay back. My family is being loaded into the back of police vans,

Purpose and Chastity along with the others, and I can smell that they're scared.

"I'm the last one," I tell the female cop they got to pat down the female congregants. That was thoughtful of them, anyway. She fluffs my bathrobe and nods at the other cops.

"This way please." A different cop tries to escort me to the police van, but Steph intervenes.

"Hold on! She's coming with me."

I glance back to the van, to the frightened faces of my family. Sheep without a shepherd. "Just a minute." I go over to the van and poke my head in. "Purpose? Great Purpose?" He responds, nodding at me with a troubled smile. "Chastity?" She also looks at me. "You guys can help take care of everyone, right? Meekness has her hands full with the littlest ones." Meekness grimaces at me, but doesn't contradict. "I know you're scared, but the police really do want to help you. And if you need help, you can—" I stop myself before saying, you can call me. Because the New Harmony plan failed to control the wolf. I'm lost, now. Wherever I'm going, they probably don't have phones. "Reach out to people."

I turn around to head back to Steph, but then I realize one person has not been accounted for. Is my father still in the Prayer Closet? Is he—a gust of wind carries his scent, the whiff of cyanide, chocolate, and death. I run after it, find a sheeted body being wheeled toward an ambulance by two uniformed EMTs, a man and a woman. "Is that my father?" I ask.

They glance at each other, then the woman nods. She turns toward me and crouches down to put us at eye level. "I'm afraid your father has passed on, sweetie."

Her cloying tones make me feel impatient, almost angry. Does she think I'm a little kid? "Look, my father was a terrible man, a sadistic abuser and a murderer. If he's gone for good, I'm not going to cry. I just want to know. Is he dead?"

A brief glance at her partner, then a nod. "He's dead."

"He killed himself with more of the poisoned chocolate?"
Another brief glance, then another nod. "Looks that way.
We'll do an autopsy."

"Can I see his face?"

The female EMT looks pained. "Oh, honey, no, you don't
want to do that. Your father—people who die from poison,
sometimes they look—it's nothing for a child to see."

"I'm sixteen, okay? I think I'm old enough to handle it. I
need to know. A part of me won't believe he's gone unless I
see him."

"All right." The male EMT pulls down the sheet, quickly,
as if hoping to get to it before his partner can object.

I see Wisdom. His face gray and distorted, eyes popping
out, mouth contorted, a drizzle of chocolate still caught in the
corner of his fading lips. It's probably an illusion created by
the poison, but he looks as if he died screaming in horror.
Maybe he saw hell as he died. I hope he did. I hope those
demons he tried to make real, I hope in his final moments he
saw them coming for him, ready to take him to his true
infernal home. I shudder, disturbed by the pure vindictive
hatred I feel. He's dead, and I still can't forgive him. Is that
wrong?

The female EMT mistakes my distress and pulls the sheet
up again. "That's enough. Are you going to be all right,
child?"

"Yes. Thank you." I smile, hope it looks appropriately
reassuring. "I'm fine."

I watch his form, hidden now, as the EMTs maneuver him
into the back of the ambulance. I'm not sure how to feel. My
father, my oldest enemy, is dead. If I want revenge, it's there,
in the terror in his face, in the knowledge that I drove him to
it, by destroying his private kingdom, threatening him with the
loss of his reputation. But the more I think about it, the more
I feel, not triumphant, but let down. Can it really be over?

No. Because Father Wisdom was not my oldest enemy.

The one that lives inside me, the wolf, she was already planted there by my real father, long before John Wise ever laid eyes on a pretty blond girl looking for help on Bourbon Street. The New Harmony plan failed to control her. She's still there, ready to destroy my life and threaten everything I ever cared about.

28

STEPH AND ABBY

I follow Steph to the rental car. She gives me a smile. "What on earth are you wearing, anyway?"

"Um. I got this from Mrs. Debord, and I'm sorry it's kind of trashed—"

She blows out her breath in a kind of half laugh. "Nobody's going to mind, kiddo. You saved about a dozen lives in there."

"Only because I endangered them in the first place by calling in the cops."

She shakes her head. "You're an idiot. Are you getting in the car?"

"Did you get my letter?"

"This one?" She takes it out of her purse, holds it up. The rosary dangles from her fingers. "Yeah, I got it. Do you want this back?"

"Did you read it?"

"Of course. It struck me as disturbingly suicidal." She holds out the rosary. "Are you sure you don't want it? I know you're not Catholic, but I thought it might give you something to focus on."

"But what about the rougarou stuff?"

She glances up at the sky, looking thoughtful. "Well, the moon's nearly full, so I thought we'd spend the next few days camping. Mama is going to be ecstatic over all the uninterrupted grandbaby time."

"But Steph, you hate camping."

"That's how you know I'm taking this seriously." She grins. "I think we'll be okay. I've got a rifle full of tranquilizer darts and a cooler full of steaks. Come on, what wolf would go to the trouble of eating me when there's practically a whole cow's worth of top-quality meat with the bones and skin conveniently removed?"

In spite of myself, I laugh. "Steph, that's not—wait, tranquilizer darts?"

"It works in the movies. I figured we could go to Barataria, that's super close to New Orleans. It's supposed to be good for bat-watching. Say, my granny said the rougarou could summon giant bats and ride on them, can you do that?"

"Steph, please. I don't want to hurt you."

"So don't hurt me. Get in the car." A pause. "Please? Maybe you can help me find that fais-do-do, that barbecue."

The rosary hangs in the air between us, twined in her fingers. I sigh, and take it, and get in the car. I stare out the window, hoping this isn't a mistake, but I don't want it to be. I want her to be right. *Don't want to hurt me? Don't hurt me.* But Steph, you don't understand, it's a wolf, an animal, a monster. She isn't me. Well, she's a part of me. But a very stupid part that can't be trusted to know the difference between friend and foe. The rosary beads cool my fingers as I pour them from one hand to another.

As promised, we go camping. We take long, slow walks through the park, and we talk. Steph says, "You'll notice I did not bring any beer along." Some time later, she asks me, "Morgan tells me you have a boyfriend? What's that all about?" And so I tell her the whole long story, including the part where I woke up in the carcass of a deer. She nods, thoughtfully, but I still can't tell if she really believes me about the werewolf stuff.

On the night of the full moon, the sun sinks, and the moon rises. With it, I feel a kind of pulling, as if tides surge within me. A scarlet veil drapes itself across my thoughts. It becomes hard to form words. I stare at my hands, clutching the rosary, and my vision doubles. Claws, deadly razors, to take life in one quick swipe like the scythe of death itself. Human fingernails: short, ragged dirty, splashed with remnants of glittering purple, reminder of the kindness and good humor of the extremely flamboyant gay couple who gave me both a ride and a makeover. My arms shiver between fur and freckles. When I close my eyes, not only my body, but the universe itself, seems infinitely malleable. Everything that exists, every moment created endlessly out of nothing.

Everyone has a universe inside of them, and mine is doubled. I am me, a girl called Abnegation, called Abby, a human suffering under regret of the past and dread of the future, that special curse that goes along with being human. At the same time, I am a wolf, newly born, without sorrow or fear, without a sense of I, a part of the world living only in the moment of action. To kill, yes, but also to sing.

In the distance, my kin are singing.

"Listen to that," Steph says. "Coyotes?"

I shake my head. "Wolves."

The nearly invisible hairs on my pale still-human arms prickle at the sound, chills racing along every nerve, up and down my back, a silver noise. It calls to me. Put down your paws and run to us, put down your burdens, your self, your fears and doubts, the human self that causes you so much pain, the trouble and heartache and confusion, all of that will fall away in an instant, and you can be the wolf and she will run in the night and wake in the morning surrounded by packmates, and you will be home.

The vision of that is so clear and strong that it feels like a memory of something that must already have happened, somewhere.

But Steph is right here, and she wants to be a family still. For her sake I can stay here, wake up in a sleeping bag, then get in a car and head up to the city, take the baby to the zoo, get that Cafe du Monde I lied about so long ago, go to Preservation Hall and listen to her father play the piano.

This vision isn't as clear. I have to work to bring it in focus. I have to anchor myself in myself, I-I-I all the time. John Wise taught that the self was the source of all pain. But my self is the only thing I have stronger than the wolf, and I will not abnegate her. For a moment anger surges in me, a defiant screw-you to my father, but anger feeds the wolf, so I have to let that go.

In my hands, the rosary breaks.

"Oh, no! Abby, can you help me find the beads?" Steph studies my face. "Abby? Are you okay?" She places a hand on my forehead. "I think you're running a fever."

I inhale once, slowly, as long as I can make it. Then I exhale and imagine that I'm blowing out the cloud of red bees swarming through my head. Blowing it out. Inhale, exhale. "I'll be okay." I start picking up beads. "Maybe we should break out those steaks now?"

She smiles. "See, that's what I thought. We'll have that fais-do-do ourselves. Why don't I put on some music?"

29

THE PEOPLE WITH WOLVES INSIDE

"Those cats have been there since Katrina," says the man with the banjo. He sits strumming it on the stoop outside the black gate surrounding Jackson Square, where Steph and I are supposed to meet. She's a little bit late. At dusk they closed the gate, and now the enclosed lawn area has filled up with pale-furred cats that stare at us, unblinking.

"Where do they go in the day?"

He shrugs. "I don't know. Keeping the quarter safe from rats and mice, maybe."

One of the cats comes near us, to drink from a dish of water left by some kind person, possibly banjo man. The cat glances at me with a wary look, then goes back to drinking.

"Well, I got to go now," says banjo man. "You got any money, miss? A dollar for cat food, maybe?"

I give him three. I have been here only a few days, but already got into the habit of traveling the quarter with plenty of small bills, for buskers and the more entertaining kind of street hustler. I don't know if banjo man will really spend any of it on cat food, but I think he might. He tips his hat to me and leaves me to watch the cats on my own time. I stare at them for a long time, picture them as little lions, lounging on the African Savannah.

Peppery sharp sweat moves through the heavy tropical air, in advance of the woman who comes to stand beside me, long fingers wrapping around the black iron gate. There's something familiar about her scent, but I can't place it. The nearest cat stares up at her in apprehension, and rises, to hiss and spit and run to the opposite corner of the garden, disappear under a bush.

"Hello, little one. I know what you are. Do you know what I am?"

She doesn't look at me when she speaks, a slight smile playing about crimson lips. Her voice is rich and low, with an accent that could be New York. But people from New Orleans sound like that too, as I've learned in the past few days.

"A stranger who talks to little girls?" I answer flippantly, but my heart is pounding. Yes, I know. I know what that black-pepper sweat means. I notice it on myself whenever I need a shower.

"Seattle, right? Abby? I'm Vivienne. Viv." She is smirking now, but still watching the cats, not me. They are drifting away from us, most not running, but all of them picking up and relocating further away. Fleeing her, but not me. What does that mean?

"I don't know what you're talking about. And how do you know my name?"

I turn, study her openly. Tall, she makes herself taller with shoes that are both thick-heeled and elegant. Chic-looking black knit sheath dress skims muscular curves. Caramel skin on her face and arms, nose and cheeks sprinkled with burnt-sugar freckles. Deep auburn hair, pinned up neatly, a few wild curls escaping. Wood smoke and very fine barbecued meat clings to her. (I refuse to let my mouth water.) The vivid lipstick is her only obvious cosmetic enhancement.

She returns my stare indirectly, eyes half-lidded. "Please,

Abby. We do watch the news, you know. It's not hard to piece certain events together, when you know what to look for. It was careless of you to infect someone like that, but it's not uncommon the first time, not for ferals. You cleaned it right up, though. Before we could even get to him. That does count for something."

Infection? She must be talking about George. I don't really want to engage with this woman, but I have to ask. She seems to know what she's talking about. Maybe I can finally get some real answers.

"Will that happen only at the full moon? When I'm not myself? Or do I always have to be careful not to—uh—not to drool on people?"

Her grin widens, displaying glossy movie-star teeth. "Only the bite of the other form can infect. Why do you ask? Are you in the habit of drooling on people?"

"I fall asleep in class sometimes. I thought it might come up."

She studies me with a thoughtful look, eyes still heavy-lidded, as if she doesn't want to quite meet my gaze. "You must be one of Leon's. You look like him. A little fragile and small, though. Were you meat-starved growing up?"

Meat-starved. You don't know the half of it. "You know my real father?"

"Knew him. Not well. He died, probably not long after siring you."

"And he was a—rougarou?"

She looks perplexed for a moment, then bursts out laughing. "Well, if you want to put it like that. That word is just a corruption of loup-garou, what the French called us."

"So what do you call yourselves?"

"Varger. Originally a Norse word, I believe. It means stranger, or outcast. But the important thing is not what anyone calls us. The important thing is what we are."

"And what is that?"

She leans down, putting us face to face, eye to eye for the first time. Her smile shows off her big, white, perfect teeth. Eyes of amber-brown flash pure molten gold.

"We are the people with wolves inside," she says, in a firm sibilant whisper, somewhere between a growl and a hiss.

I meet her gaze. "I already knew that. But I have so many questions—"

She interrupts. "Not here. I must take you back to our home in Bayou Galene, where you can meet your grandfather Pere Claude. He will answer any question you have. He can tell you all the history of our people, train you in our ways. I promise he will welcome you as his own. And he will provide well for you. We take care of our own."

"What? No way. I'm not going anywhere with you. I'm sixteen, that's creepy."

"You're a child. You don't understand. Trust me, you belong with your own kind."

Steph approaches, carrying Terry. Their scents jump out at me from the olfactory din, like a shout, like a song, a familiar voice, and I feel a surge of emotion toward them, love, protection, a feeling like family. This woman, for all her familiar peppery sweat, she's not family. Not the way Steph and Terry are. And this Pere Claude might be my grandfather, but from what I know of my real father, I'm not much interested in meeting the man who sired him.

"My people are who I choose them to be."

Viv inhales sharply, seems about to respond, but Steph rushes up to join us. "Sorry I'm late, kiddo. Emergency diaper change. Were you okay here on your own?"

"Of course."

"Who's your friend?"

"We were watching the cats," I say. "They're a little afraid of people. Well, some people."

Vivienne inhales, nostrils and eyes flaring. She's upset, but not angry. "Are you saying they're not afraid of you?"

"Not that I noticed. It might be because you're so much taller."

"Hmm. Well, that's something to think about. It was nice to meet you, Abby."

"You too, Vivienne."

"I'm sure we'll see each other again." She spins on the toes of her shoes and stalks off, heels rapping against the bricks.

"Wow, I always wondered who got to shop at Beau Travail," Steph says, watching the woman with obvious admiration, a touch of envy.

"What's that?"

"Oh, this very, very exclusive dress shop that I used to stare in the window of when I was growing up. They carried shoes and hats and handbags too. All very French. I think the name means 'beautiful work.' Of course, with a body like that, she could probably stroll down the street naked and nobody would mind."

So, my other family has money. They can track people by scent. And they know I'm here.

"Hey, Steph. When are we going back to Seattle?"

"In time for the school year. Why? Are you in a big hurry to get home?"

"I guess not." I gather her and the baby into a fierce hug, and try not to look too far into the future.

AFTERWORD

ABOUT THIS NEW EDITION, BOOK 2, AND THE TALES OF
THE ROUGAROU SERIES

The first edition of this book was released in 2015 by Per Aspera Press. At that time we planned two sequels. When Per Aspera wasn't able to release these, I decided to release them myself under the Goth House Press imprint.

I had a pretty good handle on Book 2, eventually titled *Stripping Down to Scars* (Available November 18, 2019) But once I started working on Book 3, I realized my plans were far too ambitious for a single book, unless I wanted that book to be *Lord of the Rings*.

Book 3 turned into three books, four books, and eventually five books. Since I was now the publisher, there was NOBODY TO STOP ME (bwuh-huh-huh).

This new Goth House Press edition of *Waking Up Naked In Strange Places*, has some modest changes based on fitting it into the seven-book series. It has a new cover, new chapter names, and some line-level editing that I don't expect anybody but me to notice.

ACKNOWLEDGMENTS

A huge thank you—

To my parents, who still think I could be the next Stephen King.

To my Clarion West 2006 classmates and instructors, because awesomeness is contagious.

To the members of Horrific Miscue, the Seattle critique group, who gave me great feedback on an early draft.

To Anne Mini, consulting editor, the first person to suggest that maybe the whole book needed to take place when Abby was a teenager.

To my editor Shannon Page, for helping whip it into shape.

To my husband Paul, who's always willing to drive me around the swamps of southern Louisiana looking for a good place to locate a werewolf village.

ABOUT THE AUTHOR

Julie McGalliard is a writer and occasional cartoonist. She lives in Seattle and travels to New Orleans a lot.

Photo by Andrew S. Williams

CPSIA information can be obtained
at www.ICGtesting.com
Printed in the USA
LVHW031347141019
634125LV00007B/2874/P